Together they watched the fiery sun rise

"Now you know why they call Helvellyn the Sunrise Mountain," Caan said softly in Darynthe's ear.

"I wouldn't have missed it for anything!" she agreed. They could see the valley below, shrouded in swirling veils of early-morning mist.

"It's almost like being with God, isn't it?" Darynthe said shyly, half afraid he would laugh at her fanciful imaginings. "Up here, I mean, with the world spread out below."

To her surprise, his response was perfectly serious.

"There's an old Westmorland legend that says the mountains were a place where man once could pass freely between earth and heaven.... The roots of heaven. I worship beauty," he said simply, "in nature, landscape and people. Those great green eyes of yours were meant to shine with joy, Darynthe—let them shine."

WELCOME
TO THE WONDERFUL WORLD
OF *Harlequin Romances*

Interesting, informative and entertaining,
each Harlequin Romance portrays an appealing
and original love story. With a varied array
of settings, we may lure you on an African safari,
to a quaint Welsh village, or an exotic Riviera
location—anywhere and everywhere that adventurous
men and women fall in love.

As publishers of Harlequin Romances, we're
extremely proud of our books. Since 1949,
Harlequin Enterprises has built its publishing
reputation on the solid base of quality and
originality. Our stories are the most popular
paperback romances sold in North America; every
month, six new titles are released and sold at
nearly every book-selling store in Canada and the
United States.

A free catalog listing all Harlequin Romances
can be yours by writing to the

HARLEQUIN READER SERVICE,
(In the U.S.) 1440 South Priest Drive, Tempe, AZ 85281
(In Canada) Stratford, Ontario, N5A 6W2

We sincerely hope you enjoy reading
this Harlequin Romance.

Yours truly,

THE PUBLISHERS
Harlequin Romances

Roots of Heaven

Annabel Murray

Harlequin Books

TORONTO • NEW YORK • LOS ANGELES • LONDON
AMSTERDAM • PARIS • SYDNEY • HAMBURG
STOCKHOLM • ATHENS • TOKYO • MILAN

Original hardcover edition published in 1982
by Mills & Boon Limited

ISBN 0-373-02549-1

Harlequin Romance first edition May 1983

CHAPTER ONE

'I'LL never trust another man again, not for as long as I live. I wish I'd never even met him!'

Darynthe Browne repeated the words aloud to the mountains, words which had been on her lips many times in the past few weeks. Her only living audience was a smoky-faced sheep, which, startled by the sound of a human voice in this vast solitude, rose in ungainly terror and bounded away, the thudding of its hoofs muted by the close but springy turf.

The view blurred slightly before Darynthe's wide green eyes and impatiently she blinked thick, gold-tipped lashes, annoyed with herself for spoiling this breathtaking splendour with thoughts of Mark Little.

But it was impossible not to think of Mark here, she mused, as she stood on the grass verge, looking up at the site of the Roman fort, for it was her interest in Roman antiquities which had first brought her and Mark together.

'Mark!' She whispered the name to the brooding hills, testing the name on her lips, to see if it still had the power to hurt. She found that it had, and her lips tightened in an effort to control their trembling. She had shed enough tears for Mark . . . bitter tears that no man was ever going to wring from her again.

Darynthe had left Eskdale village earlier that morning, en route for Ambleside, driving herself in her ancient but still beloved Mini. She just hoped that the small car was equal to the task that still lay ahead of it.

The gallant little vehicle had tackled the first stage of its journey gamely enough, carrying her up and around the hairpin bends on the Eskdale side of the Hardknott Pass, up gradients almost one in three . . . on her left the real mountain world of Lakeland . . . the Scafell Group, the solid grandeur of the Langdale Pikes, Great End, Bowfell; she tried the sound of their names on her tongue, imbuing them with a mystical glamour. Then, frowning over the pass itself, was Harter Fell. All of them were new to her and yet familiar, from the books and maps she had pored over in the past few days.

Out of consideration for her engine, which had begun to overheat, she had stopped here, half way up the zigzags, to take a look at the Roman fort of Hardknott, of which she had read. As a ruin, she decided, it was not as spectacular as some she had seen, but its setting was superb, a lonely situation, wild and impressive, standing as it did in the position of unparalleled impregnability, with sheer drops on three sides.

How Mark would have enjoyed seeing it! She was trying not to think of Mark, but it wasn't easy.

Although contemplating this piece of ancient history had brought back vivid reminders of her ex-fiancé, she found also a strange comfort in its very timelessness, in the thought that some things at least were unchanging. Two thousand years might have passed since the Roman legionaries had stood on this same spot, looking northwards. Two thousand years! How petty that made the last six months of *her* life seem. After all these years, this place was still unchanged; the same track wound over the pass, the same black crags loomed against the clouds . . . and in that time, how many people had loved and lost? Here, one could find comfort in solitude. People spoiled things, she decided . . . people . . . and especially men.

Darynthe sighed, turning reluctantly away from the view. She must be on her way. Over in Ambleside, her aunt, who owned a guest house there, was expecting her. However unwillingly, she must descend from the clouds, literally as well as metaphorically speaking . . . return to the world of people, of men. Well, she couldn't avoid encountering men, but she was never going to become involved with one . . . never again.

She would mix with them, speak to them, even treat them with courtesy, but no man would ever get under her guard again, would ever know the real Darynthe Browne, protected behind her determined barrier of ice-cold reserve.

But, for the present, she still had a little time left to

herself before she need assume her mask. There was still the Wrynose Pass to tackle, that undulating serpent of an ancient road that linked Eskdale with Langdale, a road once tramped by Roman soldiers, en route to Galava, the fort which had stood overlooking Windermere itself.

She returned to the Mini, which by now was cool enough for her to remove the radiator cap and top up with the water which she always carried in a plastic container in the boot. The bonnet closed once more, she started up the engine and pulled off the grass verge, where, for the sake of safety, she had been parked. The roads through these passes were exceedingly narrow, with few places where two cars might pass in opposite directions and none at all where they might overtake.

It was glorious motoring country, Darynthe thought enthusiastically, as the Mini responded to the challenge ... glorious, if somewhat wild and inhospitable, and it called for great driving skill, something on which Darynthe had always prided herself.

As she drove, she wondered idly how she would enjoy working with her aunt. They had only met once or twice, though her father, with his strong sense of family, kept in touch with his younger sister by letter.

The car had reached the summit of Wrynose and now Darynthe had a panoramic view down to the lakes, woods and meadows around Ambleside, highlighted by a dazzle of spring sunlight.

She felt a small quiver of excitement inside her at the thought of fresh territory to explore. She had always been an outdoor girl, fond of fresh air and country walks. But she had never essayed mountain climbing or fell walking. It would present a new goal to aim at, a challenge ... something which Darynthe always welcomed ... but also an outlet for the physical energy, which, once appeased, led to dreamless sleep ... a sleep in which it was possible to forget.

She changed gear for the downward descent, noticing with wry dismay that the local sheep seemed to have chosen their resting places on the steepest and sharpest corners. Several times she drew in her breath, only to release it with a sigh of relief, as yet another animal missed injury by a hairsbreadth. Perhaps their agility, their apparent ability to escape the threat posed by traffic, made her relax, become a little careless.

One bulky ewe, less brisk in her movements, did not scramble out of the way in time. Darynthe stamped hard on the brake pedal and the little car juddered to a halt, as the engine spluttered and died. She sat still for a moment, her head resting on her hands, which grasped the steering wheel, her knuckles white with tension. It would have been dreadful to kill a sheep. To her all forms of life were wonderful . . . miraculous. She knew she would never forgive herself if she were ever responsible for ending the existence of a living creature, even one so mundane as a sheep.

Apprehensively, she tried the self-starter. The old Mini could be a bit temperamental. Sometimes, after stalling in this way, it would refuse to start . . . refuse to start for her, that was. There had usually been some capable, mechanically-minded man to help. Why was it, she wondered resentfully, that machinery always responded to the male touch?

Fortunately, the engine fired at her first attempt. She was unlikely to encounter a helpful man up here in this lonely place. Not that she wanted to encounter one, helpful or otherwise, she reminded herself.

Though the engine seemed unaffected by the incident with the sheep, this was not the case with the brakes. Moving off, she tested them carefully and was appalled when her foot drove down to the floorboards, without any response. She yanked on the handbrake and sat there, trembling. Suppose she had not had the sense to test her brakes, had not discovered that the sudden stop had ejected the last of her brake fluid. She might have been on the downward slopes of the Pass, might have found herself travelling too fast, unable to stop.

For the first time since she had left Eskdale, she wished she were not alone, that there was someone to turn to for advice and comfort. Mark, with his lean, capable hands, would have known what to do. Her green eyes glazed over with tears.

Stop it, she told herself fiercely. You don't need Mark.

You don't need anyone. You're just suffering from shock. Now think! You've always prided yourself on your independence, your ability to look after yourself. There must be something you can do.

Darynthe looked at her wristwatch. The afternoon was already well advanced. Her aunt would be expecting her, worrying maybe. Somehow she had to get herself and her car the rest of the way to Ambleside.

She engaged bottom gear and with the handbrake held hard, began the descent, successfully negotiating the tight zigzags. She thanked her lucky stars that it was early in the year and that there was no heavy tourist traffic. With any luck she might complete her hazardous manoeuvre, without encountering another vehicle.

If she had been superstitious, Darynthe thought afterwards, she would have said that she had tempted the Fates by that thought, for, around the very next bend, she saw the small white car ascending the Little Langdale side of the pass at what seemed to the already nervous girl a tremendous speed. If it continued to approach at that rate, there might well be a collision. It was at that precise moment that she felt the Mini's overtaxed handbrake cable snap.

Praying frantically for time to take evasive action, she selected a spot on the nearside verge which did not look too difficult to surmount and pulled the steering wheel hard over. It was fortunate for her that the worst of the descent was over, that the ground on either side was relatively flat. If there had been a sheer drop, she thought, it would have meant certain disaster.

As it was, the Mini bounced protestingly over the uneven ground, covered with the remains of last year's bracken, and came to a jarring halt against a large grey boulder.

For the second occasion in a short space of time, Darynthe sat motionless, save for the shuddering which shook her from head to foot. As the Mini left the road, she had heard the other car screech to a halt. Now there would be explanations to be made of why she had panicked, taking evasive action in such a risky manner . . . perhaps even accusations to be faced. Wearily she lifted her head, with its sun-streaked mane of silky fair hair, and looked at the man who was striding towards her.

He was tall, with broad, square shoulders and tough, tanned good looks. Dark, wiry hair, liberally sprinkled with grey, curled closely about his head and his face was squarely cut and blunt featured.

He bent and pulled open the door of the Mini, his face, full of concern, very close to Darynthe, as she huddled in her seat. With his jeans he wore a crew-neck sweat-shirt in a vivid blue and she noticed, inconsequentially, that it matched the alert, intelligent eyes which now surveyed her appraisingly.

'Are you hurt?'

His voice was pleasingly resonant, not in the least con-demnatory, yet it filled Darynthe with an indefinable sense of panic.

A strong, muscular-looking hand grasped her arm. The fingers were firm, sure and warm, and taken off guard, Darynthe quivered in response. She had sworn never to let any man touch her again, for whatever excuse.

'Take your hands off me,' she snapped. 'If I'm *not* hurt, it's no thanks to you—blinding up that hill as if all the devils in hell were after you!'

His hand was removed immediately and the throaty, bass voice held a hint of laughter, as he replied.

'Obviously you're a very poor judge of speed. I wasn't moving that fast—it's an impossibility on these gradients. Tell me, do you make a habit of leaving the road, when you encounter another car?'

'No, I do not!' She knew exactly what he was thinking. 'I'm a very good driver. It just so happens that my brakes have failed . . . the footbrake and now my handbrake.'

She swallowed a gulp of self-pity and fearing that he might repeat his gesture of help, she slid quickly from the driving seat and straightened up to face him, her clear green eyes almost on a level with his.

He was frankly assessing her, she noticed, with a little surge of resentment. Why couldn't men and women meet as equals, without this constant need to appraise each other's appearance? After all, she thought, she was nothing special to look at, nothing that need make those blue eyes

of his narrow in that intent way which men had when a
woman excited their interest.

Darynthe had always considered her own appearance
to be pleasantly ordinary. Her colouring was clear and
vivid, owing little to cosmetics, her hair thick and straight,
with a heavy fringe over the tawny green eyes. Her mouth
she considered to be far too large, unaware that to others
it signified warmth and compassion.

'I'd better introduce myself,' the stranger suggested.

'Why?' she asked, her manner deliberately cold.
'There's no need. After all, we're never likely to meet
again. If you'd be kind enough just to help me get my car
back on the road, we can go our own separate ways.'

And the sooner the better, she thought.

He smiled and it was a curiously attractive movement,
only one corner of his finely shaped mouth curving
upwards.

'You *are* feeling prickly,' he commented.

'Do you wonder at it? I've had a difficult, demanding
drive, narrowly escaped murdering hundreds of sheep, my
brakes have failed and then, to cap everything, I encounter
a roadhog, who drives me off over the edge!'

For the first time his face lost its goodnatured expression
and she recognised that he was not a man to be trifled
with. He would only put up with so much, before asserting
himself.

'May I remind you of the unwritten rule of driving in
mountainous country? He who is climbing has priority.
He who is descending should give way.' His tone was un-
compromising.

'I know all about that,' Darynthe retorted. 'But you
missed out an important factor . . . he who is ascending
"*in low gear*". You weren't in low gear. You were driving
up that hill like a lunatic . . . and I did try to give way,
and look what happened!'

She gestured towards the little red Mini, looking
strangely pathetic, tilted to one side and leaning forlornly
against the boulder which had halted its progress.

'Hmmn!' He looked consideringly at the car and then
at her, his manner relaxing a little. 'Well, there's no purpose to be served by arguing about relative speeds. You're

obviously in a state of shock and unlikely to be reasonable.'

'Reasonable!' she echoed, anger deepening the colour of her eyes to an intense emerald. Why on earth should he *expect* her to be reasonable? 'I like that, when you . . .'

'The first thing to be done is to get you to wherever you were going . . . which is?' He quirked an enquiring eyebrow.

'To Ambleside . . . but that won't be necessary. I'll drive myself.'

'Not in that scrap heap you won't.'

Scrap heap? Her beloved Mini!

'How . . . how dare you? My car is . . .'

'Is a write-off,' he interrupted her. 'Look!'

A hand under her elbow, he steered her to the nearside, which rested against the boulder, and it was apparent even to Darynthe's prejudiced gaze that the Mini was a mess.

It was the last straw. A great sob of fury and misery welled up in her, the wide, mobile mouth trembling with the effort to control herself. Her poor little Mini, which had transported her and Mark to so many varied and interesting places. The car was filled with memories of him . . . damn him . . . and damn all men!

She shook off the supportive hand, blinking back the tears, lifting a determined chin.

'Then I'll walk.'

'Don't be so bloody ridiculous!' The set of his square jaw was as pugnacious as her own. 'What is it with you? Do you think because I'm a complete stranger that I have some dark, ulterior motive? Some designs upon your person? I assure you, nothing could be farther from the truth.'

'Oh!'

Darynthe felt curiously deflated. It was one thing to decide to abjure men for ever, quite another to hear a man, and an undeniably personable man at that, declare his complete disinterest in her.

'So shall we stop fencing? No doubt somebody somewhere is expecting you?'

'My aunt,' she confirmed.

'Right! So let's begin again, shall we?' The tolerant amusement was back in his eyes. 'My name is Lorimer . . . Caan Lorimer.'

He held out that large, tanned hand.

'Darynthe Browne,' she murmured, fingers firmly linked behind her back. She would not endure that strong, rather pleasant clasp again, a clasp which against all reason had sent a pulsating wave of heat around her body. 'Browne with an "e",' she added.

'Come on then, Darynthe Browne with an "e".' His delightful smile added crease lines to the corners of the piercingly blue eyes. 'I'll turn my car round. Have you any luggage?'

She nodded.

'Two cases . . . on the back seat.'

'Good job they weren't in the boot,' he observed, as he retrieved the cases and removed her keys from the ignition. 'We'd never have got it open.' He handed her the keys. 'Here, you won't be needing these, unless I'm very much mistaken, but you might like them as a memento.'

Darynthe stared down at the keys in her hand . . . the key-ring with its motif, shaped like twin hearts, an arrow piercing them . . . the key-ring Mark had given her. A memento? When every time she looked at it she would see his lean, blond good looks? With a sudden defiant gesture she raised her arm and flung the keys as far as she could, down the bracken-covered hillside. Impossible to find them again in that dense growth.

With a feeling almost of release, she straightened her shoulders and strode after Caan Lorimer. Apart from a questioning lift of one eyebrow, he had made no comment on her impulsive action, but had moved towards his own car, carrying her heavy cases with effortless ease.

Caan Lorimer's car was an open sports model, gleaming white, with black upholstery. He deposited the suitcases and held open the passenger door.

Darynthe relaxed into the seat, admitting to herself that it would be a relief to be driven for a change. Driving was a pastime which normally she enjoyed, but her journey today had been fraught with too many disasters . . . not least of them her encounter with Lorimer himself.

The car sped through Little Langdale and Skelwith Bridge, towards Ambleside.

'Have you visited the Lake District before?' Caan asked.

'No,' Darynthe admitted. 'But I've read a lot of guide books.'

Good manners compelled her to reply, even though she did not want to get into conversation with this man. All she wanted was to reach her aunt's house and be rid of him.

'You're in for a treat, then,' he observed. 'I was born here, so perhaps I'm prejudiced, but I believe it has the loveliest and most varied scenery in England ... mountains, valleys, rippling becks, leaping waterfalls ...'

'I'm here to work,' she said repressively, 'not to admire the scenery.'

He was not deflated, following her change of subject with the practised ease of a self-assured man.

'Work? What kind of work?'

'My aunt runs a guesthouse,' she replied unwillingly. 'My cousin who usually helps her has just had her appendix out ... and my uncle is away at sea.'

Darynthe knew that the small hotel in Ambleside could take twelve guests. They would be mostly climbers and fellwalkers, she decided, and hoped that not too many of them would be male.

Caan Lorimer, apparently, was not satisfied with the information he had elicited.

'Which guesthouse does she own?' He seemed genuinely interested. 'I believe I know every building in Ambleside.'

'The Daffodil,' Darynthe told him, 'for Wordsworth ... you know?'

'I wandered lonely as a cloud ...' he quoted in pleasantly deep tones. 'Yes, very appropriate.'

Actually, Darynthe thought it rather a ridiculous name for a guesthouse, but she was not going to criticise a relative in front of this stranger, a man who had forced his company on her.

'Well, here we are, Ambleside,' he said. 'Situs Amabilis, the Romans called it ... "beautiful site".'

The old town itself, with its stern, grey, uncompromisingly Victorian buildings, wasn't particularly beautiful, Darynthe decided, but like every other place in the Lake District, it had a picturesque setting, half buried as it was in the Vale of Rothay, encircled and dominated by the horseshoe of the Fairfield Fells.

It was just as well Caan Lorimer did know the town intimately, Darynthe thought, as he deftly steered the sports car in and out of inter-connecting back streets. She had to confess that she would never have found the Daffodil unaided.

'Here we are,' her self-appointed chauffeur announced, as he pulled up outside a tall, narrow, rather forbidding-looking building, its grey stone relieved only by white paintwork and hanging baskets of spring flowers on either side of the front door.

'I can manage now, thank you.'

Darynthe sprang from the car and began to haul her suitcases from the rear seat. She had no intention of allowing Caan Lorimer to invite himself in. She didn't want to have to introduce him to her aunt. But he forestalled her, removing the cases from her and leading the way into the dark, narrow entrance hall.

'We'll have to arrange for someone to pick up your car,' he told her. 'We can't leave it where it is, an eyesore on the landscape.'

'I had no intention of leaving it there,' she assured him, 'and I'm quite capable of arranging for its removal myself.'

'I'm sure you are,' he said cheerfully, ringing the bell on the small reception desk. 'But it's no trouble. I have to pass the garage on my way home. Shall I ask them to send the bill here?'

'Please,' she said, through clenched teeth. Really, he was the bossiest, most persistent, interfering man she had ever met! She was longing to be rid of him.

Her hope that he would take his leave before her aunt appeared was doomed to disappointment. Slender, brown-eyed and youthful-looking, Ann Forster hurried out to the desk.

'Good morning, sir . . . madam. I'm afraid we're fully booked. Oh . . . but it's Darynthe,' as she recognised her

niece. 'Fancy me thinking . . . and you've brought a boy-
friend with you . . . how nice! But I don't know where
we'll put him. You see . . .'

'Auntie Ann!' Darynthe interrupted, desperate to dispel
this embarrassing misconception. 'This is Mr Lorimer.
He's not a friend. He . . . he helped me when my car broke
down.'

For a moment Darynthe had considered repeating her
remark that he was in fact an inconsiderate roadhog who
had driven her off the road, but to do so would only cause
her aunt unnecessary concern. She would break the news
of her narrow escape when they were alone.

Ann Forster peered at Caan Lorimer in the dim light of
the hall.

'Yes . . . yes, I believe I've seen you before . . . around
the town?' She held out her hand. 'Thank you so much.
I'm very grateful to you. Heaven knows what would have
happened to the child if you hadn't come to her rescue.'

Darynthe protested, 'I'm not a child, Auntie Ann . . .
and I would have managed.'

She shot Caan Lorimer an exasperated look. If only he
would go away! But he seemed to have no intention of
leaving, leaning his large frame comfortably against the
reception desk and smiling down, with compelling male
charm, at her bemused aunt.

'Would you like a cup of tea?' Ann Forster asked him.
'I'm sure Darynthe must be dying for one, after such an
eventful day.'

Darynthe clenched her hands to prevent herself from
saying something which her aunt at least would consider
unforgivably rude and inhospitable. But to her relief, Caan
Lorimer refused, smiling again with that whimsical twist
of his mouth.

'No, thanks, Mrs Forster. I'm in rather a hurry.'

Nobody would ever have guessed, Darynthe thought
resentfully as he lingered over his farewells, his dark-
lashed blue eyes thoughtfully upon her, as he held out his
hand.

'Goodbye, Darynthe . . . for the present anyway.
Ambleside is a small place,' he observed. 'We shall
probably meet again.'

Not if I can help it, she vowed silently, reluctantly surrendering her slim fingers to his clasp, trying to ignore the pleasant sensation she received from the feel of his large hand enclosing hers.

'What a stunningly attractive man!' Ann Forster exclaimed, as she led her niece upstairs.

'Do you think so?' Darynthe said, her tone deliberately expressing supreme indifference.

Ann looked at her quizzically.

'Of course! Where are your ears and eyes, my girl? Even in that poor light . . . which reminds me, I must replace that electric lamp . . . even in that light, I could tell. He has lovely manners . . . and such looks! My word, those shoulders, gorgeous blue eyes, lovely white even teeth when he smiles . . . and that deep, velvety voice. If I weren't a respectably married woman . . .!'

'All good-looking men are conceited,' Darynthe stated flatly. 'They think that every woman they meet should be bowled over by them.'

'Don't let your experience with Mark sour you, Darynthe,' Ann pleaded. 'Not all men are deceivers. You're young . . . you'll find somebody else, one of these days.'

'I don't *want* to find somebody else,' Darynthe replied firmly. 'I'm not giving another man a chance to make a fool of me.'

Wisely, Ann Forster made no further comment, but opened the door to the room she had allocated to her niece.

'I'm sorry there are so many stairs to climb,' she apologised. 'But the guests have the first and second floor rooms during the season and we move up here.'

'I don't mind,' Darynthe assured her, moving over to the window. 'There's a marvellous view. I'm simply longing to explore.'

'I'll leave you to unpack then,' her aunt said. 'Come down when you're ready. You'll find me in the kitchen, at the rear of the dining room. Tonight I'll introduce you to the guests we have staying this week and you can start your duties tomorrow. It's very good of you, dear, to come like this at a moment's notice.'

Left alone, Darynthe remained in the window embras-
ure, kneeling on the window seat which had been built
into the recess, and watched the play of light and shade,
sun and cloud over rooftops and chimneys.

Life was a bit like that, she reflected, periods of sunny
happiness, interspersed with clouds, which sometimes
amounted to veritable storms of misery . . . as in her
case . . .

Since she had left school, Darynthe had worked for her
father, who had a small antique shop in the old Roman
town of Corbridge, and this had given her a passion for all
things ancient and for the eras in which they had existed.
Inclined to be a dreamer, Darynthe was firmly convinced
that life in the past had been less complicated, people less
mercenary . . . and far more romantic.

Perhaps it was being brought up by an elderly, widowed
and protective father, she thought now, which had given
her a rather more old-fashioned set of values than her
contemporaries, but she had no patience with modern
morality . . . or the lack of it.

Maybe her friends had been right, she thought. With
six 'O' level passes and four 'A' levels to her credit, she
could have gone on to university, or at least taken some
kind of job away from home . . . could have extended her
horizons. But her father had persuaded her that he needed
her company.

'After all, it's not as if we *need* the money,' he'd told
her.

Consequently, Darynthe knew that she was a little
naïve, a lot less broad-minded than others of her genera-
tion.

Living in Corbridge, it had been inevitable that she
should encounter visitors to the Roman site there, and
amongst them Mark Little, a university Professor of
History, spending his long vacation on a tour of historical
sites. Mark had been considerably older than Darynthe,
but already used to the constant company of an older
man, she had not found it strange that she should be immediately attracted to him. Their friendship had pro-
gressed rapidly to an engagement . . . even, to her father's
dismay, as far as wedding plans, when she had discovered

from a mutual acquaintance, a dealer in antiques, that Mark was already married.

When she had taxed Mark with her knowledge, he had assured her that he intended to get a divorce. But it was no use. Everything had been ruined, Darynthe reflected sombrely. She had tried to tell herself that there was no social disgrace these days in being divorced . . . that Mark was, so he claimed, the innocent party. No, it was partly the fact that he had not told her about his former marriage, had not intended to tell her until afterwards, when it would have been too late.

She shuddered at the memory. She could admit to herself now, though she had told no one else of this feeling, that it was more the fact that he *had been* married, had belonged to some other woman, which distressed her, rather than the fact that he had concealed it from her.

Darynthe was realistic enough to know that what she sought was almost impossible in a modern age, with its permissive society . . . knew how slender were her chances of finding a man who had never loved before, never possessed another woman. But still her romantic nature made her crave to be the first, the only woman in some man's life.

Disillusioned, she had broken off her engagement to Mark . . . an engagement into which, she considered, he had no right to have entered. It had been hard to do, but she had done it. As a consequence, she had been so unhappy that her father, though unwilling to forfeit her company, had suggested a complete change of scenery for a while and she had to admit that he had been right. It had helped.

For the past two weeks she had been staying with an old school friend, in the straggling little village of Eskdale, where congenial company of her own age and the tranquil surroundings had begun their work of easing her bruised heart.

Then had come the urgent plea, the reason for her presence here . . . a request for help from her aunt Ann, a younger sister of her father, who for the past two years had run a small private guesthouse in Ambleside.

Darynthe had a shrewd idea that her father had engineered this request, preferring her to be, if not under his eye, then under that of a member of his family; and after all, she could scarcely have imposed on her friend's hospitality much longer. Yet she did not feel ready to return home. Corbridge was too full of memories of Mark. It would do her good to stay away from familiar scenes for a while.

Despite her remarks to Caan Lorimer, that she had come here to work, secretly Darynthe was looking forward to tackling the cloud-capped hills visible above the buildings overlooked by her window. Up there, perhaps, where ravens croaked and buzzards planed, it would be possible to find solace for her recent unhappiness among the lofty crags, on the steep fellside, with its bubbling springs, as described by her favourite Lakeland author.

From where she knelt, she could just see the parish church, the cross surmounting the steeple just touching the top of the fell, which she knew as Loughrigg. She had borrowed some guide books from her friend and now she planned to explore as much as she could of the area, to see for herself the places about which she had read.

The author had painted his verbal pictures of Lakeland in glowing terms, revealing an intimate knowledge and profound affection for his subject, which was somehow infectious to the romantic, imaginative girl.

At last, reluctantly, she turned away from the window and began her unpacking. The attic room, though small, was attractively decorated; the flower-sprigged wallpaper repeating the blue of carpet and curtains. There was plenty of storage space for her clothes and the room boasted its own wash-hand basin.

All in all, Darynthe decided, she should be counting her blessings. She had a pleasant room, a new and interesting job to occupy her mind . . . and she felt that she would get on well with her youthful, attractive aunt; while, outside, was a new and beautiful world to be explored. With her love of the outdoors, she had long since discovered that fresh air and exercise were a great restorative to one's sense of proportion.

But the next few days were spent in learning the many facets to running a guesthouse, and Darynthe was filled with admiration for Ann Forster's efficiency. It only went to show, she thought triumphantly, that women *could* manage without men. Together they changed beds, cleaned rooms, prepared and cleared away meals.

One of Darynthe's tasks was to wait at table and to her surprise, she found she quite enjoyed this . . . returning the friendly badinage of the guests and overhearing fascinating, tantalising snippets of their conversation.

In the evening, between dinner and supper, she and her aunt joined the guests in the communal lounge. Tired after a full day, Darynthe was content mostly, to sit quietly and let the conversation flow over her . . . stories of the day's exploits on the fells, exaggerated no doubt, but nonetheless entertaining . . . learning the names of the various mountain ranges and the best ways of tackling them.

'But it's time you had a little first-hand experience,' Ann Forster told her niece one evening, as they were washing up the coffee cups. 'Why don't you take the day off tomorrow? The middle of the week is always slack . . . nobody leaving, no beds to change. You've worked really hard since you arrived and you've earned a break.'

Darynthe did not need much urging.

'I'll have to get some boots, though,' she said. 'I've no footwear suitable for scrambling about on the fells.'

'Oh, don't bother to buy any yet,' Ann protested. She looked down at her niece's feet. 'I'm sure mine will fit you. If you find you enjoy fellwalking that much, you can buy your own eventually.'

Darynthe tried on her aunt's boots. They were a little on the large side, but with two pairs of woollen socks, Ann assured her, they would be perfect.

'If I were you, dear, I'd go on one of the organised walks for your first attempt.'

Darynthe looked doubtful; she had been looking forward to getting right away on her own and said so.

Ann Forster shook her head.

'I don't think that would be very wise, dear. You're not familiar with the terrain. You could get lost . . . or twist an ankle. The National Park Wardens provide a wonderful service. If you enquire at the Tourist Information Centre, for a small fee they'll put your name down for one of the guided walks.'

'But there are bound to be experienced people on these walks,' Darynthe objected. 'I might not be able to keep up.'

Ann Forster laughed.

'You'll find plenty of other novices taking advantage of the service. Besides, our local guide is no greyhound over the fells; he's short, elderly and rather portly—it will be more of an amble. Do try it, dear. I know you'll enjoy it ... and I'd be far happier in my mind, knowing you weren't walking alone.'

It was this last remark of her aunt's which won Darynthe's reluctant agreement, though the idea of walking with a crowd of other people really did not appeal to her. She still had moments of nostalgia when the need to be on her own became urgent.

It rained heavily in the night and to Darynthe, in her attic room under the tiled roof, the downpour sounded particularly violent. She wondered if perhaps the weather would be too bad next day for walking.

But the morning dawned fair, bright sunlight sparkling on pools left by the overnight rain and touching the fell tops with gold. The clouds were high ... great white rolling masses, constantly changing into all sorts of shapes against a background of bright blue sky.

Clad in brightly coloured windproof clothing and her borrowed boots, Darynthe collected a packed lunch from the kitchen and made her way to the Tourist Information Centre, only a short walk from the guesthouse.

At the Centre, she registered and paid her fee, then went out into the courtyard, to join other would-be fellwalkers as they waited for their guide.

'He's late,' an elderly woman complained, restlessly pulling up gaily striped socks, retying the lacings of her boots and adjusting the straps of the light rucksack she carried.

'This must be him,' said another, as a figure approached, his khaki windcheater bearing the badge of an official guide.

Darynthe stared at him. Short, elderly and rather portly, Ann Forster had said. That description scarcely

fitted the man at whom she stared with recognition and
growing dismay.

A warning instinct of self-preservation stirred deep
within her and cautiously she began to edge away from
the group, all intention of joining the walk fading, at the
sight of that familiar square, determined face.

But the brilliant blue eyes were as observant as ever.

'Darynthe!' Caan Lorimer exclaimed, striding towards
her, his blunt, good-humoured features alight with
pleasure. 'If it isn't Darynthe Browne ... with an "e". I
said we should meet again!'

CHAPTER TWO

OH no! Darynthe groaned inwardly. Aloud, inanely, she
spoke the first words that came into her head.

'But you're supposed to be old ... short .. and fat ...'

Caan Lorimer threw back his handsome head in
genuine amusement.

'You were expecting my uncle? I'm afraid he's laid up
with 'flu, and as this job is all he has to eke out his pension,
I offered to take today's ramble for him. It seems my good
deed for the day is to have its reward.'

'Oh?' Puzzled green eyes stared back at him, their
colour intensified by the green of her waterproof anorak.

'Meeting you again,' he explained, as he subjected her
to an appreciative survey. 'I must confess I didn't expect
to see you on this walk ... but I'm delighted. Now I can
mix business with pleasure.'

Darynthe backed away a little. He was one of those
disconcerting men who had a habit of standing very close
when they talked, and as she was tall herself, it was impossible not to meet those very blue eyes and to recognise
the blatant gleam of interest in them.

'I ... I don't think I shall be able to go after all,' she
demurred. 'I've just remembered, I ... we ... that is ...'

'What are you running away from, Darynthe?'

He was certainly very direct, she thought, slightly taken

aback by the blunt question.

The look in his eyes turned to one of curiosity.

'Not from me, I hope? I assure you, I'm very harmless.'
The slow, crooked smile was disarming, dangerously so.

'Our last encounter didn't give me that impression,' she
retorted, deliberately taking the offensive, in order to
dispel the effect of that smile.

'Oh, come now!' He raised an eyebrow. 'You're not
serious? You don't really intend to go on blaming me for
the deficiencies of that old banger you were driving?
Which, incidentally, has now been towed away.'

Darynthe was saved from an indignant defence of her
car by the plaintive voice of the woman in striped socks,
who now enquired if they were ever to begin their walk.

'Yes! Coming—right now!' Caan called, then, in an
aside to Darynthe, that lopsided smile flashing wickedly at
her, 'Of course, if you'd prefer to wait until my elderly
uncle's recovered . . . if you think you won't be able to
keep up with *me* . . .'

His bold blue eyes travelled the curvaceous length of
her, from the casually cut fair hair, over her square, vivid
face and down to the splendidly proportioned long legs,
pausing there, as if to assess their potential for strenuous
exercise. Then he turned away to round up the rest of his
party.

Darynthe's warm cheeks were the result of combined
embarrassment and pique. So he didn't think she was
capable of keeping up with him . . . a typical, superior
male, he thought that a quiet amble with an elderly man
would be more in line with her capabilities.

Always stubborn to the point of mulishness, Darynthe
could not resist the implied challenge. Quite forgetting
the doubts she had expressed to her aunt, of her ability to
keep up with experienced fellwalkers, she determined that
wherever Caan Lorimer went, she would be literally right
on his heels. It was a decision she was eventually to regret.

The walk, Caan told his little group of followers, was to
take the form of a circular walk around Loughrigg Fell.
With Caan in the lead, they set out in a rough crocodile,
studded boots clattering on the pavements, as they made
for their first objective, the parish church.

'This is not a strenuous walk,' Caan turned to explain to his hearers, though Darynthe felt sure the mocking gleam in his blue eyes was directed at her. 'We try to stop at points of interest along the way, and if you have any questions . . .'

The shrug of broad shoulders denoted an open invitation.

The rest of the walkers seemed to be in parties, or pairs, and it seemed natural enough for Caan to fall into step with Darynthe . . . natural to him, she supposed, but she wished he would not single her out in this way. The constant need to keep up her guard, in accordance with her self-imposed resolve, would take any pleasure and relaxation from the walk.

'Have *you* any questions?' he asked her.

Perhaps if she were rude enough, he would be put off, would leave her alone, she thought.

'Yes, I do have a question,' she said, her voice hard and bright. 'How is it that a fit, relatively young man has nothing better to do than ramble about the countryside?'

Her emphasis on the words 'relatively young' was deliberately calculated to imply just the opposite.

'Don't you have a proper job?' she asked.

For a second his eyes narrowed, but he seemed determined not to take offence at the deliberate slight.

'Did it occur to you that this might be my annual holiday?' he asked mildly.

Darynthe felt slightly foolish, but she wasn't going to admit it . . . or to back down.

'Well, is it? Your holiday, I mean?' she challenged him. 'No.'

'There you are, then,' she said triumphantly. 'I was right. So you don't have a proper job?'

He surveyed her quizzically.

'Why this sudden flattering interest in me?' he drawled. 'A few minutes ago you couldn't turn me off fast enough.'

'I wasn't aware that you were ever "turned on",' she said unwisely, realising too late, from the gleam in his eyes, that her meaning was open to misinterpretation.

She was rescued from her own folly by their arrival at the church.

'St Mary the Virgin ... nineteenth century, neo-Gothic,' Caan recited briefly. 'But we won't spend too long here. I know you're all longing to be out on the fells in this lovely weather ... and you can come here any time to look around for yourselves. But one feature is worthy of mention, because it relates to a local custom, which some of you may witness some day ... the Rushbearing Ceremony, held here in July.' Briefly, he pointed out the salient details of a mural, painted directly on to the wall plaster of the interior. 'It was executed by an evacuated school of art, during the Second World War. For those of you who like statistics,' he added, 'the painting is twenty-six feet long and twelve feet high ... it contains sixty-two almost life-size figures, depicting scenes from the rush-bearing procession.'

As they moved out into the sunlight once more, Darynthe hoped that this short intermission would have diverted Caan's attention from their recent conversation, that perhaps he would fall into discussion with other members of the party. But, to her annoyance, he seemed strangely persistent in his attentions to her.

'In answer to your question,' he said, as they left the churchyard and walked through the adjoining park, 'no, I don't suppose mine is what *you* would term a proper job.'

'I don't see how you can possibly tell what *my* thoughts would be on the subject,' she objected.

'Oh, but I can.'

He allowed her to precede him over a narrow bridge which crossed the river.

'You see, you've made it quite obvious, right from the very first moment of our acquaintance, that you're determined to think badly of me.' He paused, then, 'He must have been a swine.'

'Who must?'

'The chap who turned you against all men. Oh, don't bother to deny it. The anti-chauvinist syndrome is all too familiar.'

'I'm not surprised *you* recognise it,' Darynthe snapped, her full lips drawn into a firm line. 'I don't suppose for one moment that I'm the only woman who's been deceived by a man. Knowing men, I don't doubt there are hundreds ... thousands of the poor girls. I expect you've encountered quite a few?'

'Encountered, yes, but don't run off with the idea that I was *responsible* for any of them.'

'You mean *you* don't make a habit of breaking hearts?' Darynthe said, disbelief in her tone of voice.

She almost had to shout, for now they were following the course of the river, a teeming torrent, fed from the tumbling becks in the hills above.

Caan looked at her, his blue eyes grave. 'Not if I can help it.' Then he gave that engaging, lop-sided grin. 'I would far rather make *one* woman happy.'

His smile played havoc with Darynthe's nerve ends and she had no doubt that he was capable of making some woman very happy indeed ... for a short space of time. But what then?

In her book, no man was trustworthy; and as for his ridiculous claim that he had never broken any hearts, it was unlikely that a man of his age had not experienced the friendship of many women. Somewhere along the way there must have been one or two to regret the moment when their relationship had ended.

She wondered, with a curiosity that surprised her, what it would be like to be made love to by Caan Lorimer, but banished the thought almost before it had formulated. She didn't want to know.

Their path turned left now, through a gate beside a cattle grid, the more daring, Darynthe among them, preferring to teeter precariously from rung to rung of the grid. Ahead of them, a well-made path curved upward, in a fairly stiff ascent, through a farmyard.

Just past the farm, an iron ladder stile surmounted a drystone wall and Caan stood on the far side, to assist the women.

Disdaining his proffered hand, Darynthe scrambled over too hastily. The stud of her boot caught awkwardly on a rung and she would have fallen but for his prompt action. Blue eyes stared mockingly into confused green ones as she rested against him, her face only inches from his, her heart thuddingly aware of the proximity.

'Pride goes before a fall,' he quoted softly, for her ears

alone, setting her on her feet once more. 'And I have a notion, Miss Browne with an "e", that your pride has a few more tumbles ahead of it.'

Furious with him and with herself, Darynthe strode on, tackling the next stretch of the walk at a punishing pace, determined to leave him behind. But once through the next obstacle, a narrow slate stile and over a small stream on to the open fell, she was forced to wait for the rest of the party, realising that she had no idea which direction to take.

'Well, it's a good way of letting off steam,' Caan observed, as he overtook her, his stride enviably effortless, his breathing undisturbed.

Darynthe was all too aware of her own flushed, moist face and gasping lungs, and literally had no breath with which to utter a retort, as they carried straight on up to a cairn. Here, mercifully, Caan called a halt, to allow his party a breather.

From the cairn it was possible to look back over their route and to obtain a good view of Ambleside, and of the upper reaches of Windermere.

Once again, as if by accident, Caan appeared at Darynthe's elbow.

'It's as well, when on a stiff climb, to take short steps,' he observed casually. 'It helps your breathing too, if you whistle or sing.'

She glared at him. Whistle, indeed! Did he take her for some kind of fool, to be gulled by a schoolboy's trick like that?

'I'll save my breath for walking, if you don't mind,' she said irritably.

He raised his eyebrows.

'Just as you please, of course.'

After the short respite, they moved on, down a dip in the fell and up a rise to the crags, where once again they paused, this time for the benefit of keen photographers, who took advantage of this opportunity to take snapshots of the lake, with its river-like character . . . and for the historians to exclaim over the square foundations, spread out below them, of the Roman fort of Galava.

To Darynthe's relief, their way lay steeply downward now, past a small tarn. She had not realised how unused she had become to walking and she was glad to note that

Caan now seemed to feel he should converse with others in the party, leaving her to conserve her energies for the walk. She had received quite enough of his disturbing attentions and ridiculous advice. After all, she thought, he wasn't the proper guide . . . only a substitute.

For a while she was only conscious of putting one foot before another, watching the feet immediately in front, as they followed the course of drystone walls and passed through gates. Both heels were beginning to chafe and she had a shrewd suspicion that a blister was forming on one.

On Loughrigg Terrace itself there were several seats, and Caan suggested that here the party might eat their packed lunch.

This was what one came walking for, Darynthe thought, quite content to sit alone and munch the delicious cheese and tomato rolls her aunt had provided . . . to reach a viewpoint and sit, absorbed in the beauty of nature, to watch the wind stirring the bright green tracery of the larches, already starting to clothe the woods beneath them. Young lambs, enjoying their first taste of life, looked from above like badly wound bundles of wool. Only nature was capable of true serenity, Darynthe thought, but perhaps, for a while, she might borrow from its tranquillity.

She was not left for long in peaceful contemplation. A slight protesting sound from the wooden bench upon which she sat indicated that someone had come to join her and reluctantly, she turned away from the view, to find Caan at her side, his bright, wide-apart eyes . . . the squint lines of an outdoor man at their corners . . . watching her expressive face.

'Enjoying it?'

'I was.' She left the implied 'until you came along' to lie uneasily between them.

A slight tightening of his lips showed that he had taken the point. He rose.

'Ready to go on?'

His tone was suddenly brusque, and though she had deliberately engineered it, the disappearance of his friendly manner left Darynthe feeling curiously bereft.

She was appalled to discover how much her legs had stiffened up, during even such a short rest. She knew this would ease as they moved on, but before long she was limping from another cause, the pain in her right heel.

'Blister?' one of the other women asked sympathetically.

Darynthe nodded. ' 'Fraid so.'

Caan overheard the exchange.

'Let me see. Sit on that rock over there,' he ordered, his voice cool, commanding.

Darynthe tried to protest, but for once he was standing no nonsense, and to her humiliation she found herself lifted like a child on to a rocky outcrop, while hard, sure fingers removed her boots and socks.

'I don't suppose you thought to bring any plasters?' he enquired.

She shook her head.

His well-defined brows lifted in exasperation and he removed his rucksack, delving into its capacious depths.

'Lesson One,' he informed his hearers. 'Never go fell-walking without the proper equipment.'

Darynthe felt still more mortified.

'Why don't you tie a label on me, marked "Exhibit One"?' she snapped.

Deft fingers anointed her sore heel and applied a plaster.

'Let me see the other one, while I'm at it,' he commanded.

'No, really, there's no need. It's perfectly all right.'

She was inexplicably afraid of the insidious enjoyment which had stolen over her at the touch of his hands.

'I'll be the judge of that.'

He inspected her other heel.

'As I thought! Do yourself a favour next time and buy yourself some boots that fit you. There's far too much space in these . . . they're bound to slip and slide.'

'They're not mine,' she said, unwisely, as it turned out, for it was the prelude to yet another lecture.

'Never borrow boots, always have your own . . . break them in to suit *your* feet. No two people have feet the same.'

While he spoke, he had treated the second foot and put back the offending boot.

'No more walking for you today,' he ordered.

'What do you mean?'

Surely he wasn't proposing to carry her? She bristled at the totally unacceptable idea.

'What I say. When we get down to the Ambleside to Keswick road, you're taking the bus back.'

'I most certainly am not!' Her eyes flashed green fire.

'If you don't,' he told her grimly, 'you'll be crippled for a week at least . . . longer if those blisters turn septic.'

To her fury, he insisted on taking her arm for the rest of the descent to the main road. Forced to accept his help, Darynthe submitted in a mood of silent, prickly hostility. But she had to admit to herself that even this short distance was fraught with pain. She would never have managed the remainder of the trek, around Rydal Water and back to Ambleside.

'I don't know how long you'll have to wait for the bus,' Caan told her. 'Have you any money?'

'Of course.'

What kind of an impractical idiot did he take her for? Probably he treated all women as feckless, irresponsible creatures.

'Please don't bother to wait,' she added stiffly. 'Believe it or not, but I am quite capable of catching a bus on my own.'

Nevertheless, she felt a pang of loneliness as she watched the rest of the party dwindle in her sight, led by that confident, stalwart figure, well-carried head and shoulders visible above all the others.

'My, you're back early!' her aunt exclaimed, as Darynthe limped painfully in through the rear entrance of the guest-house. 'Old Jack must have set a cracking pace for once. Did you have a good day?'

'No, I did not,' Darynthe said emphatically. 'It was not old Jack, it was his bossy, overbearing, know-it-all nephew, Caan Lorimer . . . and he did set a cracking pace, and I'm back early because I have blisters, and the hateful beast put plasters on them and then made me catch the bus!'

Then, to her own horror, she burst into tears.

Ten minutes later, her boots removed and a cup of tea in her hand, she was able to review the day more realistically.

'I suppose there were some good moments,' she admitted, recalling that time of serene contemplation on the Terrace. 'But I wish the guide *had* been your elderly, portly Jack.'

'It doesn't sound to me as if Mr Lorimer was *too* unkind to you,' Ann Forster remarked. 'Some guides wouldn't have bothered to enquire about your feet . . . or sensibly send you home.'

'Bossily send me home, you mean,' Darynthe muttered. She was still seething at the embarrassment of being treated like the tyro that honesty told her she was.

Ann laughed.

'I can see there's no defending Mr Lorimer to you! A pity, because he appears to be such a nice man . . . and he does seem to take an interest in you.'

'I don't want his interest . . . or any man's!'

Darynthe met her aunt's shrewd brown eyes squarely.

'You're afraid of him, aren't you?' Ann accused. 'Afraid that he'll penetrate that chain mail your heart's encased in. Subconsciously you must be attracted to him, my dear, or you wouldn't fear his effect upon you.'

Darynthe looked at her aunt in appalled silence. Was it true? Could her aunt possibly be right? *Was* that the effect Caan Lorimer had upon her . . . was that the catalyst which had made her pulse race with irrational fear from the very first moment of their acquaintance? She had sworn never to let another man come close to her emotionally; but wasn't her violent antipathy to Caan Lorimer in particular an unusually strong reaction . . . a tribute to that powerful aura of his, his flagrant masculinity . . . and some other indefinable attribute, which eluded definition and puzzled her . . . something in his character, his personality, which owed nothing to his undoubted sexual attraction.

She looked at her aunt, her green eyes wide in terrified appeal.

'I don't want to get involved,' she whispered, 'with him, or with anyone else. I . . . I wish I need never see him again . . . but this town is so small . . .'

As she had foreseen, her wish was doomed to disappointment . . . but sooner than she had feared.

'There's a visitor for you, Darynthe,' Ann Forster told
her niece after dinner. There was a note of satisfaction in
her voice. 'Fortunately, the guests are either out or
watching T.V., so I've put him in the lounge.'

'Him?' Darynthe didn't really need to ask the question.
She knew only one man in Ambleside. 'Couldn't you have
told him I was out, or something?'

'No,' Ann said firmly, 'I couldn't. If you're so determined to reject his friendship, you must make your own
excuses. Personally, I can't see what you've got against
the man.'

'That he *is* a man.' Darynthe's reply was bitter.

Ann looked at her niece, exasperation in her pleasant
face.

'You can't lump people into categories, Darynthe.
There are decent men, just as there are wrong'uns. Why not
give him a chance, love? Judge him on his own merits. Don't
spend the rest of your life using Mark Little as a yardstick.'

'Since Caan's here, and you won't send him away, I'll
have to see what he wants,' Darynthe said. 'But I shall get
rid of him as quickly as possible.'

Leaving her aunt to shake her head in despair, she
stalked into the residents' lounge.

Caan Lorimer's tall, broad figure dominated the small,
comfortable room, and though Darynthe herself was of no
mean stature, she felt diminished by his physical presence.
He had remained standing while he waited and his blue
eyes met hers challengingly, as she paused in the doorway.

'How are the blisters?' he asked, before she could speak.

'Sore . . . but I'll live.'

She remained poised in the doorway, deliberately not
sitting down, lest he took it as an invitation to seat himself.

'Was that all you wanted?' she asked pointedly, her
voice coolly dismissive.

'No, damn it, that was not all I wanted.' His out-thrust
chin was assertive, determined. 'Come in, shut the door
and sit down!'

'Charmingly put,' she murmured, but nevertheless, something in her responded to his air of command and almost before she realised that she had done so, she had obeyed him, perching on the extreme edge of a chair, as far away from him as possible.

But it seemed that this too did not suit him. A forceful hand grasped her wrist, pulling her from the chair and depositing her, none too gently, upon the two-seater settee, where he promptly joined her.

Again that primeval sense of warning, the knowledge that, against her will, something in her responded to his male dominance stirred deep inside her and she could feel her body vibrating to the panic-stricken beat of her heart.

His fingers shaped the curve of her cheek, forcing her to look at him, his eyes on her in a deeply personal appraisal.

'It's time someone talked to you like a Dutch uncle.'

Oh no, Darynthe groaned inwardly. She had received enough lectures to last her a lifetime. Aloud, trying to make a jest of it, she said:

'Thank you, but I've just been through a session with my "Dutch aunt".'

'So she agrees with me,' Caan observed with satisfaction.

'How can I possibly know if she agrees with you, when I haven't the least idea what you're talking about?' Darynthe said crossly. But she was afraid that she knew all too well what Caan Lorimer wanted to discuss.

'Why don't you ever relax?' Caan said, one large hand pushing her firmly against the back of the settee. The piece of furniture was so small that it was impossible for her to avoid the brush of his thigh.

How could she relax? Darynthe thought frantically. Oh, why didn't her aunt, one of the guests ... anyone ... come in, release her from this perilous situation, and why did Caan Lorimer have to interfere, be so domineering? He needn't think she was going to let him ... or any man ... rule her life. What she did, what she thought, was none of his business.

'Who *was* this man, and what did he do to you?' Caan asked bluntly. It was as if there had been no interval between their conversation on the fells and this moment.

Resentment flared up within her.

'What the hell has it got to do with you? Why should I tell you the details of my private life?'

'You make it my business, when you treat me as if I were as bad as this rotter who turned you into a man-hater. If you like, you can say I'm standing up for myself ... and for men in general.'

'Men in general!' Darynthe's enticing upper lip curled in a sneer. 'Men in general make me sick!'

'And what about the individual?' Caan asked.

'The individual?'

'Yes, the poor sap who doesn't fit your sweeping gener-alisation, the good guy ... the one you're going to meet some day ... that you'll drive away by your bigoted atti-tude.'

'B—bigoted?'

Darynthe's wide eyes were even more enormous with the sense of outrage she felt. He had the nerve to call her bigoted, but he himself was prejudiced ... he was pre-judging her. How could he know what she had suffered ... what she still suffered sometimes, in the depths of the night, when her half-awakened senses clamoured for something, she scarcely knew what ... only knowing that an ingredient was lacking in her life, something that she had looked to Mark to supply, until she had found out the depths of his deception.

'Hasn't anyone tried to tell you that not *all* men are rotten?' Caan persisted.

'Practically everyone I know,' she said bitterly. 'It's easy to preach, when you're not the one who's been hurt.'

'But they can't *all* be wrong ... your friends ...'

'I don't care who's right and who's wrong,' Darynthe told him wearily. 'I just know what's right for *me*.'

'And you think it's right for you to go through life as an embittered man-hater?'

She stared down at her clasped hands, lips set mulishly, refusing to answer him ... unable to answer him, for sometimes a small, swiftly smothered inner voice asked the same question.

With a sound of exasperation he stood up, pulling her with him, then marched her across the room, to where an oval mirror hung above the fireplace. Firmly but gently he turned her to face the mirror, then stood at her shoulder.

'Look in the mirror, Darynthe,' he commanded. 'Look at yourself.'

Reluctantly she raised her eyes to confront her own reflection, square face flushed with resentment, green eyes enhanced by the bright emerald sweater-dress she had donned for the cool evening.

'What do you see?' he demanded.

'Myself, of course.'

'Yourself,' he agreed. 'Study yourself, Darynthe. Study yourself closely.'

Reaching over her shoulder, with one finger he outlined the square, attractive face, the determined chin. Darynthe quivered as his hand toyed with the silky mane of hair which framed her vivid face.

'Those great green eyes of yours were meant to shine with joy.' Fleetingly, he touched her lips. 'Your mouth is meant for kissing.' His voice became husky, caressing. 'You're beautiful, Darynthe, but it's more than looks. You have a kind of sparkle, when you forget to be miserable . . . a magnetism that's going to attract men to you, wherever you go. How long can you go on fighting them off, scowling at them, until those cat's eyes of yours are narrowed and bad-tempered, that sweet mouth sulky and drooping?'

Mesmerised by the sound of his deep voice, the touch of his hands, his warm breath fanning her cheek, Darynthe stared obediently at herself in the mirror. Was she really beautiful? she wondered. Mark had told her she was, but Mark was a liar.

As though released from a sorcerer's spell, she turned upon Caan.

'What is it to you how I look, what I do with my life?'

'I worship beauty,' he said simply, 'beauty in nature, landscape and in people . . . and I hate waste. You're wasting yourself, your youth, your beauty.'

'Wasting them! Wasting them, because I'm not bestowing them on some insensitive man who only sees one purpose for them?'

Darynthe choked on her anger, now almost a physical lump in her throat.

'Yours is a typically male attitude! You men, you ... you think women were made just for your pleasure. You seem to forget we're people, with our own rights, not "things" for you to ...'

'Be quiet!' His deep voice lashed at her.

Shocked into silence, she obeyed. No man had ever spoken to her like that.

'Don't give me any speeches on women's rights. It's totally unnecessary. Of course women have rights ... but so have men. Yes, I do think that women were made for man's pleasure ... just as I think man was made to please women. What makes you think it's a one-way thing?'

His voice softened seductively.

'Have you never felt pleasure in a man's arms, or were you just a passive "object" allowing yourself to be used?'

'No ... no ... no!' Darynthe was close to tears. 'I was not an "object". Yes, I have felt pleasure, only I call it love, which seems to be something men don't understand. To men, pleasure is physical fulfilment, the satisfaction of their baser natures. I want to be loved because I'm me, not because I'm a body with two arms, two legs, two breasts ... and whatever else it is that men look for when they look at a woman.'

'You forgot the head,' he told her gravely ... a gravity belied by a betraying twitch of his lips.

Despite herself a bubble of laughter escaped with the sob.

'Don't make fun of me! You don't understand. You're like all the rest ...'

'I disagree. If I were like all the rest, as you put it, wouldn't I be employing their methods? Instead of reasoning with you—which, incidentally, doesn't seem to be any more effective—you'd be in my arms right now, receiving a practical demonstration of how it should be between a man and a woman.'

'You see! You see!' She was almost hysterical. 'You *do* think that would solve everything.'

Caan led her back to the settee.

'Sit down!'

It was quietly said, but his manner brooked no denial
She did so; all will to resist had fled. She felt confused,
unreal. What was she doing in this room, with this man,
almost a total stranger, letting him talk to her in this ...
this *intimate* way. She felt as if she were in the middle of
some strange nightmare, trying to beat her way through
an impenetrable barrier.

Caan took her face between his hands, a long tremor
invading her body at the warmth, the intimacy of the
gesture.

'Darynthe, I *do* understand. I haven't lived thirty-eight
years without learning something about women.'

So he *was* experienced, she thought, like all the rest. The
thought should have filled her with triumph, but it didn't.

'I realise that women expect more of a relationship than
the average man ... that they want to be mentally and
spiritually committed before they'll give themselves to a
man ... unless they're promiscuous. But you can't separate the physical from love, Darynthe. They are two halves
of the same apple. There has to be physical attraction
between a man and a woman, from the very beginning, if
the mental and spiritual affinity is to grow.'

She opened her mouth to tell him that she knew all this,
that this was not the battleground upon which she was
fighting her own personal war, but he swept on remorse-
lessly, intent on making his point.

'Did he frighten you, this other man of yours? You
mustn't ever be afraid of the physical side of love,
Darynthe.' His blue eyes softened, and his fingers moved
down to caress her throat.

'But I'm not ... I'm not!'

She denied the accusation strenuously. Did he think she
was frigid? The very idea that he might believe that of her
was humiliating.

He seemed unconvinced.

'Your fear shows in your every reaction to a man's
touch. I wish I could lay hands on the swine who's done
this to you.'

Tormented by the implication of his words, dizzied by
conflicting emotions and still weary from the day's un-
accustomed exertions, Darynthe lost her temper.

'Shut up! *Will* you shut up! Suppose *you* just listen for a change? I'm not an ignorant child. I'm twenty-one, and ... and I'm not frigid, which is what you seem to be implying. I don't intend to tell you about my fiancé ... what happened was between him and me and it had nothing to do with the physical side of our relationship.'

But was that strictly true? Always painfully honest with herself, even as she spoke the words, she knew it was not the whole truth. Wasn't it the fact that Mark had been married, had physically possessed another woman, which had appalled her romantic nature? Because she was uncertain of the veracity of her words, she spoke with assumed assurance.

'I'm not afraid of physical love, or of you ... or of any man. I just don't ...'

'Aren't you, Darynthe ... aren't you really?'

The provocative tone of his voice, the question, filled her with panic. She was aware of danger, aware that her words could be construed as a challenge.

There was a moment of charged intensity, before he said:

'I'm tempted to demand that you prove that assertion.'

'B-but you won't?'

There was a cloudy gleam in the blue eyes, which she understood only too clearly, had seen in other men's eyes. At the thought that he might be contemplating kissing her, the nerves in the lower part of her body fluttered, but she met his eyes squarely, defying him. The look they exchanged was long, deep and infinitely disturbing. Then the spell was broken, as Caan rose from the settee, looking down at her with that oddly twisted smile which gave character to a face otherwise too uniformly handsome.

'I shan't demand anything of you, Darynthe, until you're ready to give it of your own free will.'

Overwhelming relief was tinged with a curious sense of deflation.

'You ... you're not going to k-kiss me?'

He shook his head.

'Not until *you* want me to.'

She gathered the tattered shreds of her pride, rising the better to outface him.

'Well, that will be never . . . do you hear me? I shall never want you to kiss me.'

'I wonder,' he said softly, blue eyes half closed now, sleepy, seductive. He seemed bent upon provoking her.

'I mean it,' she cried, desperate with the need to convince him . . . to convince herself?

'And yet I think that if I tried to kiss you now, you might put up a fight at first, but you wouldn't resist for long.'

He made the statement with what she considered to be odious assurance. The vain, complacent, bigheaded . . . Did he really think he was that irresistible, that she was so weak, so easily conquered?

'You're starved for affection, did you know that?' Caan said softly. 'You *need* love, Darynthe.'

She backed away, putting the width of the room between them.

'Don't you dare . . . don't you dare!'

'Oh, I *dare*,' he said, voice and smile still mocking her. 'But I don't want to.'

'Y-you don't?' she said, only half believing him.

'No. I never bestow my favours where they aren't wanted.'

His favours! The typical male arrogance of the man!

'That's just as well,' she told him, her voice icy, 'because they never will be wanted . . . not by me.'

'I think we've covered all that ground.' He sounded suddenly, utterly bored. 'I'll say goodnight, Darynthe. I think we understand each other now.' He sketched her a derisive salute. 'Until we meet again.'

'I never want to set eyes on you again!' she hissed. She was bewildered by the turmoil which possessed her . . . anger, frustration, depression, longing, chagrin. Which was uppermost?

'Never!' she repeated.

'But you will see me again, Darynthe. Oh yes, you'll see me.'

The door closed quietly and she was alone at last, as she had desired. But there was no peace now in solitude. All her self-assurance, her certainty had been swept away. She had been so sure of her future course, the pattern that

her life would follow. Now she was certain of nothing . . .
not even the present state of her feelings towards Caan
Lorimer.

CHAPTER THREE

IRRITATINGLY, Darynthe found it quite impossible to put
Caan out of her mind, to dismiss the memory of their
disturbing conversation.

As she went about her tasks at the Daffodil, she found
his words repeating themselves over and over, in a dreary
litany.

'Bigoted . . . wasting your youth, your beauty . . . your
fear shows in your every reaction . . . you *need* love.'

Uppermost, however, was her resentment of his accusation of frigidity . . . all the more so because she feared it
might be true . . . now. Once she had believed that, with
the right man, she would be capable of deep passion, of
selfless, joyful giving. But Mark had destroyed that confidence.

Though it was too late now, she found herself imagining
the cool ripostes she could have made to Caan's provocative remarks, the dignified aplomb with which she might
have discouraged him. She should have made it quite clear
by her speech and by her attitude that persistence on his
part would be of no avail.

Yet, as the days passed and he did not redeem his promise to seek her out, she felt a growing sense of chagrin. It
was all very well to determine to resist all male advances,
but how could one resist a challenge which did not exist?
She knew that she ought to feel relief, but, contrarily, she
found herself hoping for another opportunity to do battle
with him. Only because, she assured herself, she felt that
Caan had completely misunderstood her and she longed
to justify herself, to state her case, her reason for her distaste for men, logically and clearly, without any of the
tension and turmoil of their former meetings.

'That nice Mr Lorimer hasn't called again,' Ann

Forster observed one morning, as they were tidying bed-rooms. 'I rather thought we'd be seeing a lot of him.' She looked suspiciously at Darynthe's averted face. 'You didn't say anything that might have put him off, I suppose?'

'Yes, I did,' Darynthe said defiantly. 'And it seems to have worked, doesn't it?' she added, wondering why she did not feel the satisfaction this outcome ought to have caused.

She had been wondering what to do with her next full day off. She dared not spend it roaming around Ambleside and its environs, for fear of encountering Caan Lorimer. He had not sought her out, so she certainly did not want it to appear as though she was engineering another meeting.

'I think I'll go over to Windermere on the ferry,' she told her aunt, when Ann enquired how she intended to spend her time.

'All alone?'

'Of course. I prefer my own company.'

It was true, she told herself defiantly, trying to banish from her memory, the times when pleasures shared had been pleasures doubled.

Determinedly mustering up her former enthusiasm for the hours of freedom ahead, Darynthe strode briskly the three-quarters of a mile to Waterhead, where the River Brathay carried the tumbling, accumulated waters of rivers and becks into Windermere itself.

Windermere ... the expanse of water seemed impressively vast to Darynthe, the surrounding mountains dignified in their apparent inaccessibility, almost like heaven, offering a challenge that was irresistible and which she hoped soon to meet.

She chose a seat on the upper deck of the ferry, the better to enjoy the passing scenery. A more glorious environment she could not imagine. On her right the mountains, on her left the landscaped gardens of large houses sloped down to the water ... many of the houses having their own private piers and landing stages; bays and promontories bustled with smart yachts and other craft.

As the ferry made its unhurried journey, quarrelsome, squalling gulls kept pace, taking food from the hands of the passengers.

Darynthe lingered a while at the landing stage, to watch the steamer leave with its new consignment of passengers.

From there it was almost a two-mile walk into the town, up a very long, very steep hill, running between shops, grey, slate-built houses, boarding houses and cafés. She took her time . . . the whole day was hers, wandering in and out of any shop which took her fancy.

She was greatly drawn to the rural craft shops, and in one such shop, possessed by a mood of affectionate gratitude, she purchased a beaten copper pendant for her aunt.

As she left the shop, tucking purse and gift into her handbag, she almost collided with a figure barring her path, and looking up to apologise, she met the bright, amused eyes of Caan Lorimer.

There was no justice, she reflected bitterly. She had come here on purpose to avoid such an encounter and this was the result . . . her reward.

'F-fancy seeing you,' she said tritely.

She moved to one side, intending to pass on, but he barred her way.

'I told you we should meet again. Now that we have, how about lunching with me?'

He certainly didn't beat about the bush, she thought. Nothing could be blunter, or more direct, than his invitation.

'Oh, I . . .'

About to refuse, Darynthe caught back the words. Wasn't this the opportunity she had wanted . . . a chance to talk in civilised surroundings, where Caan could not overpower her, confuse her by the mere aura of his personality?

'Very well,' she acceded.

To her dismay, he immediately tucked a proprietorial hand under her elbow, steering her towards the nearest large hotel.

'What have you been doing with yourself?' he enquired.

'Helping my aunt. Wh-what about you?'

She didn't really want to know what had kept him from seeking her out, she told herself. It was merely a polite attempt to return his enquiry.

'More guided walks,' he said. 'My uncle didn't recover too quickly from his bout of 'flu. But he's all right now, so I thought I'd give myself a day off.'

A day off . . . from what? she wondered cynically. By his own admission, he had no job . . . he could scarcely call filling in for his uncle an onerous task. She was filled with a tinge of regret that a man like this should be wasting his undoubted potential in idleness.

They entered the restrained elegance of the hotel and at a glance from Caan, an attentive waiter indicated a table for two in a secluded corner. Darynthe would have preferred something a little less intimate, a place where she would be less conscious of Caan's proximity, but even so early in the season, the dining room was almost full.

The waiter having pulled out their chairs, they were left to study the menu.

Somehow, with Caan's appearance, Darynthe's mounting appetite had vanished. She chose a salad, but merely toyed with it, hoping he would not notice her lack of enthusiasm. It was a vain hope. She might have known, she thought exasperatedly, that he would not miss any opportunity to lecture her.

'You're not eating,' he observed, making heavy inroads upon the substantial meal he had ordered for himself . . . how could he afford to eat like that? 'A big girl like you can't exist on fresh air alone.'

Darynthe seethed. She was tall, but she was slender. He made her sound like an ungainly Amazon!

'I never eat much at lunchtime. I have my main meal at night.'

But he was already off on another tack.

'Have you thought about what I said to you the other evening?' he enquired abruptly.

The entire conversation had repeated itself monotonously in her brain ever since, but she wrinkled her brow as though in an effort of recollection.

'I don't think I recall . . .'

'Rubbish! You remember very well. Have you come to your senses yet? Got over your little fit of pique . . . decided to start treating men like members of the human race again?'

Pique! Little fit of pique! She felt like hurling the mangled remains of her salad at him. How dared he attribute such petty motives to her? What did he know of the anguish she had suffered?

'You . . . you don't know what you're talking about . . . just because I don't swoon every time you appear, don't choose to involve myself . . .'

Where were all her rehearsed, reasoned arguments now, her cool self-justification? She was stammering, confused, resenting his inquisition.

Caan sipped at a glass of water, regarding her thoughtfully over its rim.

'You definitely need someone to take you in hand,' he said at last. 'Someone to show you just how fine a relationship between a man and a woman can be.'

'I most certainly do not!'

She realised, from the surprised, staring faces around her, that she was shouting. She lowered her voice.

'I know what I expected . . . needed from such a relationship, but what I wanted just doesn't exist.'

'Perhaps you expect too much,' he remarked between mouthfuls.

'Yes . . . too much from a man.' Her tone was bitter.

His blue gaze was uncomfortably penetrating, as though he sought out the innermost recesses of her mind, tested the truth of her convictions.

'I wonder?' he murmured.

Stubbornly Darynthe kept her eyes on her coffee cup, abstractedly stirring the contents, long after the action had ceased to be a necessity. She refused to question him, to ask just what perplexed him.

But of his own accord, he decided to enlighten her.

'I can't help wondering about you . . . whether you really have been hurt, badly treated, or whether you're just one of these ultra-perfectionists, someone who would find a flaw in a saint.'

'Then you'll just have to wonder,' she snapped, downing the remains of her coffee in one swift, angry movement. 'Whatever I told you, you'd be bound to take a typically male attitude about it. But I don't intend to tell you anything. As I told you before, it's none of your business.'

He rose with her.

'And as I told you before, I'm making it my business. For your own sake, someone has to sort you out, and . . .'

'Why you? What gives you the right . . .?' Unknowingly, she had raised her voice once more.

'We can't discuss this here.' Abruptly, he interrupted her indignant flow of words. 'Come on, I'll drive you back to Ambleside.'

He paid the bill and followed her into the street.

Darynthe glared at him, wishing he'd stop ordering her about, trying to run her life.

'I'm not ready to go back yet. I've got the whole day off and I intend to go back the same way I came . . . on the ferry.'

'There's nothing else to do here,' he said, with positive assurance. 'You'd be bored within ten minutes of my leaving you.'

The conceit of him! she thought. Why should he imagine his company was a talisman against boredom . . . and besides, how did he know what she had or hadn't done?

Yet, somehow, she found herself sitting beside him in the little white car, one of a line of slow-moving vehicles en route for Ambleside.

Darynthe had expected Caan to be a fast, impatient driver, edgy with the necessity of forming part of this leisurely procession of sightseers, who were more concerned with the scenery about them than with reaching their destination. But he seemed quite content, whistling tunelessly under his breath, his hands lightly grasping the steering wheel, hands which against her will drew her attention . . . broad, tanned and strong, the fingers slightly spatulate, nails short and well tended. They didn't *look* like the hands of an effete, lazy man.

She had expected an immediate continuation of their discussion, but it was not until he pulled the car off the road, on a slight rise overlooking the lake, that he turned to her once more.

'I thought you were taking me back to Ambleside,' she said, immediately on the defensive.

'There's plenty of time' Caan said lazily, stretching out his arms and, as if by accident, allowing one to rest along the back of her seat. He was not quite touching her, but he might as well have been, for the electrifying effect the movement had upon her senses.

She stiffened perceptibly and heard his soft chuckle.

'Relax, Darynthe . . . enjoy the view.'

She tried to take his advice, thinking that, fully occupied as she had been in the last few days, she had not noticed the imperceptible change from spring to summer. The fells, the gardens overlooking the lake were newly, lusciously green. There was plenty to admire. But it was no use.

'How can I relax,' she asked him peevishly, 'When I know you're sitting there just waiting for another opportunity to lecture me? Why are you so curious about my . . . my . . .'

'Because I'm interested in *you*,' he said calmly.

'M-me? But you hardly know me!'

Sometimes it isn't necessary to "know" people, not in the sense you mean. You can be acquainted with someone for years and yet feel no closer to them. But when I met you, up there . . .' He gestured vaguely in the general direction of Wrynose, 'I had a feeling of . . . of instant recognition, as if my whole life had been moving towards that point in time . . . our encounter part of some plan.'

'Rubbish,' Darynthe said deflatingly, forgetting that it was not so long since she had indulged in similarly romantic fantasies.

'Why is it rubbish?'

'Because . . . because . . .' she said in a rush, 'I don't believe in such things as love at first sight . . . not any more.'

'Who mentioned love?' he drawled.

A painful flush encompassed her.

'You . . . you did,' she stammered.

'Oh no!' He was odiously cool, in contrast to her own warm confusion. 'I was talking about chemistry, that moment of awareness . . .'

'What you're talking about,' she said bluntly, 'is sex.'

Anger and disappointment made her suddenly icy-cold. Just for a moment, she'd imagined that she had actually met a romantic man, the kind she had once believed existed.

'A physical attraction . . . that's all men think about, isn't it? Love as an emotion means nothing to them.'

'Now you're generalising again,' he told her. 'That may be true for some men, I won't deny it. But you have your priorities in the wrong order. There has to be an initial physical attraction for love to grow. You can't seriously tell me that you would fall in love with a man who didn't first attract you in some way?'

'Why not?' she said defensively. 'There's such a thing as affinity of mind . . . you know, shared interests.'

'Bunkum!' Caan demolished her theory with the one derisory comment. 'You can share affinity of mind, as you call it, common interests, with someone of your own sex.' He looked at her curiously. 'Is that all you expected of your ex-boy-friend? Is that what turned you off him? If he was any kind of a man, I bet he expected more than an intellectual relationship.'

Darynthe was steadily growing more furious.

'Of course that isn't all I expect. Of course I was attracted to Mark . . .'

'Mark, hmm? So that was the blighter's name.'

She ignored the interruption.

'So you can stop implying that I'm some kind of a frigid freak! I wanted all the things that marriage implies . . . wanted them desperately. But I also wanted to be able to respect and admire the man I married . . . to trust him, to . . . to be first with him . . .'

'Two-timed you, did he?'

She hesitated before answering him.

'I suppose you could call it that.'

Let him think that if he liked. After all, what did it matter?

'He must have been mad,' Caan said softly.

'Wh-what do you mean?'

His eyes were blatantly caressing.

'To risk losing such a lovely creature.' He leant closer and his warmth, his masculinity seemed to envelop her in an aura of trembling awareness. 'I told you that you were beautiful, Darynthe, didn't I?'

She shook her head, not denying his words, but the truth of them. She was not beautiful. She didn't want to be just beautiful in any man's eyes. She would rather be ugly, she tried to convince herself now, so that she might be admired for herself, her beauty of mind, of personality, rather than for her outer veneer, for physical attributes which were hers only by an accident of birth. And yet, despite herself, the knowledge that Caan thought her attractive was balm to her wounded heart . . . comforting but dangerous knowledge.

'P-please take me back to Ambleside,' she begged.

She didn't want to be alone with Caan like this, in the close confines of his car . . . to feel her resolve crumbling, melting before the warmth in those blue eyes. She would not give in to the physicality which she despised. She didn't know this man, or anything about him . . . didn't want to know. He might even be married, as Mark had been. He could have girl-friends by the score . . . with his looks and magnetic charm that would hardly be surprising.

He shot back a cuff and consulted his wristwatch, then nodded.

'Yes, we'll go. I promised your aunt I'd have you back by teatime.'

'My . . . my aunt? But when . . . how . . .?'

'I called at the Daffodil this morning and we had quite a chat. Mrs Forster told me where you'd gone.' He chuckled as if at a private joke. 'I was at Windermere before the ferry.'

So their meeting hadn't been a coincidence. He had followed her. No wonder he had seemed so sure that she had exhausted the possibilities of the town! It gave her an uneasy feeling to think that she had been watched, followed. His certainly seemed to be more than a casual interest . . . just what did he want, expect of her? The shock of his disclosure rendered her speechless for the remainder of the journey and outside the Daffodil, she slipped hastily from the car, eager to be alone with these new, disturbing reflections.

'Thanks for the lift,' she said.

'You're not getting rid of me that easily,' he informed her. 'I'm invited for tea.'

This was a conspiracy, she thought indignantly, between Caan Lorimer and her aunt. Ann Forster was deliberately throwing her into this man's company. What on earth did she hope to achieve by it?

Darynthe had hoped that her aunt's presence at the tea-table would act as a bar to any further discussion of her feelings, but she had reckoned without the call of duty, which kept her aunt busy, preparing the evening meal for the guests.

Darynthe fidgeted.

'I ought to be helping my aunt,' she said, seeking an excuse to escape this further tête-à-tête.

'She has a woman in, on your day off, doesn't she?' Caan asked.

'Yes, but . . .'

'There you are, then. You're not needed. Drink your tea.'

'All right,' she conceded defeat, 'But on one condition . . . that we don't talk any more about me. You can talk about anything else under the sun, but if you start on me again, I shall walk out and leave you!'

He laughed at her intensity, but nodded.

'Agreed. Well now, what shall we talk about? You said "anything under the sun". Would "sunrise" be appropriate, do you think?'

Teacup uplifted, Darynthe looked at him, green eyes wary, not catching his meaning.

'You can't be said to have seen Lakeland in all its moods if you haven't watched a sunrise,' he explained.

'Oh, that!' She dismissed the idea with a wave of her hand. 'I'd have to be up far too early.'

'Or not go to bed at all,' Caan suggested. He turned to Ann Forster, who had come in at that moment, to see that they had all they needed. 'Mrs Forster, would you have any objection to my taking Darynthe up Helvellyn, to see the sunrise?'

Ann Forster looked as surprised as Darynthe felt . . . but for a different reason.

'She doesn't need *my* permission, Mr Lorimer. She's over twenty-one, you know.'

They were talking above her head, as though she didn't

exist, and Darynthe's eyes deepened to the emerald which
betokened anger.

'You may not need my aunt's permission, Mr Lorimer,
but you certainly do need *my* agreement . . . and I wasn't
aware that I'd given it, or even that I'd been consulted!'

Caan turned towards her, outwardly apologetic, and
only Darynthe could see the amusement, the challenge in
the blue eyes.

'My apologies . . . please may I have the pleasure of
your company on Helvellyn, tonight?'

'T . . . tonight? But you said sunrise!'

He nodded.

'It's the custom to go up at night and sit on the mountain, waiting for the sun to come up.'

'Do go, dear,' Ann Forster urged. 'You'll enjoy it. It's a
never-to-be-forgotten experience.'

Between the two of them, Darynthe felt harassed,
cornered.

'But I'd be tired,' she objected. 'I'd be of no earthly use
to you in the morning.'

'You can sleep in,' Ann said blithely, unaware that
Darynthe was desperately seeking for an excuse to refuse.
'I can manage quite easily until lunchtime.'

Darynthe contemplated saying that she didn't want to
go, had no particular desire to see a sunrise. But she knew
such an excuse would sound utterly feeble . . . especially
as she constantly enthused to her aunt about her desire to
learn as much of her new surroundings as possible.

'Oh, very well, then,' she said, knowing that she
sounded as ungracious and unwilling as she felt.

But Caan did not seem offended.

'Right,' he said. 'I'll call for you at half-past eleven.
Wear warm clothing and bring a blanket. I'll provide a
hot Thermos.'

With a word of thanks to Ann for his tea, he was gone,
leaving Darynthe to confront her aunt.

'Why didn't you get me out of it?' she asked indignantly.
'You could tell I didn't want to go . . . at least, not with
him.'

'Well, you certainly couldn't make that climb alone,'
Ann defended herself, busily clearing away the tea things.

'It's no climb for a novice, even in daylight . . . and to my knowledge, no one else has offered to take you.'

As Darynthe moved to help her aunt, another thought occurred.

'Oh yes, and why did you tell him where I'd gone today? I was trying to avoid the wretched man and instead I end up spending nearly the entire day with him . . . and now the night as well!'

She flushed, as Ann laughed mischievously.

'Well, you know what I mean.'

Together they carried the crockery into the kitchen.

'I knew you'd be annoyed with me,' Ann admitted, 'but I'm not happy about this urge you have, constantly wanting to be alone. Oh, I know that occasionally everyone needs a little time to themselves, but not all the time. It's not healthy. It . . . it seems morbid to me.'

Darynthe smiled.

'I've no intention of becoming a recluse, if that's what you're afraid of. But I'm in no hurry to rush into a new relationship . . . in fact I don't suppose I shall ever get married now,' she said with an air of unconscious martyrdom.

Ann looked at her fondly.

'That's nonsense, and you'd know it, if you could see yourself from where I'm standing. You're an extremely attractive girl . . . very domesticated too.' She indicated Darynthe's efficient economy of movement, as she swiftly washed and dried the crockery.

'Why is it that everyone else thinks they know what's best for me?' Darynthe pushed aside her heavy silken fringe in an irritated gesture. 'Surely that's for me to decide. But even Caan . . .' She stopped.

'Yes?' Ann said interestedly. 'Even Caan what?'

'Oh . . . oh, nothing. But he scares me, Aunt Ann.' She turned towards her aunt, her eyes widening. 'I just don't want to get involved with him.'

Ann took the dry crockery and put it into a cupboard.

'If I'm any judge of character . . . and I think I am . . . you meet all sorts in this business, I don't believe you'll come to much harm with Caan Lorimer. We had quite an interesting chat this morning, and he told me quite a lot about himself. You would have been very interested. Fancy him being . . .'

'I'm not a bit interested,' Darynthe interrupted.

Ann, diverted from what she had been about to say, shut the cupboard with an air of finality.

'Darynthe Browne, I'm ashamed of you! All right, so you've had one unfortunate experience . . . maybe it won't be your last, but you can't hide from life. You can't always be your daddy's little girl . . . sheltered, protected. I've always thought Arthur made a mistake, keeping you at home like that. Perhaps, in one sense, it's a good thing Mark did happen to you.'

'Auntie!'

Shocked, Darynthe stared at Ann Forster. How could her aunt, her own flesh and blood, think it was a good thing that she had been hurt?

But Ann was nodding firmly, quite unrepentant.

'As I said before, your life before you met Mark was too sheltered . . . and then he was far too old for you, in my opinion. Marrying him would have been like transferring your dependence from one father figure to another. You would never have had an opportunity to grow up.' She smiled at her niece. 'I don't think I'm wrong about you, Darynthe. I believe that as a woman, as a wife, you have great potential. Don't let one unhappy experience sour the whole of your life.'

It was then that Darynthe decided to confide fully in her aunt . . . something it had been impossible to tell her father, or even her closest friends.

'I couldn't bear the thought that I wasn't the first for Mark,' she explained. 'It wasn't even that I'm narrow-minded, or prejudiced. I know lots of people get divorced these days. That's all right, for them . . . but not for me. I wanted . . .'

'I know exactly what you wanted,' her aunt said slowly. 'You wanted a marriage like your parents had. But they were exceptional, you know. They met at school and never even looked at anyone else, right up until the day your mother died.'

She perched on a kitchen stool and regarded her niece with understanding.

'But, my dear, you're pursuing a romantic dream, a myth. Unless you can find a youth of your own age . . . as your mother did . . . to whom you're his first and last love, then you're bound to be disappointed.' She paused, then continued, 'But somehow I can't see you being happy with a completely callow, inexperienced lad. It was different for your mother, but you've been too much in the company of older men . . . your father, his friends, then Mark.'

Reluctantly, Darynthe had to admit that there was some truth in what her aunt said . . . and certainly she had found men of her own age tedious, uninteresting in their conversation, their kisses inept.

'What shall I do?' she asked Ann, all her heart in the green eyes, lustrous with unshed tears.

Ann smiled encouragingly.

'That's my girl! You've made a start already, by realising that you do have to do something . . . that you can't hide from life. Well, for a start, come out of that protective shell you've grown around yourself . . . and secondly, why not go up Helvellyn with Caan tonight willingly, not reluctantly? Make up your mind to enjoy yourself. Keep it lighthearted and don't treat him like the big bad wolf.'

Caan was punctual. Dressed warmly, as instructed, in slacks and anorak in her favourite shade of emerald green, Darynthe ran out to the car, carrying her blanket.

After a short drive they parked in the wooded valley beside Grisedale Beck.

'My uncle's cottage is not far from here,' Caan told her, as they turned their steps up the fellside, towards Striding Edge.

As they climbed, the moon rose from behind a crag, lighting their steps; from the valley below them came the sound of a dog's bark and, closer at hand, the soft hoot of owls from shadowy woods, the eerie sound making Darynthe suddenly glad of Caan's firm, warm clasp at her elbow.

Higher up, passing the vague shapes of sleeping sheep and lambs, they trod the craggy edges, above black, unseen depths.

'Is it true that people have been killed up here?'

Darynthe asked her companion nervously.

'Only the unwary, or the inexperienced.' His deep, reassuring voice was strangely comforting. 'Don't worry, I shan't let anything happen to you.'

Since she had unburdened herself to her aunt, had made up her mind to follow Ann Forster's advice, Darynthe had felt curiously lighthearted, aware of a sense of release, a way out from the prison she had manufactured for herself.

Her aunt was right, she decided. The fact that Darynthe had been bitterly disappointed in Mark should not be allowed to blight her life, but should be looked upon as a salutory experience. It did not occur to her how inconsistent it was to accept Ann's view, while strenuously resisting identical advice from Caan Lorimer.

In future, she resolved, she would allow herself the company of men, and she would enjoy it, with a light heart, as Ann had suggested. But nevertheless, an inner core of caution remained ... she still did not intend to become romantically involved, not unless some man could win her trust, prove himself worthy of all that she felt she could offer to such a one.

They had reached their goal and from the flat plateau on the summit of Helvellyn, they could see the moonlight glistening on the distant reaches of Ullswater. To their left, the light flooded the Coniston fells and beyond glimmered on a narrow glimpse of the sea.

Caan led Darynthe to a sheltered spot, a T-shaped stone windbreak, just below the eastern edge of the plateau. With their backs against the rock and their blankets snugly enfolding them, Darynthe experienced a sensation of being cocooned in security.

When Caan put his arm around her, to draw her closer for greater warmth, she stiffened momentarily, then, remembering, deliberately let herself relax.

'That's better,' he said approvingly.

'It doesn't mean I've changed my mind,' she told him hastily.

'About men?' he sighed. 'No, I didn't suppose you had ... not so quickly.' He looked at her, his eyes in the moonlight silvery blue. 'I suppose you wouldn't let me try an experiment?'

'An . . . an experiment?'

'Would you scream and run away from me if I kissed you?'
Her whole body tensed again.

'That wouldn't be fair,' she objected. 'You know I can't
run away . . . not up here. Oh, please, don't . . . don't
tease me!'

'I'm not teasing you. I really do want to kiss you, very
much.'

'But . . . but why?'

Against her better judgment, she felt herself weakening,
insidiously tempted by the warmth of sincerity in his
velvet-toned voice. After all, what harm could there be in
one kiss?

'Oh, Darynthe,' he said softly, 'do you really need to
ask why? It's a beautiful night . . . you're a very lovely
girl. I'm only human, and we're quite alone.'

This was what she had feared.

'Please, Caan,' she begged. 'Don't . . . don't take advantage of me! You made me come here with you, when I
. . . I didn't really want to, and . . .'

He repeated the question which she had asked herself.

'What harm is there in a kiss? If I promise to stop the
moment you ask me, may I kiss you?' he persisted.

She shrugged helplessly, afraid to give him her permission, strangely reluctant to refuse.

'I don't understand you. You're . . . you're different
somehow. Nobody has ever asked my permission before.
They usually just . . . just take hold of me, and . . .'

'Like this?' he murmured, his encircling arm tightening,
his free hand exploring the contours of her face, as his lips
came down to brush hers, gently . . . oh, so gently. Yet, for
all his gentleness, making her tremble with the puzzling,
unfamiliar sensations his kiss had evoked. Why was this so
different, so much more disturbing than any other kiss she
had ever received?

Caan lifted his head and looked down into her moon-
dazzled eyes, as if to gauge her reaction. She stared helplessly back at him, unable, unwilling to move, powerless
to resist him. As he gazed, her eyelids fluttered down and
she swayed towards him of her own accord, offering her
lips to his.

Darynthe did not know what she had expected, in that moment of submission; perhaps a deepening of his kiss, an attempt perhaps at further intimacies. But with an exultant little laugh Caan touched her lips again, warmly but fleetingly, then settled her once more into the circle of his arm.

She was aware of a sense of disappointment, of anticlimax ... aware that she would not have resisted, would not have objected, if he *had* prolonged his caress.

But it was just as well, she told herself firmly. The very fact that she had enjoyed his kiss was dangerous enough in itself. To allow him greater influence over her was to put her new-found peace of mind in jeopardy. She just wanted to be friends with Caan Lorimer, she assured herself ... nothing more, and fortunately he did not seem inclined to demand more. So she mused, unaware of the rigid control exercised by the man at her side.

For two hours before the dawn they alternately dozed, talked and drank coffee from the thermos Caan had provided, while the light in the east grew steadily brighter.

Just before five, the eastern sky gained in intensity, glowing rich orange, gradually deepening to flaming red, until the flaring tip of a fiery sun, swelling into a great ball, almost intimidating in its proportions, lifted over the distant Pennines.

'Now you know why they call Helvellyn the Sunrise Mountain,' Caan said softly in Darynthe's ear.

'Well, was it worth it?' he asked, as finally they rose, folding their blankets and preparing to descend from their vantage point.

'Oh yes,' Darynthe breathed, referring to the sunrise, 'I wouldn't have missed it for anything!'

'Nor I,' said Caan, with an ambiguity which escaped her, his eyes warm as he studied her unconscious profile.

It was light enough now to see the valley below, shrouded in swirling veils of early morning mist.

' "I climbed the dark brow of the mighty Helvellyn," ' Caan quoted, ' "Lakes and mountains beneath me, gleamed misty and wide ..." '

'It ... it's almost like being God, isn't it?' Darynthe said shyly, half afraid that he would laugh at her fanciful imaginings. 'Up here, I mean, with the world spread out below.'

To her surprise, his reply was perfectly serious.

'Yes, there is a feeling up here ... of being close to heaven. We're not the first ... or the last ... to sense it. There's an old Westmorland legend, which speaks of the mountains as being a place where once man could pass freely between earth and heaven ... they called it "The Roots of Heaven." '

Darynthe breathed a sigh of satisfaction.

'I think that's perfectly lovely!'

Caan took her hand, as they made their way down the path, which dropped sharply over rough scree, then rose again, followed by an easy walk along a ridge. After crossing a grassy slope, their way fell steadily in the direction of Ullswater, finally emerging near the foot of Grisedale Valley.

The sheep were stirring now, the contralto voices of the ewes mingling with the shrill soprano sounds of their new lambs.

'Are we going home now?' Darynthe asked.

Strangely, considering her earlier reluctance for this expedition, she now wished that it need not end ... at least, not yet.

'I thought we'd call in on Uncle Jack,' said Caan. 'That's if you've no objection? I could cook breakfast for us, then run you back to the Daffodil.'

The thought of a hot breakfast made Darynthe's stomach groan in delightful anticipation. Besides, she was curious to meet the guide whose illness had been responsible for her second encounter with Caan.

'Breakfast would be lovely,' she agreed.

Still hand in hand, they crossed the springy turf, leapt the beck and made their way up a narrow track to where a sturdy stone cottage sheltered under the lee of the hillside.

Thick walls supported a heavy slate roof and the small porch was protected by flat stones reared against each other. A few yards from the back door, the ground rose steeply to the hillside, and beyond, the mountain extended upwards, open, barren and rocky, to the pale sky. Through the front garden ran a rocky gill, full of minute noisy waterfalls.

Hearing footsteps, a black and white Border collie dog ran to meet them, his warning bark turning to whimpers of joy as he recognised Caan.

'Here boy, then . . . here, Scipio! Where's your master, then?'

The back door was unlocked and, the collie preceding them, they stepped straight into a flag-floored kitchen, strewn with brightly coloured rag rugs, where Jack Lorimer was already busy with frying pan and whistling kettle.

A small, tubby man, with a thatch of grizzled hair and a twinkle in his eye, Jack's round face creased into a welcoming grin.

'Saw the pair of you coming down the hillside, and I guessed you'd be hungry.'

Introductions over and seated opposite Caan at the scrubbed wooden table, Darynthe thought that bacon and eggs had never tasted so good. She was filled with a sense of wellbeing which had not been hers for a long time. Whatever happened to you, she thought, with a newly-acquired philosophy, there were always the good memories to look back on, and this was one of them.

She would never forget the pageantry of the sunrise, the keen morning air, followed by the cosiness of this cheerful little room and the mouthwatering, welcoming smell of bacon frying. A small inner voice wondered if she would also remember Caan's tentative, experimental kiss.

CHAPTER FOUR

'YOUR first time in the Lakes, I believe?' Jack Lorimer placed a large, fragrant mug of coffee in front of Darynthe. 'Like it?' His friendly blue eyes were a faded edition of Caan's.

'Oh yes,' she assured him. 'If it wasn't for Dad, back in Corbridge, I think I'd like to stay here for ever!'

Jack grinned and again Darynthe was aware of the strong family resemblance, as his mouth quirked up sideways.

'When he retires, maybe you can persuade your dad to move up here? I went away to work when I was a young man, but I've made my way back north, and here I am, within spitting distance of my old home over at Grasmere.'

'I love your kitchen,' said Darynthe, looking about her appreciatively, at white walls, colourful rag rugs, crisp gingham curtains and solid wooden furniture.

Bright copper pans gleamed on the wall above an old-fashioned black-leaded range and the collie, Scipio, who had greeted them when they first arrived lay in the aura of its warmth, nose on paws, an ear flicking from time to time at the sound of voices. When Caan's deep tones registered with Scipio, the plumed tail moved also, in frenzied, affectionate recognition.

'Would you like to see the rest of the cottage?' Jack asked.

'Could I?'

Darynthe was genuinely eager. During her brief time in the district, she had already come to admire the sturdy little whitewashed buildings which seemed to nestle with reassuring security in unsuspected folds of the fell country.

'It must be marvellous to live somewhere like this,' she told Jack, as she followed him into the living room.

Tastefully but sparsely furnished, it was surprisingly large . . . larger than one would suppose from the outside. It was essentially a man's room . . . well-worn slippers by the shining fender, a pipe-rack comfortably to hand, a shelf of regularly-thumbed books, mostly about the Lake District, she noticed. There were no ornaments, save a single potted ivy on the windowsill and a few family portraits. Darynthe had no difficulty in recognising Caan as a boy and could not resist studying the photograph.

Jack noticed her interest.

'He's a good lad,' he said, as though his nephew were

still the fresh-faced lad of some fifteen or sixteen years depicted in the snapshot. 'Always my favourite nephew, he was . . . and he's grand company to have about the place.'

'He lives with you?'

Darynthe was surprised. She had not pictured Caan in quite such primitive surroundings. Despite his obvious love of the countryside, she sensed a certain sophistication about him which did not tally with the life-style epitomised by this simple stone cottage.

'Aye, he's living with me at present,' Jack confirmed.

Somehow Darynthe was sorry to receive such disquieting information. Out of work and living with his elderly uncle, whose only subsistence was his pension . . . and his part-time work as a warden . . . it didn't seem right, or fair.

Jack showed her the two diminutive bedrooms which comprised the rest of the cottage, but, absorbed in her thoughts, she barely glanced at them, unable afterwards to recall their appearance or contents . . . though why she should be so concerned about Caan's apparent vagrancy, she could not fathom.

'All mod cons, too!' Jack demonstrated, flicking electric light switches off and on. 'We have our own generator out back, in the outhouse.'

In the kitchen, Darynthe hovered uncertainly.

'I really ought to be going,' she told Caan.

He nodded, wiping his mouth and rising from the table, where he had consumed a portion of bacon and eggs which, in Darynthe's opinion, would have fed two men. She wondered how Jack could afford to feed him, if he ate like that all the time. Still, there was probably Caan's dole money, she thought.

She eyed him a little scornfully, as he bent to pat Scipio in farewell. Surely a big, strong, muscular man like that could find work of some sort. If he had any pride at all, he'd be willing to do anything, even labouring work, rather than sponge off his elderly relative.

With genuine warmth, she thanked Jack for the breakfast and for the tour of his cottage, then, feeling rather subdued, she followed Caan out to the car.

'Come and see me again soon, love,' Jack called after her. 'Nice to see a pretty face about the place!'

She waved and nodded, though she thought it extremely unlikely that she would visit Caan's uncle again. The fact that she had taken such a strong liking to the portly little man made her indignation against his idle nephew all the stronger.

'You're very quiet. Tired?'

Caan shot a look at her as they drove back along the quiet road towards Ambleside; the daily build-up of traffic had not yet begun.

'Yes,' she admitted, 'I suppose I am.'

Tired and a little depressed, she thought. Suddenly she wished that she had not agreed to last night's excursion. She had enjoyed it . . . had begun to enjoy Caan's company, to trust him even, albeit reluctantly. Now she felt that she had again laid herself open to disillusion. Once you got to know someone too well, inevitably, you learnt the bad with the good. The strange thing was that Caan just hadn't struck her as the type to be an idle sponger, which only went to show you couldn't judge by appearances.

The car pulled up outside the Daffodil.

'I won't come in this time,' said Caan. 'I expect you'll want to rest for a few hours. When do you expect to be off duty again?'

Darynthe did not intend to tell him, but she had no hard and fast hours of work . . . not as if she were a genuine employee. Her aunt was grateful for Darynthe's help, but she was also anxious that her niece should get out and enjoy her surroundings; thus her free time was quite flexible.

'I really don't know,' she said mendaciously. 'Perhaps not for ages.'

'Oh, come now!' His blue eyes twinkled. 'I can't believe your aunt's that much of a slavedriver. Now, when can I take you out again?'

He leant over, as if for a farewell kiss, and Darynthe fumbled for the door handle.

'I . . . I don't want to go out with you again,' she told him, as she scrambled from the car.

He reached out, in an effort to grasp her wrist, to detain her, but she was too swift for him.

She ran across the narrow pavement and into the guest-house, as though pursued by demons. She dared not look back, terrified that he might follow her, demand an explanation of her impulsive words.

But, as she gained the sanctuary of the hallway, she heard the roar of the car's engine and an excessively noisy gear change, as it moved away.

She leant against the inside of the front door, suddenly feeling tearful and utterly dejected. What had possessed her, to be so abruptly dismissive ... and after he had taken so much trouble to give her a memorable experience!

She knew the answer, without too much heart-searching. She had panicked ... panicked because she *had* enjoyed last night ... and Caan's company ... far too much. Then, to find out, as she had feared, that he had feet of clay ... what her father would call 'no moral fibre' ... had been the last straw. Oh, he was kind, gentle, considerate and compellingly attractive, but none of these things made up for a deliberately indolent, parasitic character. Probably Jack Lorimer *did* enjoy having his favourite nephew under his roof, but that didn't mean it was right for Caan to take advantage of his uncle's partiality.

No, she decided, as she toiled wearily up the stairs to her attic bedroom, she should have clung to her resolve, instead of allowing herself to be persuaded. Fortunately, this time, she had discovered the man's defects before she had had time to become irretrievably attached to him. Which didn't quite explain why she then cried herself to sleep.

Darynthe appeared in time to help her aunt serve lunch and, in spite of carefully applied make-up, a little heavier than she normally affected for daytime wear, she knew Ann Forster was not deceived, and she dreaded the consequent enquiries.

Her aunt did not make any direct reference to her drawn face and shadowed eyes, but that she was curious was betrayed by the question she asked, with attempted casualness, as soon as they were alone.

'When are you seeing Caan again?'

'I'm not,' Darynthe said shortly.

It was an effort to maintain her hard-won composure. Even the sound of his name seemed to have a strange effect upon her.

'Didn't you enjoy yourself last night?' Ann pressed gently for information.

'Yes . . . yes, it was . . . was a tremendous experience, but . . .' She turned to her aunt with a pleading gesture of her slim hands, 'but I don't want to go out with him again. Oh, please, Auntie, don't try to throw us together again . . . and if he calls . . . if he wants to know where I am, please make some excuse . . . don't tell him.'

Despite herself, a sob escaped with these last words.

'Why, child, whatever's wrong?' Ann was immediately concerned. 'What's he done to upset you?' She bristled indignantly. 'He didn't try to . . . to . . .?'

'No . . . no!' Darynthe gasped out a laugh, a pitifully strangled sound. 'He was a perfect gentleman. It . . . it's not that.'

'He didn't even kiss you?'

Ann was incredulous. She had imagined that, given the right conditions and a beautiful girl like her niece by his side, Caan Lorimer was too essentially masculine for such rigid abstention. She had hoped that he was the right man to break through Darynthe's reserves.

'Oh yes, he kissed me,' Darynthe admitted. Tears welled into her eyes, which became limpid green pools, at the remembrance. It had been such a gentle, restrained kiss, more on a par with the romantic caress of her imagination.

'And . . . and you objected?'

'No,' Darynthe said dully, 'I didn't object. I . . . I enjoyed it. That's the whole trouble.'

Ann Forster sat down abruptly.

'This is going to take some understanding. Let me see if I've got it right. Caan kissed you, in a perfectly acceptable, gentlemanly manner, and you didn't stop him . . . you even enjoyed it . . . but you never want to see him again?'

'Ten out of ten,' said Darynthe, though she had never felt less like humour.

'But why?' Ann Forster sounded frustrated almost to the point of screaming. 'Why, for goodness' sake? It doesn't make sense!'

'It does to me.'

Darynthe wandered over to the kitchen window, looking out over the small, gravelled car park that backed on to the guesthouse. 'You see,' she said softly, so quietly that Ann had to lean forward to hear her, 'I enjoyed it too much. I wanted him to go on, to . . . to kiss me again.'

'And what's wrong with that?' Ann asked. 'It sounds like a perfectly normal reaction to me.'

Darynthe swung round and advanced upon her aunt, her tone fiery because it was the only way she could restrain her tears.

'Because I've sworn never to fall in love again. Oh, Auntie, how is it that some girls are fated always to pick rotters? I could fall in love with Caan quite easily, I know I could, but I'm afraid . . . partly because it might just be on the rebound, after Mark, and yet Mark never made me feel . . . But anyway, it's mostly because Caan's no good either.'

Ann stared at her niece in stunned amazement.

'However do you work that out? What has he ever done to give you that impression?'

'It's not what he's done,' Darynthe said impatiently. 'It's what he *hasn't* done . . . isn't doing.'

'What he *hasn't* done?' Ann was still puzzled. 'You mean because he *didn't* kiss you again. You're afraid he doesn't care for you?' she hazarded.

'No.' Darynthe sat down, shoulders drooping dejectedly. 'I don't know *how* he feels about me . . . that's true enough. But I do know how I *could* feel about him, and he isn't worth it. Auntie, he . . . he's just a layabout. By his own admission, he hasn't a job. He just idles about the Lakes, lives off his old uncle and . . . Why are you laughing?' she asked indignantly, as Ann Forster suddenly collapsed in helpless mirth.

'Oh dear!' Ann wiped away tears of merriment. 'Oh, I'm sorry, Darynthe, honestly. I'm not laughing at you,

love, not really. It . . . it's just the idea of Caan, Caan
Lorimer of all people being an idle good-for-nothing!'

Another fit of laughter threatened, but with an heroic
effort Ann suppressed it.

'Don't . . . don't you know who Caan Lorimer is?'

Perplexed, Darynthe shook her head.

'No . . . should I?'

'He's only about the best-known authority on the Lake
District, with literally hundreds of reference books and
guide books to his credit. That's why he's here now . . .
he's working on an up-to-date version. He told me, the
day he followed you to Windermere.'

Darynthe stared at Ann, frozen into horrified im-
mobility. Then she leapt to her feet and Ann could hear
her running feet on the stairs. She rose anxiously, intending
to follow her niece, then relaxed, as she heard Darynthe
returning at the same breakneck speed.

In either hand Darynthe held a book, both of which she
thrust under her aunt's nose.

'Look at these!' she gasped in self-accusation. 'I've read
both of them, from cover to cover, and never even noticed
the author's name. Even if I had, I don't suppose I'd have
connected C. G. Lorimer with Caan.'

Ann nodded.

'I've seen them in your room. That's why I didn't say
anything. I assumed you knew by now, that he would
have told you himself.'

'What a fool I've been!' Darynthe said shakily, sitting
down again with a sudden thump, as if her legs had
suddenly refused their support. 'To think I've been despis-
ing him, and feeling sorry for Jack Lorimer! No wonder
he's so proud of his nephew! His books are just beautiful
. . . the descriptions are wonderful. I fell in love with the
idea of Lakeland before I ever saw it. Oh . . .' she covered
her eyes with her hand, 'whatever must he think of me?'

'You didn't tell him what you thought?' Ann asked.
'You didn't accuse him of . . .'

'Not exactly.' Darynthe tried to remember just what
she had said. 'I didn't say anything last night . . . this
morning, I mean . . . only that I didn't want to see him
again . . . but once before, the second time I met him, on

that guided walk, I asked him if he had a job.'

'And he didn't tell you?'

'He just said it wasn't what I would call a proper job. I didn't even want to know him then, so I didn't question him. I just assumed ...'

'Why not ring him up?' Ann suggested gently, brown eyes sympathetic. 'Apologise ... say you were overtired, that you didn't mean ...'

'I can't. His uncle's cottage isn't on the telephone,' Darynthe said hopelessly. 'Besides, I couldn't ... I wouldn't want him to think I ...'

'To think what?' Ann prompted. 'That you're running after him? I'm sure he wouldn't think that.'

'Well, it's probably just as well,' Darynthe said. 'In a way, knowing he's someone famous only makes it worse.'

'I can't see how.'

'Don't you see,' Darynthe explained, 'he's a well-known author, probably quite rich and used to intelligent, sophisticated company ... probably has dozens of smart, clever women friends. I ... I couldn't compete. I'd only end up getting hurt again.'

Ann looked at her shrewdly.

'If the truth be known, I believe you're more than half in love with him already!'

Though Darynthe strenuously denied her aunt's accusation, in the days that followed, she began to wonder if it wasn't true. Certainly life seemed more dull, she herself more dispirited at the thought of never seeing Caan again. Oh, probably she would encounter him, see him from afar, but that would only add to the torture of knowing that he existed, but not for her. Wantonly, foolishly, because of a stupid assumption on her part, she had tossed his proffered friendship aside, and with it the chance that it might develop into something deeper. Almost she felt like packing up and going home to Corbridge. At least she would no longer be haunted by its reminders of Mark.

This brought her up short in her musing; with a feeling of wonder, she realised that she could think about Mark Little now with no sense of hurt. Was she so shallow, so fickle that his memory could be erased so soon, supplanted already by another man's image?

No! She shook her head, unaware that her aunt was watching her with understanding eyes, quite able to imagine Darynthe's inner turmoil, the endless, conflicting dialogue with herself.

No, she wasn't that capricious. This feeling that she had for Caan was quite, quite different from the sensations she had experienced after her parting with Mark. She knew, though she could not explain even to herself how she knew it, that nothing could ever dispel Caan's effect upon her mind and heart. Unwillingly and against all reason, she had fallen in love . . . only this time it was the real thing. The only similarity between the two emotions was that once again her longing was futile, doomed to be frustrated.

'Letter for you!' Ann climbed up the attic stairs one morning, a few days later, as Darynthe was brushing her hair. 'Looks like a bill.'

'Oh, lord,' Darynthe groaned. 'It's probably for the car. I'd almost forgotten about it,' she added, with a sense of wonder. 'So much seems to have happened.'

'I hope it isn't going to cost you too much,' Ann said anxiously.

Darynthe ripped open the envelope and scanned the contents.

'They say the car's a write-off, only fit for scrap. The bill is just for towing it away and . . . oh . . .' she exclaimed, half dismayed, half indignant . . . 'and it's stamped "paid in full"!' Over the piece of paper, her green eyes regarded her aunt. 'It wasn't you,' she said slowly, 'so it must have been . . .'

'Caan Lorimer?'

'Yes.'

'It's very good of him,' Ann said doubtfully, 'but . . .'

'But I can't allow him to foot my bill,' Darynthe agreed. She looked at it again. 'It's not too exorbitant. I can just about afford to pay him back, but that means . . .'

'That you'll have to go and see him!' Unsuccessfully, Ann tried to conceal her satisfaction at the prospect.

But Darynthe was shaking her head.

'No,' she said curtly. 'I'll write, enclose a cheque.'

'Wouldn't that seem rather ungracious?' Ann objected.

'I don't care. I . . . I won't go looking for him,' Darynthe said a trifle wildly.

'How about popping over to see his uncle, then, at the Tourist Centre, before he goes off on one of his walks? If you give him your cheque, with a verbal message, it wouldn't seem quite so brusque and ungrateful.'

'That is an alternative,' Darynthe admitted. 'You do see?' she said pleadingly. 'I have to repay him. I couldn't possibly . . .'

'Of course I understand,' Ann reassured her, 'and I'm sure he will, if you go about it the right way.'

Darynthe was at the Tourist Information Centre early, before Jack Lorimer could possibly set off on one of his daily guided tours. But in the end it was a strange man, wearing the emblem of the National Park Warden, who arrived.

'Oh, I was expecting to see Mr Lorimer . . . Jack Lorimer,' faltered Darynthe.

The man grinned at her all-too-evident disappointment.

'Won't I do for you, then, love? What's old Jack got that I haven't?'

Darynthe flushed scarlet.

'It . . . it's not that. I . . . I wanted to give him a message for . . . for someone else.'

He nodded kindly.

'O.K., love, only teasing! But I'm afraid if you want to see Jack, you'll have to go out to his place. He's on the sick list again, since the weekend. Caught a chill, I reckon . . . and not long after that nasty bout of 'flu. Can't be too careful at his age.'

Darynthe was concerned. Yet she did not feel inclined to go out to Grisedale Beck, for fear of encountering Caan.

'I suppose his nephew will be looking after him?' she ventured.

The man shook his head.

'Young Caan's down in London . . . been gone for over a week. He won't even know the old boy's laid up.'

Darynthe hurried back to the Daffodil; quickly she

explained the situation to her aunt.

'Would you . . . would you trust me with Uncle Bob's car?' she begged. 'I wouldn't ask you for any trivial reason, but I really think someone ought to go and see if Jack's O.K. up there, all on his own.'

Ann nodded understandingly.

'I'm afraid I can't spare the time to come with you, though. Can you cope on your own?'

'Yes . . . yes,' Darynthe said breathlessly. 'If he's all right, I'll just leave my cheque and the message . . . but if Jack's ill, he may need a doctor. It's so isolated where he lives.'

Five minutes later she was on her way, thankful that Bob Forster's car was well maintained, ready for his next leave ashore.

She parked by the beck and climbed the narrow track to the cottage, making her way round to the back door, where a dejected-looking collie lay, nose on paws, eyes listlessly watching her.

'Scipio? Hallo, boy.' She bent to pat him.

The collie rose, wagging his tail, diffidently at first, then in rapturous greeting as his doggy memory recollected her scent. Darynthe opened the unlocked door for him and he led the way into the house, plumed tail waving to and fro.

'Jack—Mr Lorimer! Are you there? It's me, Darynthe.'

A muffled assent from one of the bedrooms guided her.

Jack Lorimer looked extremely sorry for himself, heavy-eyed and seeming strangely old and shrunken, as he sat up in bed, a patchwork quilt drawn up around his shoulders.

'Goodness,' Darynthe exclaimed with more truth than tact, 'you do look awful!'

'I don't suppose you expected to find me in bed?' he said ruefully, rubbing a hand over his stubbled jaw.

'I did, actually. They told me at the Centre that you were ill, so I came to see if there was anything I could do.'

'That's good of you, lass,' Jack said gratefully. 'If you could feed old Scipio, he'll be your friend for life. He was out all night, poor lad. I tried to get up this morning to let him in, but my legs just wouldn't seem to hold me.'

'Of course I'll feed Scipio,' she said, 'and then I'll feed you. After that we're going to send for the doctor. Don't argue,' as he seemed about to protest. 'I'm sure Caan would agree with me, if he were here. What's your doctor's name?'

Fifteen minutes later Jack looked more cheerful, tucked in with two hot water bottles and with a bowl of steaming soup on a tray before him. Scipio, his lean belly now comfortably full, followed at Darynthe's heels with abject devotion.

Jack jerked his head towards the dog, with an amused, twisted grin, so heart-tuggingly like his nephew's.

'He knows where he's well off, that one . . . not like some people. I told our Caan he was daft, not seeing you again . . . nicest girl he's ever brought to see me . . . not like the last one . . . stuck-up, dressed-up little madam. What went wrong between you two? I could've sworn . . .'

'I'm afraid that was my fault,' she told him hastily. 'A—a misunderstanding on my part, and . . .'

'And your pride wouldn't let you apologise?' His faded blue eyes were shrewd.

She nodded. 'Something like that.'

'Daft! The pair of you. Hey, where are you going?'

'Only to the nearest phone-box,' she assured him, 'to call the doctor.'

The doctor, when he called, was reassuring. Only a heavy cold, he told Darynthe, adding that a couple of days in bed, plus the drugs he had prescribed, should see Jack Lorimer up and about again.

'You a relation?'

'No,' she admitted. 'Just a friend . . . a friend of his . . . his nephew's.'

'I see.' The doctor's brows drew together consideringly. 'The old fellow ought to have someone here, to see that he does as he's told, takes his medication, stays in bed, keeps warm . . . that sort of thing. Would you be prepared to stay here for a day or two?'

'I'm sure I could manage that,' Darynthe agreed. As long as I'm well away before Caan returns, she added silently to herself.

Not unnaturally, Jack was delighted and a little relieved that he was not to be left alone.

'Having Caan here for the last six months has spoilt

me,' he admitted. 'You get used to having someone about the place.'

Ann Forster readily agreed to release Darynthe from her duties and with sufficient clothes for a few days' stay, Darynthe was soon on her way back to the cottage.

It was rather fun, she thought, to have a house to run, albeit on a rather diminutive scale. Since her mother's death, her father had employed a housekeeper, so that his daughter could be in the shop with him, and somehow Darynthe had never liked to interfere with the rather stern woman's management.

After only a few hours the fine veil of dust which had settled during Jack's illness had been banished and the interior of the cottage wore its customary air of shining comfort.

'You're a grand lass,' Jack repeated. 'Our Caan might do a sight worse for himself.'

Darynthe flushed, as she placed a daintily arranged tray before him and uncovered the light but appetising meal she had prepared. She felt bound to disabuse Jack of any conception he might have formed concerning her and Caan.

'There's nothing like that between us,' she said firmly. 'We're . . . we're just acquaintances.'

Jack laughed at the rather old-fashioned term.

'What they call "just good friends" nowadays? Pull the other one, girlie! I saw the way that nephew of mine was looking at you.'

Wistfully, Darynthe wished she could believe in the accuracy of his observation.

She had been prepared to curl up for the night on the comfortable old sofa in the living room, but Jack insisted that she make use of Caan's bedroom.

'He'll be away for a bit . . . gone down to see his publisher . . . and I'm sure he'd have no objection to you being in his bed,' he added with a twinkle.

'You're a wicked old man,' she told him in mock reproof. But nevertheless, she allowed herself to be persuaded. She was glad, she told herself, that Caan hadn't gone away for good.

It was strange, she mused, as she relaxed on her back in

bed that night, staring up at the crazed pattern on the distempered ceiling . . . strange to think that Caan usually slept in this bed, that his dark head, with its distinguished sprinkling of grey, had rested where hers lay now. A little tingle of sensuality, hastily suppressed, ran through her at the thought, as she fancied she could still inhale some lingering traces of his occupation.

She diverted herself from these disturbing reflections by looking around the room, seeking some further clues as to the personality of its owner.

The furnishings, she guessed, were Jack's taste. They had the some old-world, home-spun simplicity as the rest of the cottage decor. But there were definite traces of Caan's occupation. On the old-fashioned dressing table were a row of expensive-looking male toiletries which, when she had investigated their contents, exuded a pungent, essentially masculine fragrance which vividly recalled Caan to mind. A table under the window bore a sturdy portable typewriter and several reference books, amongst the other minutiae of the writer's craft. So he typed out his own manuscripts . . . that would account for the curiously spatulate fingertips she had noticed.

With guilty curiosity, she had peeped into the massive oak wardrobe, inserting a tentative hand to touch a tweed jacket, which she remembered Caan had worn on the day they had met in Windermere. Like the bottles on the dressing table, the clothes were redolent of his favourite cologne.

Climbing into the bed, wide enough for only a single occupant, she had wondered momentarily if she would find a pair of Caan's pyjamas beneath the pillow. But there were none to be seen. Perhaps he didn't wear them . . . some men didn't, she believed. At the thought that she might be lying in a space once occupied by his naked muscularity, a warm glow suffused her from head to foot and she became aware of unfamiliar sensations which both disturbed and excited her.

She sat up, searching the bedside shelf for something to read, something sufficiently absorbing to distract her thoughts from their dangerous preoccupation, but all the books seemed to have been written by Caan himself and

inscribed for his uncle. There was no distraction to be
found that way. With a sigh, she extinguished the over-
head light and endeavoured to compose herself for sleep.

How well she had succeeded was proved by the start
with which she woke from profound slumber. Mouth dry,
heart thudding, she wondered what had woken her. All
very well to tell herself that, despite the remote situation
of the cottage, she was not alone, that she had a man and
a dog for her protection. Jack Lorimer was sick, probably
by now in a drugged sleep, and dogs could be overcome.

She stayed motionless, yet every nerve was tensed as
though for action.

Someone was definitely moving about in the cottage.
She relaxed suddenly, smiling at her own ridiculous imaginings. Of course, it would be Jack, unable after all to
sleep. He might need a hot drink. She was about to reach
up for the pull cord above the bed, intending to investi-
gate, when the door to the bedroom opened and someone
operated the wall switch, dazzling her with the sudden
intensity of light.

Before her eyes had time to focus, she knew who stood
in the doorway.

'What the hell are *you* doing in my bed?'

With an instinctive—self-protective gesture, Darynthe
hauled the sheet up to her neck, aware that the scanty
nightwear she affected offered very little in the way of
cover for her splendidly proportioned breasts.

'This is an unexpectedly warm welcome home, considering our parting . . . unexpected, but decidedly pleasant.'

The deep voice was uncharacteristically sardonic, quite
unlike the friendly humorous tones she had remembered
so wistfully during the past days.

Huge emerald-green eyes, wide with nameless fear,
surveyed him over the flimsy barrier of the sheet.

'Please . . . you don't understand. I . . .'

'No,' he agreed, 'I certainly don't . . . but understanding
isn't always essential to enjoyment. Wouldn't you agree?'

He put down the suitcase he carried and closing the
door behind him, moved towards the bed. Aghast,
Darynthe stared at him. The blue eyes which had always

been gently mocking were almost steely grey in their cold, intent survey.

'Caan, if you'll just let me explain . . .'

Her voice faded away, as he sat on the edge of the bed, not touching her, just staring at her in a peculiarly riveted manner, which made her heart thud and her pulses flutter. For a long moment he held her eyes with his own, and Darynthe had to reject a shameful and ignoble impulse to fling herself into his arms, against that broad chest, to beg his forgiveness for her recent churlish behaviour, her hasty words of rejection after their night on Helvellyn.

Still he did not touch her, but he was close enough to sense the trembling of her slender body beneath the covers and she saw his cold eyes warm into the unmistakable gleam of desire. The atmosphere of charged intensity lasted a moment longer, then, with a sudden exclamation that was almost a groan, Caan flung away from her, standing with his back towards the bed, one large hand rearranging the items upon the dressing table with fingers that trembled slightly.

'All right,' he said, his voice husky, 'you'd better explain.'

She did so, seeing his taut shoulders gradually relax as she spoke. Finally she referred to the manner of their parting.

'I'm sorry about that, Caan. It . . . it was unforgivable, after you'd taken so much trouble . . . sacrificed a night's sleep. I . . . I made a dreadful mistake about you. I won't insult you by telling you what it was, but I know now how terribly wrong I was. Please, will you forgive me?'

He turned to face her, his eyes sparkling with a light not entirely due to the reflection of the lamplight.

'I think,' he said, in a voice which was slightly unsteady, 'I could forgive *you* almost anything.'

He moved slowly towards her, as one drawn by an irresistible force, his nostrils slightly flared, his breathing erratic. Of their own volition her hands went out to him, forgetful of the sheet they held, which slipped back to waist level, revealing her firm, splendid curves to his aware, penetrating gaze.

'Darynthe!' His voice held a sensual resonance, as he

leant across the bed, gathering her up to him, her body
pliant, unresisting, curving against him.

'Caan,' she whispered, as his lips came down, closing
her own over his name.

Starved senses, suppressed too long, came alive in rapturous acceptance of his kiss and she wound her fingers
into the thick, vibrant, close-cropped hair which curled
about his head. His mouth crushed hers hungrily, while
one strong hand began to follow the curves of her body,
cupping her breasts in a caress which provoked an intense
response in her warm, pulsing flesh.

Just as she felt herself beginning to drift on the sweet
tide of sensuousness, she was aware of a sudden stillness in
him; with an effort which seemed to call for superhuman
strength, he pulled himself free of her entwining arms,
then stood swaying slightly, eyes glazed, a curious expression of anguish on his face.

She gave a little gasp of protest at the shattering of the
moment of intimacy, all its promise unfulfilled, and as he
moved towards the door, she found her voice.

'Wh-where are you going?'

He answered her without turning his head.

'To bed, of course. I'll sleep on the settee for tonight.
There'll be no need for you to stay here, now that I'm
back.'

To her sensitive ears, his voice sounded harsh, angry.

The door closed firmly behind him and she sank back
on the pillow, her trembling beginning to subside, as she
strove to regain the poise the last few moments had destroyed. But instead, intense humiliation began to take
possession of her, as she recalled her own violent reaction
to Caan's lovemaking, the obsessive need which had possessed her, a need of which he could not help but be
aware. For a short while she had been oblivious to everything but the pleasure induced by his kiss, his caress. But
wasn't it all too obvious, from his sudden coolness, that he
had been disgusted by her eager submission, wildly at
variance with her former behaviour in his company?

Where, he must be wondering, was all her vaunted dislike for members of his sex? Drearily, she asked herself the
same question . . . what had become of her distaste, mis-

trust, when her very first encounter with another man had dispelled all her resolution? It was no credit to her that these last few moments in his arms had not had a different outcome . . . had not resulted in a deeper intimacy, from which she would have emerged shamed and disgusted by her own wanton behaviour.

How Caan must be jeering at her now, triumphing in his successful demolition of her defences, in having proved to her that she was no more immune to masculine wiles than she had ever been.

Sleep was impossible now. Darynthe knew she could not possibly face Caan in the morning . . . encounter the sexual mockery in those brilliant blue eyes. She rose, pulled on jeans and sweater and moving quietly about the room, began to pack her few possessions. At first light, before Caan and his uncle awoke, she would leave the cottage and drive back to Ambleside.

She rummaged in her handbag for the cheque she had made out, to reimburse him for the removal of the Mini, then she scribbled a message, leaving cheque and note propped against the dressing table mirror. Now all she had to do was to wait for the dawn.

To Darynthe, eager to be gone, to erase her own despicable behaviour from her mind, it seemed a very long wait. Curtains drawn apart, she sat watching the sky for the faint smothered flush in the greyness, which held the promise of sunrise. At last, slowly at first, then with increasing intensity, colour drenched back into the landscape.

She opened the window and peered out. It was only a short drop to the springy turf beneath and the window was just large enough to facilitate her escape. She lowered her suitcase to the ground, then scrambled after it.

She picked up her case and began to make her way across the uneven, dew-drenched garden. Only a few more seconds and she would be in her uncle's car, making good her escape.

'I don't suppose you have our family heirlooms in that case, but isn't this a rather unorthodox way of terminating a visit?'

A shiver of fear zipped down Darynthe's back as she

turned to face Caan Lorimer, and she stood, suddenly cold and rigid, as he stepped from his place of concealment in the front porch.

'You're . . . you're up early,' was all she could think of to say.

Caan's mouth quirked in lopsided derision.

'We have that much in common at least,' he remarked.

Darynthe began to edge towards the path, the route to the car, to safety, to sanity. But with a smooth, fluid movement he intercepted her, a detaining hand on her arm.

'We don't allow our guests to leave without their breakfast.'

'I . . . I don't want any breakfast,' she told him, aware of a certain difficulty in drawing breath.

That much was true. She felt as if food at this moment would choke her.

Caan inclined his head.

'Very well. But at least you won't go without saying goodbye to my uncle? It would be very churlish, not to give him the opportunity to thank you.'

'I don't suppose he's awake yet. I . . . I wouldn't want to disturb him.'

It was a feeble excuse and received the success it merited.

'As you've already observed, we rise early in this house. Come on!'

Firmly, the suitcase was removed from her nerveless fingers and a strong hand, which brooked no resistance, turned her towards the cottage.

'Shall we use the more conventional entrance?' he asked.

He was laughing at her, and in a more rational frame of mind Darynthe would have laughed with him, knowing how ridiculous her stealthy exit must have appeared. But now fury mingled with her miserable awareness of his proximity and its devastating effect upon her. An unwilling captive, she was marched indoors. In the kitchen she attempted to release her elbow from his grip. Tight-lipped, she said:

'I'll just go and see your uncle and then I really must go.'

'No rush,' he told her lazily. 'Uncle Jack was still asleep when I looked in on him.'

Darynthe's green eyes blazed.

'But . . . but you said . . .'

'I didn't actually say he was awake,' Caan reminded her.

'No, but you implied . . .'

'Never mind Uncle Jack for the moment.'

Suddenly he seemed impatient of their fencing and propelled her into the living room, forcing her to sit on the settee, which still bore traces of his overnight occupation . . . a restless one, if the rumpled state of the rugs and cushions was to be believed.

'You still have some explaining to do,' he told her.

Bewildered, she refuted his suggestion.

'I explained everything to you last night . . . I told you why I was here . . . and . . .'

Almost roughly he pulled her into his arms, silencing her protests with a kiss which bore no resemblance to the gentle, sensuous caresses of the night. It was brutal, punishing, as if he meant to hurt her, and a moan of pain escaped her as she attempted to fight him off.

'You explained a lot of things last night,' Caan murmured between kisses, 'but not the things that I most wanted to know.'

'Wh-what do you want to know?' she whispered, one shaking hand pressed to her bruised, pulsating lips.

'Presently, presently.' His voice was husky. 'First things first.'

As gentle now as he had been cruel, one strong hand stroking her sun-streaked hair, Caan soothed her into quiescence, as he repossessed her mouth.

CHAPTER FIVE

At last Caan released her, though by now Darynthe would have been willing to remain indefinitely in his embrace ... in arms, where, for a while, she had experienced a sense of security, a kind of wild but sweet peace.

'Now,' Caan insisted, 'that explanation. Friends shouldn't hide things from each other ... and we *are* friends now, aren't we?' His blue eyes were beguiling.

Wordlessly Darynthe nodded, though friendship was scarcely a strong enough word for the feelings she now knew that she entertained for Caan Lorimer.

'What was this dreadful mistake? The one you wouldn't insult me with?' he persisted.

Darynthe shook her fair head, her green eyes imploring him. 'Don't make me tell you, please. I ... I'm so ashamed.'

But Caan was gently insistent, and inevitably Darynthe found herself confessing all her former disgust with him ... her belief that he was just an idle sponger, living off his uncle. The words poured out of her in a jerky, incoherent stream, while she stared fixedly at the repetitive pattern of roses on the carpet, tracing the outline of one bloom with her toe.

She finished her pitiful little tale and sat with her head still lowered, her flushed face obscured by a thick fall of hair, as she waited for the moment when his completely justifiable wrath would descend upon her ... when he would tell her to get out of his life.

He was silent for so long that, at last, Darynthe could bear the suspense no longer. She risked a swift upward glance, only to find him racked by silent laughter.

It was too much. After all the pangs of guilt she had endured, the ignominy of having to confess her error of judgment, he was actually laughing at her!

She jumped up, her face, which earlier had been coloured by embarrassment, now white with angry humiliation. But he forestalled the furious words that trembled on her lips.

'Steady now! I'm not laughing at *you*.'

'What, then?' she said disbelievingly.

'My own conceit, I suppose,' he admitted. 'My mistaken belief that I was so well known. I remember you once asked me if I had a job, but since I'd told your aunt, I thought she would have enlightened you long before this.'

'But why didn't you tell me yourself?'

He shrugged.

'Mainly because, in spite of my apparent vanity, I really don't care to blow my own trumpet . . . and then you didn't seem particularly interested in me, or in anything about me.'

If only he knew! Feeling very small and petty, Darynthe just wanted to get away. Surely he wouldn't want her company any longer, not now he knew the worst of her, her insulting readiness to think ill of him.

'Please . . . can I go now?' she asked.

'Why go now . . . now that everything is cleared up to everyone's satisfaction?' Caan said in surprise.

'You're really not angry with me?'

'Angry? Do I look as if I'm angry?'

Green eyes met bright blue and were hastily lowered, before the impact of that glance. There was strong emotion in Caan's eyes, but it certainly wasn't anger.

'How long were you planning to stay with my Uncle Jack?' Caan asked, when the silence had become almost unbearable.

'Two or three days . . . as long as it seemed necessary.'

She was able to meet his eyes now, relieved by this change of subject.

'So no one's expecting you back at the Daffodil today?'

Slowly Darynthe shook her head, half reluctant to make the admission.

'There you are, then,' Caan said triumphantly. 'There's no need whatsoever for you to go yet.'

'B-but I can't stay here! N-not now that you're here.'

'Not overnight, I agree,' said Caan. 'Not that I'd have any objection,' he added, a wicked gleam lighting his eyes, 'except that I doubt my self-control would be equal to the strain.'

'Please . . . please don't talk like that,' Darynthe pleaded tremulously.

She hated what she thought of as cheap, sexual innuendo. Because that was all it could be . . . because Caan was only flirting with her, encouraged by her unexpected readiness to accept his kisses . . . accept and return, she thought, her cheeks colouring. It would be different, of course, if he really meant it . . . that he was irresistibly, irrevocably attracted to her, that he loved her . . .

'You shall go safely home to Auntie tonight,' he said gravely, though his eyes had not entirely lost their teasing glint. 'But, in the meantime . . .'

'Yes?' she prompted a little nervously.

'It does seem a pity to waste this early start to the day.'

Darynthe looked at her wristwatch. It was only six o'clock. Incredible that so much emotion-charged action could have been packed into so short a time.

'Windermere is a wonderful place to be, at this time of day,' Caan suggested enticingly.

'But we can't leave Jack . . . I mean Mr Lorimer . . . alone.'

'He's on the mend, I promise you,' said Caan. 'He's a tough old bird . . . he has to be, to live his kind of outdoor life. Besides, if we go now we can be back by lunchtime.'

'Lunchtime!' Darynthe squeaked protestingly. 'Never mind lunch, what about breakfast?'

The burden of her guilt removed, her appetite was suddenly miraculously restored.

'That too will be taken care of, madame!' Caan said grandly. He crossed the living room and looked round Jack Lorimer's door.

'I'm taking Darynthe down to the boat for an hour or so. Will you be O.K.?'

The sounds of assent came from the other room and Caan rejoined Darynthe, smiling with satisfaction.

'There you are . . . you've no excuse now to refuse my company.'

Far from wanting to refuse it, Darynthe alone knew how eagerly she would seek his company. If only she did

not have this uncomfortable conviction that this way lay
certain danger to her peace of mind.

To Caan, she was sure, she had only been a challenge
. . . a lame dog, whom, in his good nature, he was helping
over her particular stile . . . mistrust of his sex. What he
could not realise, she thought hopelessly, was that in
endeavouring to reinstate men in general in her good
opinion, he was establishing himself far too firmly in her
heart.

Down at the lakeside, Caan handed Darynthe into a
small dinghy.

'This is the best time of day, while Windermere is all
ours,' he said, and indeed there was no other craft to be
seen on the long reaches of the lake, or in its bays and
inlets.

He rowed slowly towards the moorings, the wake of the
dinghy ruffling the placid surface. The only other disturbance of the water was the barely perceptible movement
of hundreds of darting minnows in the shallows and the
noiseless diving of coots in pursuit of an early breakfast.

The air still held the shivery feel of the dawn, a chill
which would not be dispelled until the hazy sun climbed
higher above the lingering mist, which encapsulated them
in silence, while giving promise of a still, warm day.

The world of Lakeland seemed all asleep. No breeze as
yet stirred the trees on the margin of the lake and even the
swans still had their long necks curled, heads buried beneath their wings.

Darynthe's eyes were drawn irresistibly to the sight of
Caan's bare, muscular forearms, as long steady strokes
brought the dinghy alongside a cruiser which bore the
name *Serenity* in white letters on its dark green hull. He
made fast the dinghy and helped her to step aboard.

The cruiser was well fitted out, with cabins fore and aft
and a spotless galley, where Caan soon had breakfast
under way; and before long the delicious smell of grilled
bacon mingled with the fresh scents of the summer morning.

As they ate, the sun climbed steadily over the ridgeline
of the Troutbeck fells and on the far shore, lakeside cam-
pers could be seen emerging from their tents, the hardier

among them taking a chilly pre-breakfast dip into the water.

The remains of breakfast cleared away, Caan started up the engine and headed south, threading a way between the numerous islets and the many craft moored behind Belle Isle, with its oval Georgian house. Some of the islets seemed to be no larger than rocky points, barely above water level and just big enough to give roothold to a tree or a foothold to a roosting bird.

Caan indicated to Darynthe that she might take the helm and stood close behind her, one arm around her, hand resting lightly over hers, correcting any errors. The brush of his bare arm against hers, with its sensuous caress of hair-roughened skin, filled her with a heightened awareness and she found it difficult to concentrate upon the task in hand, experiencing a wild, compulsive yearning for both of his arms to come around her, to crush her backwards against his hard frame.

The ferryboat was making its first crossing of the day.

'Hard to imagine, on a day like this, that one of the early ferries actually sank,' Caan observed, 'with no survivors either.'

Darynthe, watching the ferry's steady progress, with its load of cars and people, en route to Hawkshead, shuddered at the thought.

'You must know just about everything there is to know about this area,' she observed.

Caan shrugged.

'One tends to think one does . . . then suddenly, during a day out on the fells, one can discover an entirely new facet, a new mood of this countryside. After all these years, after all the books I've written, I still like to think there's something more to be learnt.'

'I wish I knew it as well as you do,' Darynthe said wistfully.

'No reason why you shouldn't some day . . . if you stay here long enough.'

That was the whole trouble, Darynthe thought. She wouldn't be here long enough. She couldn't run away from the past for ever. Besides, her father would be missing her and, if the truth were known, there was no real reason why she should not return to Corbridge immediately. This sojourn in the north-west had effected its cure. No trace remained of the hurt inflicted by her break with Mark.

The only snag, she mused wryly, was that the panacea had resulted in unexpected side-effects, namely the present state of her feelings towards Caan Lorimer.

'I'll let you take the helm again on the run back,' Caan said, interrupting her reverie. 'I want to get up a bit of speed while I have a chance.'

He opened up the throttle and began a fast run down the lake.

'We won't be able to do this later,' he told Darynthe. 'Once the lake gets crowded, I'll have to make too many changes of course.'

The note of the engine deepened, the bows of the craft lifting, their wake creaming out behind them, the rush of their progress exhilarating. Relieved of her need to concentrate, Darynthe studied the eastern shoreline, with its privately owned villas and hotels.

'Where did you live before you came to stay with your uncle?' she asked.

Caan darted her a sideways look.

I don't live with him permanently, you know. I have a flat in London. I live there for half of the year . . . but when I'm researching a new book, I usually come up and stay with Jack.'

'I'm surprised you don't live here all the time, since you love it so much.'

'Strange you should say that,' Caan told her, 'because recently I've been thinking seriously about buying a house in this area and giving up the flat. As I get older, I find city life palling somewhat. I miss the freedom of the fells . . . the clear air.'

'Wouldn't a move affect your career as a writer?'

'Not really. I do most of the writing during the six months I'm up here anyway and I only need to see my publisher occasionally. It would be just as easy to go down to London once or twice a year. That's where I've been for the last week, incidentally, delivering the finished manuscript.'

By Silver Holme, an island off the western shore of the

lake, Caan eased the throttle, slipped into reverse and stopped at its rocky flank.

'How about a dip?' he suggested.

'I've no costume.'

'You'll find one in a locker in the cabin. I should think it will about fit you ... though Ozanne's a mite skinnier than you.'

'I don't think I'll bother,' said Darynthe, her tone chilly. She wasn't going to wear a bikini belonging to one of his women friends; who was this Ozanne, who was sufficiently familiar with Caan to have left her swimwear in his cabin?

Caan shrugged, unbuttoning his shirt.

'Suit yourself. You don't mind if I go in?'

'Not at all,' she replied frigidly.

With a swift movement, which gave her no time to avert her eyes, Caan whipped off his thigh-hugging jeans and stood before her in close-fitting trunks which left very little to the imagination.

Darynthe had long been aware of his broad shoulders and muscular torso, but now she was in possession of further knowledge of his pyhsical attributes ... the lean waist, taut firm hips and buttocks, which merged into the strong muscularity of sun-bronzed legs.

With a fluid, effortless movement, Caan went over the side, his smooth dive scarcely disturbing the calm, flat surface of the lake.

Darynthe leant over the side of the boat to watch him cleaving through the water with a strong overarm stroke. She could admire his technique and being a powerful swimmer herself, she would have dearly loved to join him in the water. But she had made that impossible now, by her instinctive fit of pique at the mention of another woman.

She looked around at her peaceful, solitary surroundings and wondered just how many other girls Caan had brought here, whether this Ozanne was the latest in a line of them.

Jack Lorimer had given the impression that Caan had brought quite a few girl-friends to see him. She tried to imagine Caan with another girl ... particularly the type that the name Ozanne conjured up. What was Caan like when his companion was not inhibited, as she herself was, by a mistrust of men? Had he made love to any or all of his girl-friends? And by that, she admitted to herself, she was thinking of lovemaking in the fullest, deepest sense of the word.

What would it be like? she wondered, her eyes glazing over as she deliberately allowed her thoughts to rove sensuously, picturing two bodies locked in intimacy ... Caan's, and hers.

Being tall herself, she had always liked big men, and physically she knew Caan was the most arresting man she had ever met. Where Mark had been lean to the point of angularity, Caan was broad ... a large man, but rangy rather than bulky, with big bones and powerful, well-carried shoulders, giving an impression of latent strength, but strength combined with gentleness. There was something about him, too, which inspired confidence. He had a compelling personality, straight and forthright, totally frank, about everything, except for one thing ... his feelings for her ... mental, emotional feeling; for there could be no doubt that he found her pleasing in the physical sense. That had been all too clearly revealed in the moments of exquisite tension between them, and most recently, in the early hours of that morning, when he had found her in his bed.

But he had never put anything into words. Darynthe felt that he was not a man to speak lightly of love where he did not feel it, and too honest to pretend.

So where did that leave her ... a temporary amusement, a substitute for the missing Ozanne, who had staked her claim to Caan by leaving her swimwear behind?

Caan was returning to the boat, heaving himself effortlessly on to the deck, water streaming from him, moulding the material of his trunks to the flat, firm belly, while the vital, springy dark hair, with its tell-tale traces of grey, was plastered closely to his head. He shook himself, much in the manner of a water spaniel, then disappeared in search of a towel.

When he came back on deck, he wore the towel sarong-like around his middle, and from the fact that he carried a damp pair of trunks in one hand, Darynthe gathered that the towel was all that protected him from her mesmerised gaze.

'Was . . . was the water very cold?' she babbled inanely . . . anything to conceal the fact that his near-nakedness disturbed her.

'You'll never know, will you?' he said tantalisingly. 'Why didn't you come in? Can't you swim?'

'Yes, I can swim,' she replied, then, 'who is Ozanne?' she asked, unaware just how revealing the question was to the man watching her so intently.

He shrugged.

'A friend.'

'Girl-friend?' she hazarded.

She was trying desperately to make her manner casual, so that he should not sense the painful jealousy which had gripped her at the mention of Ozanne's name.

He neither confirmed nor denied her supposition.

'Why do you want to know?'

Casually, he moved closer to her, so that she could smell the faint but pleasant scent of his damp skin.

'I . . . I just wondered. Just making conversation, I suppose.'

'We know each other too well by now for that to be necessary,' he said. 'Something is bothering you . . . I can tell.'

Oh, something was bothering her all right . . . the knowledge that somewhere in his background was a girl called Ozanne, a girl who was more slenderly built than herself, who probably lived in London and would therefore be more sophisticated than herself. But more disturbing than any of this was his proximity, in that towel, which looked all too insecure to her.

She backed away, until the cabin stopped her retreat, then found she could not move in any direction, as he effectively blocked her way, a hand resting either side of her head, against the cabin wall.

'Why do you want to know about Ozanne?' he persisted.

'I don't want to know anything about your . . . your women friends,' she snapped. 'It's a matter of supreme indifference to me whom you go around with, bring out on your cruiser . . .'

'Evidently,' he said with dry sarcasm, 'but do you always show so much rancour about things that are of no interest to you?'

'I'm not jealous, if that's what you're thinking.'

She stopped, appalled by such gauche naïvety. Her very denial must make it evident to him that she was in fact burningly, miserably jealous of this unknown Ozanne, indeed of any woman he knew. She waited for him to taunt her with this fact, for the smug, knowing look which would cross his face.

'Of course you're not jealous,' was all he said. 'Why should you be? After all, you don't even like men very much, do you? Am I supposed to be grateful that you even tolerate me?'

'I . . . I don't just tolerate you,' she stammered. 'I . . . I quite like you, in fact. It . . . it's just that . . .'

'That you're still afraid, still terrified to show any feeling, to admit that you *have* normal feelings. Tell me something, Darynthe, purely academically, of course . . . just what *do* you feel when I kiss you?'

Wordlessly she stared up at him. His question was impossible to answer. With Machiavellian cunning, he had trapped her. If she stated now that she enjoyed his kisses—enjoyed, what an understatement—he would take that as permisssion to make love to her, here, now, in a state of undress, the very thought of which made her throat close up with panic. On the other hand, if she denied his effect upon her, pretended that his kisses left her unmoved, that she disliked them even . . . being male, he would undoubtedly see that as a challenge, an excuse to prove both to himself and to her that she had lied. From past experience he knew only too well what his caress did to her, how she had responded. Both alternative answers were fraught with danger. Was there a middle road open to her?

Caan repeated his question, pressing closer to her as he spoke.

'What do you feel when I kiss you?'

'I . . . I'm afraid I couldn't say,' she faltered. 'I . . . I've never really thought about it.'

And that must be the biggest lie you've ever told,

Darynthe Browne, she chided herself. Hadn't she spent at least ten minutes, while he had been swimming, imagining her reactions to an intimacy far more thought-provoking than a mere kiss?

Caan was looking at her quizzically too, as if he did not believe her, and the incredulous twinkle in those blue eyes, the very fact that he seemed to think she could not possibly be indifferent to him, stung her out of retreat into taking the offensive.

'Why do you want to know, anyway?' she challenged him. 'Does it boost your ego . . . do you keep a sort of kissometer and ask all your girl-friends how you rate?'

'*All* my girl-friends,' he mused. 'Now I wonder what makes you say that? You seem to have some very strange ideas about me. Am I supposed to have a harem tucked away somewhere?'

'According to your Uncle Jack, you. . . .'

'Ah—Uncle Jack! So you've been quizzing him, have you?'

'Certainly not!' she snapped. 'I'm not sufficiently interested in you, or your love affairs. He just happened to mention . . .' She broke off, biting her lip. She couldn't very well repeat exactly what Jack had said . . . that she was the nicest girl Caan had ever brought to meet him.

She endeavoured to change the subject.

'Aren't you going to get dressed again?'

Immediately she knew the question had been a mistake. The ironic gleam in his eyes intensified.

'Do I make you nervous, like this?'

'Oh no,' she lied, 'of course not, but . . .' With sudden inspiration, she glanced at her wristwatch. 'oughtn't we to be getting back? Your uncle's all alone, and . . .'

He gave his slow, crooked smile, curiously tender and understanding.

'Don't worry, Darynthe. Surely you know me well enough by now to know that I wouldn't deliberately do anything to alarm your susceptibilities?'

She turned her head aside, avoiding his questioning gaze, unable to answer. It was all very well for him to deny that he was alarming, but he still hadn't moved. She was still trapped, imprisoned between him and the cabin wall ... close enough to him to feel his breath on her cheek. Though he was not actually touching her she could feel his strength enveloping her. She seemed to be in a sentient state, waiting ... waiting for what? Waiting for the inevitable?

She was afraid of what might happen, if he touched her now ... kissed her ... yet she felt an obsessive need for his kiss.

It was as if he sensed her thoughts, for he leant forward slightly to brush his lips against the side of her neck, just below her ear, making her shudder with pleasure. His mouth trailed its insidious, seductive path across her cheek, to the corner of her mouth and she was lost ... instantly all fire, turning eagerly, fusing her mouth to his in a wild response, which seemed to take him by surprise, for his breath caught momentarily, before he hauled her into his arms, his lips parted to consume her suddenly eager, seeking mouth.

Her hands, which had remained clenched at her side throughout their conversation, relaxed, lifting to run caressingly over the muscular strength of his naked back, as she shifted against him in a sudden frenzy of arousal.

Beneath the towel the muscles of his thighs were hard against hers, and for an instant she was wholly aware of his desire.

Gently, Caan released himself from her wildly caressing hands ... firmly holding her away from him.

'No more, Daryhthe,' he said, his mouth twisted in wry self-abnegation. 'I'm only human, after all.'

She was aware of aching disappointment, as he turned resolutely away, announcing in abrupt tones his intention of getting dressed.

'You're right,' he said, over his shoulder. 'It *is* high time we were getting back.'

Left alone, Darynthe wound her arms tightly about her fluttering stomach, her emotions in tatters ... a terrible, unfamiliar craving unassuaged. For a moment or two she had been like a creature possessed, clinging, grasping, her nails scoring Caan's bronzed, naked back. She did not recognise herself in this wanton, passionate creature. She had never felt this way with Mark ... had no idea that she was even capable of such a feeling. Such a quivering, violent need had never presented itself . . . the problem of this aching desire for a man's total possession.

Despair tore at her. Was she doomed to unhappiness yet again, just as the dark clouds of her broken engagement had lifted?

When she had parted with Mark, in the depths of her misery she had cried out, wishing that they had never met, that she had never felt love for a man. But strangely, in spite of the foreboding, which told her that this love for Caan could prove many times as painful, she could not express the same wish . . . that she had never known him.

Not to have experienced a sensation so sublime, revealing a hitherto unimagined promise of bliss, would have been tantamount to sacrilege. She felt as if she had matured, aged in wisdom, in an incredibly short space of time. Love might be hurtful, but it was the very breath and essence of life. Not to have experienced it would be not to have lived at all.

When Caan returned, fully clothed, she was able to face him with only the slightest trace of selfconsciousness, and to her relief he followed her lead, his manner friendly but self-contained.

On their return journey up the lake, the water was considerably busier, with waterborne activities of all kinds, canoeing, sailing, rowing and water-skiing. Threading a careful passage between the other craft, jockeying for position in the bay, they picked up the cruiser's moorings once more and made all ship shape.

As the dinghy bobbed shorewards, Darynthe re-examined her feelings. She was in love with Caan, of that there could be no doubt, and she had learnt to trust him. After all, not many men, excited, as she had excited him by her eagerness, could have exercised such ruthless self-control . . . would have wanted to control themselves. But he had not lost his consideration for her, despite the very obvious fact that he had returned her desire.

Darynthe's mind was made up. She would stop running away from Caan, from the danger he posed. She would no longer try to avoid the occasions of hurt. Suddenly it seemed important to make the most of every moment with him, regardless of what the future might bring. Perhaps, she thought optimistically, if she stopped fighting him he might find something to love in her . . . real, lasting love. For the first time in a long while, hope seemed to lie in wait.

'You'll come back with me for lunch?' Caan asked, as he beached the dinghy.

Darynthe nodded. She would not be refusing any more invitations from Caan; besides, she had to collect her uncle's car.

The day had lived up to its early promise, the mist having completely disappeared and the clear air gave sharp definition to the mountain tops. It was a day of promise, of sunshine, and Darynthe felt as if the sunlight had penetrated to the gloomiest corners of her mind, making it as cloudless as the blue arc of the sky above.

Hand in hand they returned to the car.

'Come climbing with me tomorrow?' Caan suggested, as they drove slowly back through Ambleside and on towards Grisedale Beck. 'Just the two of us . . . a whole day's outing?'

'I don't know,' Darynthe demurred. 'Oh, I want to,' she added hastily, seeing his oblique, questioning glance. 'But I don't know if I ought. I feel a bit guilty about Auntie Ann. I'm supposed to be here to help her.'

'Are you really needed that much?' Caan asked curiously. 'I thought perhaps the whole thing was a polite fiction, while you got over your unfortunate romance?'

'That's probably true in part,' Darynthe admitted. 'But my aunt is shorthanded with my cousin away convalescing.'

'Well, perhaps the next day, then,' he said, 'when you've caught up on your chores . . . eased your conscience?'

'That would be lovely,' she said happily. 'As soon as we've had lunch, I must get back to the Daffodil and let Auntie know that everything is all right. She was quite concerned about your uncle.'

'She's a delightful woman, your aunt,' Caan said, then, hesitantly, 'I shouldn't imagine she's very much like her brother . . . your father?'

'Whatever makes you think that?'

He shrugged.

'Oh, just things she's said ... things that you've told me. Mrs Forster doesn't seem as ... as possessive about her family. Her husband is away at sea, and she postively encourages you to go out.'

Darynthe was silent for a while, resentful at his implied criticism of her father. At last she said quietly, with no wish to renew the conflict between them,

'I don't think you should make assumptions like that. After all, you don't know my father.'

With a slight inclination of his head, he accepted the rebuke.

As they drove on in companionable silence, Darynthe wondered whether it was likely that Caan and her father would ever meet. What they would think of each other. She had always been aware of a certain veiled hostility in her father's attitude towards Mark ... and afterwards, she had put it down to an intuitive feeling on Mr Browne's part, that Mark was not all that he seemed. Now she couldn't help considering the possibility that her father had resented Mark, that he might resent any man who wanted to marry her and take her away from Corbridge. Then she shook her head. She was allowing Caan's insinuation to colour her thoughts. Her father had only ever wanted what was best for her, had denied her nothing.

'Where shall we go ... climbing, I mean?' she asked Caan.

'I wondered when you were going to come out of that brown study,' he commented. 'You were thinking so deeply, I could almost hear the cogs turning. Worth sharing?'

'Not a bit,' she said hastily. She couldn't tell Caan she had been wondering how he would get on with her father. He might think she was assuming too much ... hearing wedding bells, as one of her friends had once put it.

'I thought we'd try Old Man Coniston,' said Caan. 'It's not too stiff for a novice, yet still gives you a sense of achievement. All right by you?'

'Fine,' she nodded.

Caan pulled the car off the road, across the bumpy, rutted track, and parked next to Bob Forster's car.

'New car?' he asked.

'No ... no, it's my uncle's. But that reminds me. I'd forgotten all about the bill for the Mini. I ... I've left a cheque on the dressing table in your room.'

'Oh, there's no need for that,' he said airily. 'That small amount won't break the bank.'

'I know you're probably very rich,' said Darynthe, with a return of her old stiffness, 'but I can't let you do it.'

'Why not?' He tucked an arm through hers, as they moved towards the cottage. 'It was my fault, you said, that you went off the road.'

She stopped in her tracks, facing him squarely.

'You know I only said that because ... well, because you were a man, and at that time I felt vicious towards any man I met.'

'But you don't now?'

'I ... I don't think so,' she prevaricated, unwilling to confess the full extent of her changed feelings.

'That's good.' He steered her forward again.

'Then ... then you'll accept my cheque?' she asked.

He sighed.

'If I must. You're a very stubborn, independent young woman, Darynthe Browne with an "e". '

She laughed. She didn't mind him teasing her now about her haughty insistence on that final 'e'.

As soon as they stepped into the cottage, Darynthe sensed something different in the atmosphere. The kitchen, normally a place of warm, inviting cooking smells, had been invaded by a heavy, sensuous perfume; and from the open door to Jack Lorimer's bedroom came the murmur of voices.

As Caan shut the outer door, Jack Lorimer called out to him.

'That you, Caan? You have a visitor.'

Darynthe would have hung back, but Caan propelled her forward into the room, where Jack was sitting up, looking considerably better.

But it was the figure rising from the chair by the bed which held all of Darynthe's attention.

The girl who had been talking to Jack was a tall, willowy brunette, very tall, very languid and very glossy, with an air of arrogant self-assurance. Elaborately coiffured hair lay in a heavy swathe from right to left of her broad forehead and high, dramatic cheekbones tapered to a finely pointed chin.

'Caan!' this apparition drawled. 'Wherever have you been? I've been waiting simply ages!'

Her narrow, slanting, feline eyes took in Darynthe, standing at Caan's side, and her assessing glance made Darynthe acutely aware of her faded jeans and sweatshirt.

The other girl glided forward, her seductive body sheathed in elegant black, her mouth a moist, crimson pout, inviting Caan's kiss. He obliged, with a swift brush of his lips.

'Darynthe, this is Ozanne Hanson ... Ozanne, Darynthe Browne. But this is a surprise, Ozanne. What brings you here?'

As if he didn't know, Darynthe thought scornfully, as the secretive golden eyes looking into his widened in assumed amazement.

'Why, darling, don't you remember? When you were in town last week you mentioned that you were thinking of buying yourself a pied-à-terre in these parts. Someone has to keep an eye on you, to see that you don't choose anything too ridiculously primitive.'

As Ozanne spoke, the tawny gold eyes swept around Jack's homely bedroom and it was all too obvious that this was her idea of primitive accommodation.

So Ozanne Hanson had come to help Caan choose a house, had she? That implied a considerable degree of intimacy. Perhaps it was intended that she should share his home.

Darynthe shot a surreptitious glance at the girl's left hand, then she relaxed a little. At least she didn't wear a ring ... yet.

'It's very good of you to concern yourself with my comfort,' said Caan. His tone was so even that Darynthe could detect neither irony nor enthusiasm.

Finely pencilled, arching brows rose still further, as Ozanne slipped a possessive arm through Caan's.

'Darling, it's the least I can do, after all you've done for me.'

Imperceptibly she was edging Caan away from Darynthe, away from his uncle and towards the door of the living room.'

'This is such a terrible place to get at,' she exclaimed in her loud, drawling voice. 'The taxi fare was out of this world!'

'If you'd let me know you were coming, I could have met you at Windermere station,' Caan observed.

'But you're not on the phone here, lover . . . and a letter takes far too long. You know what a creature of impulse I am. I just threw a few rags into a suitcase . . . and here I am.'

Darynthe, regarding Ozanne's retreating back view, in the elegant black skirt, wondered cynically what the girl's other 'rags' were like.

Turning away, she met Jack's shrewd eyes and he grinned conspiratorially.

'That's the dressed-up little madam I was telling you about,' he whispered. 'Pain in the neck, isn't she?'

Darynthe nodded, then briskly changed the subject. She didn't want to think about Ozanne Hanson until she was alone, for fear the bitter jealousy she felt would show itself in her expressive face.

'Lunch!' she said. 'What would you like? I'll get yours, then I'm off.' She jerked her head towards the living room. 'She can get her own . . . and Caan's.'

Jack looked at the determined set of her face, an anxious frown wrinkling his weatherbeaten brow.

'Not going to run away again, and leave her a clear field, are you, love?'

'I was going home this afternoon anyway,' Darynthe pointed out, as she plumped his pillows and straightened his quilt. 'So an hour earlier isn't going to make much difference.'

All the time she had been talking, she had been aware of something different about Jack's room, something missing. Then she realised.

'Where's Scipio?'

Usually the collie draped himself across the foot of his master's bed.

Jack pulled a wry face.

'Outside. Ozanne's allergic to dogs.'

'Does . . . does she stay here, then?'

Darynthe was filled with jealous horror at the thought that Caan might give up his bed to the other girl . . . for somehow she couldn't see Ozanne on the capacious but lumpy settee.

'Lord no . . . thank goodness. She'll expect to be put up in a hotel in Windermere or Grasmere. Nothing but the best for Lady Ozanne.'

'Lady?' Darynthe paused at the door.

Jack nodded.

'A real live lady . . . makes you sick, doesn't it?'

It certainly did, Darynthe thought, as she heated soup and buttered wedges of wholemeal toast in the bright, cheerful kitchen. She had suspected that Caan moved in intellectual and sophisticated circles, but a 'lady'! How could she possibly compete in that league? she wondered drearily.

As she passed through the living room, tray in hand, Ozanne looked up from her animated conversation with Caan . . . a long, hard, cold stare.

'I hope *we* don't have to eat here, Caan darling? I was rather hoping that you'd take me out to lunch . . . preferably somewhere exotic.'

Caan hesitated before he replied and Darynthe kicked the bedroom door shut behind her. Let him take his precious Ozanne out to lunch . . . see if she cared!

She sat on the edge of Jack's bed, watching him as he spooned up the soup with relish. He looked at her over the bowl, blue eyes pleading.

'Don't throw in the towel, love. Stick around . . . see her off. You can do it, you know. You're worth a dozen of my lady.'

Darynthe shrugged.

'That's all very well, but I presume Caan has some say in the matter. Obviously he prefers Lady Ozanne.'

Jack shook his grizzled head.

'Not his type. Oh, she may be fine at these swagger do's they have up in London. But can you see her in old jeans and gumboots, out on the fells?'

Darynthe laughed with him, immensely cheered by this

unflattering picture of the other girl.

As they laughed, Caan came into the room. For a large, normally self-assured man, he looked almost diffident.

'Darynthe, would you mind very much if I took Ozanne out to lunch? I know we planned to lunch here, but . . .'

'But it's not good enough for *Lady* Ozanne,' Darynthe said. She stood up and moved towards the door.

'Darynthe!' Caan's voice was curiously pleading, but she ignored him, speaking instead to his uncle.

'Bye Jack . . . see you some time . . . maybe.'

As she opened the back door, she found a despondent Scipio, lying across the step. He rose, as if to enter the cottage and, about to prevent him, Darynthe paused, a sudden mischievous smile illuminating her face. Jack had urged her to fight back . . . well, so she would!

She opened the door wider.

'Go on in, Scipio,' she invited, in a low voice. She giggled. 'I'm sure *Lady* Ozanne will be delighted to see you!'

CHAPTER SIX

Somehow, although she had postponed their outing to the following day, Darynthe had expected Caan to make contact with her next morning . . . perhaps to apologise for breaking their luncheon arrangements, and certainly to settle the time when he would call for her.

But he did not call in at the Daffodil, nor did he telephone; and the sense of injustice she had felt mounted steadily. In all probability, she thought resentfully, he was out with the glamorous Ozanne, house-hunting.

Jealousy lent power to her elbow and she attacked her tasks around the guesthouse with energetic fury.

'My word, you're certainly making up for lost time!' her aunt observed. 'There's no need to kill yourself, you know. I did do *some* work while you were away. I must say I'm glad Caan's back to look after his uncle. I wasn't too happy about you being over there, so isolated and with no telephone if anything had gone wrong.'

She looked keenly at her niece's flushed face. 'When are you seeing Caan again?'

'I . . . I don't know,' Darynthe prevaricated, giving the cutlery a final vigorous polish. 'He . . . he has a friend staying with him, so I shouldn't think he'll have much free time at present.'

'A friend?' Ann queried. 'What's he like?'

'*She* is about my height, though much slimmer . . . extremely chic and a member of the aristocracy!'

'Oh!' Ann looked doubtfully at her niece. 'Competition?'

'I don't know what you mean,' said Darynthe, adding mendaciously, 'In no way am I in competition for Caan Lorimer's favours. She's welcome to him. In fact, it seems as if she's got him, since she's here to help him with his house-hunting.'

'Oh dear!' Ann's pleasant face wrinkled with concern. 'What a pity. I did think . . . but there, perhaps you're mistaken. She may be just a good friend.'

'Pouf!' Darynthe expressed her breath in a sound of disgust. 'She's not the type that men make good friends of, and you wouldn't think so either, if you'd seen her oozing sex appeal all over him.'

Purposely Darynthe refrained from telling her aunt about Caan's suggestions for the next day; because she didn't intend to be around when and if he arrived to collect her. Most probably he wouldn't turn up anyway, she thought. But if he did, he wasn't going to have the satisfaction of finding her meekly waiting . . . not after he'd so readily abandoned their plans to have lunch at Jack's cottage, preferring instead to escort his sophisticated lady friend to a hotel meal.

'We've had some new arrivals while you were away,' Ann told her.

Darynthe nodded.

'Yes, I noticed them at breakfast. A man and woman, and their son . . . or is he their grandson? They look rather old to be his parents.'

'Mmm, that's what I thought. But they're his parents all right.'

'I shouldn't have thought they were up to fellwalking,' Darynthe commented, as she arranged new flowers on the reception desk.

'They spend their time sightseeing,' Ann said, 'while their son goes on the walks. He's a nice lad. I feel a bit sorry for him. He'd probably get more enjoyment from this type of holiday if he came with friends of his own age.'

Darynthe had an opportunity that evening to make the acquaintance of the Griffiths and their son. While his parents were enthusing to the other guests about Beatrix Potter, Wordsworth and Ruskin and their pilgrimages to the places connected with them, he engaged Darynthe in conversation.

A tall, stringy young man, with an untidy straggle of beard and moustache, impudent brown eyes and a shock of fair, untidy hair flopping over his forehead, he was a cheerful extrovert.

While he enjoyed fellwalking, he told Darynthe, his main obsession, a hobby as well as an essential part of his work, was botany, and he was using this holiday to combine the two interests.

'I go abroad for most of my holidays,' he continued, 'but the aged parents like me to spend one holiday a year with them. I do most of the driving coming up, to make things easier for Dad, then he just tootles round on these day trips of theirs.'

He seemed a nice, uncomplicated sort of person, Darynthe thought, genuinely fond of his parents and with a very proper concern for their welfare.

'Do you get any free time?' he asked Darynthe.

'Goodness, yes! Mrs Forster is my aunt,' she explained, 'so I work pretty flexible hours.'

'That's great,' he exclaimed. 'Then how about coming on a walk with me tomorrow? It's a bit tedious talking to oneself.' He grinned engagingly. 'A pretty girl could do a lot to relieve the boredom.'

Darynthe considered the idea. Why not? she thought. She rather liked young Mr Griffiths, who, she guessed, was not very much older than herself. Agreeing to an outing with him would provide her with a golden opportunity to be unavailable, should Caan decide to keep their date.

'By the way,' the young man added, 'I know your name's Darynthe, and a jolly pretty name it is, but I don't think you know mine. It's Marcus . . . though my friends call me Mark.'

Darynthe stared at him. Mark! Even though it was only an abbreviation of his full name, it was an unpleasant coincidence. She had long since recovered from her period of unhappiness over Mark Little, but still felt that she should automatically dislike anyone who bore that name.

'What is it?' Marcus asked, his brown eyes concerned. 'Are you annoyed? I mean, it probably sounds pretty fast work, asking you to go out with me when we've just met. But we're only here for a few more days, and I assure you, I'm the soul of respectability.'

'It's not that,' she assured him. 'It's just that I used to know someone called Mark. I . . . he . . . well, I won't go into details, but it's not exactly my favourite name at the moment, and it was a bit of a shock, that's all.'

'You can call me Griff instead, if you like,' he offered. 'Some people do.'

'No . . . no, really.' Darynthe shook her head. 'I'll call you Mark.'

It would be ridiculous after all, she thought, to get a hang-up over a name, just because it had belonged to someone who had let her down. With a little pang she wondered if the sound of the name Caan would some day produce the same unpleasant effect.

'I'd thought of going up the Old Man,' Marcus Griffiths said, bringing her wandering thoughts back to the present.

'Coniston?' Darynthe said doubtfully.

The very place where Caan had promised to take her. But it was unlikely he would still go up the mountain, once he discovered she had not waited in for him.

'Too stiff for you?' Marcus asked.

'No . . . no, of course not. I'd love to come, but . . . but could we make a *very* early start?'

Although, in her own mind, she was firmly convinced that Caan would be too occupied with the glamorous Lady

Ozanne to recall his promise to her, Darynthe was determined to be away well before he was likely to call at the guesthouse.

As they cleared away the guests' supper things, Darynthe told her aunt of her plans.

'I'm going to climb Old Man Coniston tomorrow, with Mark Griffiths. We'll need two packed lunches. I'll make them up myself, before I go to bed, and leave them in the fridge.'

Darynthe woke to the sound of torrential rain. Uttering a little cry of dismay, she leapt out of bed and ran to the window. The clouds hung low and heavy, with no visible sign of breaking, as the rain fell unrelentingly on subdued, sullen gulls, roosting on slick, dark grey rooftops.

Marcus had ordered an early breakfast and Darynthe joined him, though there no longer seemed any point in hurrying.

But Marcus was an optimist.

'It'll break later, you'll see,' he said cheerfully. 'By the time we get over to Coniston, the weather will have changed.'

'But we'll be soaked long before we get there,' Darynthe objected, with a dismal vision of waiting in the rain for public transport.

'No, we won't. The parents have chummed up with another couple and they're all off to Keswick together this morning, so we can have the car.'

They set off as planned. Other intrepid folk, disconsolate huddles of rucksacks and wet-weather gear, were emerging from the grey Victorian buildings of Ambleside, which looked even more forbidding under matching slate-grey skies.

'Since we've made such an early start,' Mark suggested, 'how would it be if we went the long way round, via Windermere and the ferry? A least it will give the weather a chance to clear up.'

Darynthe agreed readily to this suggestion. Cat-like, she was not over-fond of getting wet.

'Are you hoping to collect any botanical specimens today?' she asked, as they drove out of Ambleside.

'You never know your luck,' Marcus told her. 'I'm

always on the look-out, of course, wherever I go. I found some pretty good specimens of liverwort yesterday ... and Coniston should be a good spot for lichens.'

The actual site of the vehicle ferry was beyond Bowness and when they reached the narrow road, which led down to the crossing, Marcus and Darynthe had a considerable wait, owing to the long stream of traffic, all bound for the ferry.

Marcus seemed unperturbed and chatted on gaily, filling in details of his job as a laboratory assistant in a large comprehensive school in the south of England.

'Normally I only get school holidays ... but Mum's not been too well and the doctor ordered her away for a break. So I put in for an extra week off. Fortunately, the head's a decent sort ... backed my application to the Education Department. Part of my job is to prepare the specimens for all the botany students,' he continued, 'mount them on slides, etc.'

As he talked, requiring no real response from Darynthe, she allowed her thoughts to wander, from time to time interjecting a 'yes' or a 'no' in appropriate places.

As their car moved nearer and nearer to the crossing, she could not help comparing the lake in its present mood with the aspect it had worn two days previously, when she and Caan had traversed its length in *Serenity*; and as they drove on to the chain-operated ferry she remembered, with a shudder, Caan's mention of a ferry of earlier years which had sunk with much loss of life.

Marcus, distracted from his monologue, looked at her in concern.

'Cold?' He ran up the window, lowered earlier in an effort to reduce the internal condensation.

'Not really. Just remembering something someone told me, about a ferry that sank.'

Darynthe knew it would be more sensible to try and banish all thoughts of Caan from her mind, for today at least, but there was so much to remind her of him. There was no scene, no aspect of Lakeland that he had not written about.

Had he called at the Daffodil? she wondered ... and if so, what had been his reaction to finding her gone, and with another man? For she had no doubt her aunt, who thought Caan could do no wrong, would give him chapter and verse of her niece's whereabouts.

She found herself wishing that she had not been quite so explicit, had not mentioned their destination to Ann Forster. Suppose, just suppose Caan did come in search of her, as he had on the day she went to Windermere? But no, she thought. This was different. Then, he had felt sorry for her, had been trying to break down the barriers she had erected around herself; but he could only recognise today's action for what it was ... a deliberate avoidance of his company. Pride and annoyance would probably deter him from seeking her out ever again. She found herself half regretting the pique which had prompted her flight, then took herself to task for presumption.

Whatever makes you think he'll remember to come calling for you, Darynthe Browne, when he has a beautiful, sultry, wealthy woman like Lady Ozanne Hanson hanging on his every word? Illogically, she felt relieved by the thought that, in all likelihood, Caan would never even know of her ill-mannered behaviour in deliberately cutting their date.

The rain was still heavy, lashing the lake with cold, merciless lances, while the wind from the hills whipped the surface into a seething fury; and Darynthe was relieved when they drove safely off the ferry on the far side and took the road signposted 'Near Sawrey.'

'My parents were here yesterday,' Marcus told her. 'My mother was determined to visit Hill Top and wallow in Beatrix Potterism. I think she was bitterly disappointed the day she discovered I'd grown out of Peter Rabbit!'

Darynthe laughed. Marcus's light conversation was a sure antidote for gloomy thoughts ... thoughts which, inevitably, included visions of Caan and the sophisticated Ozanne, hunting for their future home.

The route Marcus had chosen took them along the side of Esthwaite Water to Hawkshead, a quaint, picturesque old village, and Darynthe, who had read about the place, with its timber-framed buildings, coaching inns and narrow cobbled streets, would have liked to stop and explore, but the glowering, sulky clouds were lifting slowly, the rain decreasing in intensity, and Marcus seemed anxious to reach Coniston.

'You don't need a lot of mountaineering knowledge for the Old Man,' he told Darynthe blithely. 'I've been up once before, when I was only a kid. It shouldn't take more than a couple of hours, and if this weather clears you'll get a smashing view from the top.'

Marcus parked the car and by the time they had walked the length of the village street, a watery sun was struggling through the clouds.

Just past the church, the road began to climb, continuing for about half a mile to the bank of a beck, which was shown on Marcus's map as Church Beck. They crossed a small bridge over the beck, then continued on their way upwards, over the close-knit springy, emerald surface of the fell, with its delicious damp earth scents. Around them, gorse bushes were bright with gold and high above them towered the proud, much scarred contours of the Old Man.

'Glad you came?' Marcus asked.

Darynthe nodded, but a small inner voice persisted in hinting that she would have enjoyed it even more had she been with Caan.

'Great! Rhizocarpon Geographicum!' Mark exclaimed, halting suddenly in his tracks. 'Sorry,' he apologised, as Darynthe cannoned into him. 'Look, on this rock . . . this green lichen. See the black lines, making it look like a map?'

Carefully he collected a sample before they walked on, another mile bringing them to the beautiful little tarn of Low Water. From the tarn it was a fairly hard pull of roughly a thousand yards, their feet slipping and sliding over very loose scree, to the cairn on the summit.

Seeing Darynthe paused for breath, Marcus held out a helping hand.

'Take short steps,' he advised, 'and try whistling. It really helps your breathing.'

She stopped, riveted to the spot by the familiar words. 'Where did you get that idea from?'

'Oh, I read it somewhere . . . probably one of C. G. Lorimer's books. He's quite an authority.'

Darynthe, remembering her indignant rejection of this advice from the author himself, began to giggle infectiously, and Marcus joined in, though quite unaware of the cause of her mirth. Sheep below them on the hillside, nuzzling the new crop of bracken, lifted their heads momentarily to seek the cause of the disturbance.

As Marcus had promised, the view from the summit was impressive . . . the spectacular grandeur of mountains, the sylvan beauty of lakes and dales. To the south were the woods and fields of the Furness Fells, with Morecambe Bay shimmering in the distance; to the west, the Irish Sea, with the Isle of Man on the horizon. North lay Scafell, Skiddaw and Helvellyn, with Ambleside and a large part of Windermere clearly visible. Eastwards rose the Yorkshire hills and directly below them they could see Coniston Water.

'I wonder why they call it Old Man?' Marcus mused aloud.

This was a question Darynthe could answer with confidence, based on her own reading of Caan's books.

'Apparently 'old man' is a local term for a miner, and this mountain is riddled with old copper mines.'

They ate their sandwiches, then began their descent. As they did so Marcus laughingly pointed out a solitary sheep, which had become separated from its brethren and was bleating disconsolately, stranded on a ledge overhanging a seemingly vertical drop.

Darynthe was immediately concerned.

'We must try and rescue the poor thing,' she said.

Marcus shook his fair head dismissively.

'Far too risky. I shouldn't worry about it if I were you. The creature probably knows its way about on this hill better than we do.'

The sheep continued to bleat mournfully.

'But it's only a lamb,' Darynthe protested. 'It might fall and kill itself.'

Marcus shrugged with what Darynthe considered to be appalling callousness.

'Golly, Darynthe, what's one sheep more or less? There are hundreds of them in Lakeland.'

Oh, if only it were Caan she was talking to! He, she felt

sure, would have no hesitation in attempting to rescue the lamb.

'It's a living creature, Mark!' To Darynthe all life was sacred. 'I *must* try and help it. You can please yourself.'

Gingerly she made her way across the face of the hillside, her boots slipping on the rough scree, until she was directly above the stranded lamb. She was not a little relieved to find that Marcus, although reluctant, had followed her.

'I think I could scramble down there,' she told him.

'But what are you going to do when you get down there?'

'You have a rope,' she pointed out. 'I could tie it round the lamb and you could pull it up.'

Marcus shook his head.

'It won't work Darynthe. It won't let you near it, you know.'

'I have to try,' she said stubbornly.

'Then let me go down,' he offered, 'since you're so set on rescuing the creature.'

Darynthe shook her head.

'It would be better for me to go down,' she pointed out. 'I'm lighter than you ... far easier for you to pull me back up than for me to pull you.'

In the end she made her descent in a sitting position, an uncomfortable and undignified procedure, as she held on to any tuft of growth or small outcrop of rock that offered a handhold; until, with a last breathtaking skid, she landed on the ledge only a few feet from the lamb.

'Let down the rope,' she called up to Marcus.

The rope came snaking down, a loop already formed at one end. So far so good. Cautiously Darynthe approached the lamb, which was now regarding her activities with obvious suspicion and mistrust in its boot-button eyes.

To her dismay, she found that Marcus's prognostication had been all too accurate. As she drw closer, so the lamb retreared, nearer and nearer to the edge of the drop below.

Darynthe was just comtemplating risking everything in a headlong dive at the lamb, hoping to take it by surprise and effect its capture, when she was halted by an infuriated roar from above.

'What the hell do you think you're doing down there?'

As she looked up the lamb, with that irritating instinct for survival often displayed by the most irretrievably marooned creature, bounded away, descending the mountainside on footholds indiscernible to the human eye.

Though relieved tp see that her erstwhile protégé had safely rejoined its mother on the slopes below, Darynthe had no time for undue rejoicing. Like the lamb, she was faced with what appeared to be an insurmountable problem, that of facing a furiously condemnatory Caan Lorimer, glaring down from his vantage point some twelve feet above her head.

To her horror, he was now venting his ire upon the hapless Marcus.

'What were you thinking of, you young fool, letting Darynthe go down there . . . and why the hell didn't you put the rope on her *before* she went down? Have you so little regard for her safety?'

'I . . . I . . .'

Darynthe could see Marcus crumbling beneath Caan's verbal onslaught.

'Mark!' she shouted. 'If you hold the rope firm. I'll hang on to it as I climb up.'

'He'll do no such thing!' Caan roared. 'Tie that rope round your waist. I'm going to haul you up.'

'Mark is quite capable,' she began icily.

'Is he? I take leave to doubt that.'

In the end, it took the combined efforts of both men to haul her up, for Darynthe, though slim, was tall and well made; and she could not help wondering what would have become of her had Caan not come along.

As she floundered pver the edge, relief at her safety mingled with fury at the man who had encompassed it. Having envisaged him happily house-hunting with Ozanne, blithely unaware of her own defection, it was a shock to encounter him here . . . having so obviously come in search of her. But trust him to arrive at an inopportune moment too, catching her at a disadvantage.

'What are *you* doing here?' The words issued ungraciously from between her tightened lips, as he disentangled the rope, the task bringing him far too close for comfort.

'I think I'm entitled to ask you that,' he returned. 'I was under the impression that you were supposed to be here with me.'

'Oh, I felt sure you'd be far too busy,' said Darynthe, sweetly venomous, 'with *Lady* Ozanne.'

'Green eyes are the right colour for you, you little cat,' he said evenly, but there was a lurking trace of amusement in his voice. He was laughing at her again. He was always laughing at her, even when she was in deadly earnest. The conceited pig probably thought she was jealous. She'd show him!

She slipped her arm through that of Marcus, who had been standing tongue-tied, abashed before the wrath of the older man.

'Come on, Mark,' she said cheerfully, 'let's get on with our walk . . . at least the lamb's safe now.'

'Which is more than you are,' Caan interrupted, 'loose up here with this idiot.' His contemptuous gaze flickered towards Marcus.

'Oh, I say, sir!' Marcus was finally stung to protest. 'I'm not such a tyro. I've done a considerable amount of mountaineering and Coniston is hardly the Alps . . . scarcely a hazardous climb.'

'Maybe not,' Caan said grimly, 'but it does present hazards of a kind, chiefly to impulsive and reckless females. What possessed you, to let her go down there?' He gestured to the ledge, now below them.

'Mark couldn't stop me,' Darynthe interposed defiantly. 'It was my idea . . . my decision.'

'Any *man* worth his salt would have prevented you!'

Darynthe stared at Caan, open-mouthed. He was being extremely hard on Marcus. What had got into the man? He could be overbearing and bossy, but she had never before encountered this streak of unkindness . . . maliciousness even. He sounded . . . he sounded as if he actually disliked Marcus . . . no, even stronger than that . . . as if he detested the younger man. Surely he couldn't be jealous, because she had chosen Marcus's company in preference to his? It was a heady thought, but she dismissed it almost immediately as being highly improbable, in view of his undoubted relationship with Ozanne Hanson.

She turned her back on him.

'Shall we be going?' she asked Marcus.

'I . . . I suppose we'd better.'

Marcus looked slightly strained and decidedly unhappy, and Darynthe felt a surge of compassion. His day had been ruined by the unfortunate incident, and it wasn't even his fault. She urged him away from Caan and down the mountainside; uncomfortably aware of the heavy tread dogging their steps.

They descended in silence, and Darynthe became more and more furious at the oppressive sensation of Caan Lorimer's eyes boring into their backs. She turned on him.

'There's no need for you to come any further. If you wish to continue your own walk, we're quite capable of finding the way back to our car.'

'I came here expressly to find you,' said Caan.

'Well, you've found me,' she said flippantly.

They had reached the cars now, Caan's white sports model parked close beside the Griffiths, more homely family saloon.

'I'll drive Darynthe home,' Caan said to Marcus.

'Oh, I say, but . . .' Marcus protested.

'I came with Mark and I shall go back with him,' Darynthe announced.

To her utter astonishment, making no reply, Caan lifted her bodily, dumping her without ceremony into the open sports car, and vaulted in beside her; and before she had time to gather her scattered wits, the engine roared into life and the little car was accelerating away in the direction of Coniston village.

A swift glance over her shoulder showed a dejected Marcus staring after them, Caan's high-handed move having taken him completely by surprise.

Tempestuously, Darynthe turned on Caan.

'How dare you? How dare you treat me like this? You had no right to break in on my date with Mark! Whatever must he be thinking? You're the most rude, abominable, detestable man it's ever been my misfortune to meet!'

'Worse than your fiancé?' he enquired drily.

'My *ex*-fiancé.'

'Oh?' He lifted a sardonic brow. 'I thought perhaps it was all on again.'

She puzzled for a second or two over this incomprehensible remark, then light dawned. He had heard her calling Marcus Griffiths by the shortened version of his name. Caan thought that Marcus was Mark Little! The humour of the situation struck her forcibly and an irrepressible giggle escaped.

'I see nothing to laugh at.' Caan's deep voice revealed submerged, dangerous icebergs of anger. 'I can only assume your levity is caused by triumph . . . that you've succeeded in bringing your cavalier back to heel. How *did* you accomplish it, as a matter of interest?'

'That's none of your business.'

Darynthe had made a swift decision. Let him go on believing that Marcus was Mark Little. Caan had his Lady Ozanne. Marcus would be a good camouflage for her own pride, for the callous way Caan had abandoned her, immediately upon the appearance of his svelte lady-friend.

'How long do you intend to preserve his *ex*-fiancé status? May we shortly expect an interesting announcement?'

'Funny,' said, Darynthe, in a swift counter-attack, 'I was just going to ask you the same question. In fact, I thought you and Lady Ozanne were looking at houses today.'

He darted her a quick glance.

'You really believed I'd break my date with you, just like that?'

'Well, you jumped to her bidding pretty quickly the other day,' Darynthe reminded him. 'When she demanded to be taken out and fed.'

'Ah, yes . . . well,' his manner was suddenly evasive, 'I did have my reasons for acceding to that particular request.'

'I bet!' Darynthe's tone was scornful. 'Anyhow, you needn't have missed your house-hunting on my account.'

'I didn't,' he assured her. 'I had absolutely no intention of looking at houses today. I'd arranged to go to Coniston with you and as far as *I* was concerned that arrangement still stood.'

'How did you explain *that* to your girl-friend?' Darynthe asked.

'I didn't have to explain anything. By now Ozanne is back in London.'

After one startled glance at his rugged profile, Darynthe sat in silence, assimilating this unexpected intelligence.

'That was a short visit,' she volunteered after a while.

'Yes, wasn't it?' he agreed pleasantly.

A further silence ensued, before Caan asked:

'So, how long is your fiancé staying?'

For a moment Darynthe contemplated telling him the truth; but she had a sneaking suspicion that Marcus might still be needed as a safety valve.

'Just till Saturday,' she said evenly. 'He has to get back to work next week.'

'Saturday, hmm? So after that you'll be a free agent again . . . or were you thinking of going back with him, now that all is forgiven?'

Oh dear, she thought. This was getting more and more complicated, which only went to show that small lies grew into larger ones, until one was entangled in a very complicated web of deceit. Still, it was Caan's fault, not hers, she assured herself. She hadn't actually *told* him that Marcus was her ex-fiancé Mark Little. He had assumed it.

'I . . . I shan't be going back just yet,' she said at last.

Caan braked outside the Daffodil and looked at her, blue eyes shrewd.

'The course of true love not running smoothly again yet?'

She shrugged. Impossible to confirm or deny his assumption.

Caan leant across her to open the door, his arm brushing accidentally against her breasts as he did so. She drew a quick, deep breath, to steady the flutter of nerves the contact induced. She half expected him to make some comment, but instead he sat, obviously waiting for her to get out of his car.

Darynthe felt a sense of anti-climax. Why had Caan bothered to drive all that way, climb Coniston just to find her, only to bring her back here and then leave her, with no indication of whether he intended to see her again?

Slowly, reluctantly, she slid from the car and stood looking down at him.

'Well . . . er . . . goodbye,' she offered.

He barely glanced at her.

'Goodbye. Make sure you shut the door firmly, will you?'

Darynthe took the opportunity his command offered of venting her feelings. She slammed his car door, with a force which ought to have made him wince. But beyond a fractional lift of an eyebrow, there was no reaction, as the car glided smoothly away.

Ann Forster greeted her in the rear porch.

'Was that Caan?'

'Yes.'

Ann seemed pleased.

'Good. I'm glad he found you. He said you two had a date for today. I said I felt sure you must have forgotten . . . or got the day wrong.'

'I didn't forget and I didn't get the day wrong,' Darynthe said shortly, as she bent to unlace her boots.

'You mean you avoided him deliberately?' Ann said incredulously. 'But why? I thought you two were getting on so much better.'

Darynthe sat on a kitchen stool to strip off her woollen socks.

'Not really,' she said with an attempt at indifference.

Ann shook her head in comic dismay.

'I don't understand you, Darynthe Browne. Here you are, with one of the most personable, eligible men imaginable interested in you, and . . .'

'He's not the least bit interested in me, except as a sociological experiment,' Darynthe said bitterly. 'Now that he thinks I'm cured of disliking men, he hasn't even mentioned seeing me again.'

'Are you surprised?' Ann asked, uncharacteristically sarcastic.

'No.'

Honesty made Darynthe admit it.

'As to being interested,' Ann continued, 'when he arrived this morning and asked where you were and I told him you'd gone out with Mark, I thought he'd burst a blood vessel ... Oh!'

Dawning realisation in her aunt's eyes made Darynthe nod her bright head.

'Yes,' she said drily, 'he thinks Marcus Griffiths is Mark Little.'

'And you didn't enlighten him?'

'No. Why should I? You seem to forget, he has his Ozanne.'

'You want your brains tested,' Ann said crossly.

'You're not to tell him, Auntie,' Darynthe insisted. 'Promise me? I'll never forgive you if you do.'

Ann sighed.

'It's impossible to help you, love, even by stealth, isn't it? Why don't you put up a fight for what you want, before it's too late? All right, all right. I promise ... under protest, not to tell him anything.'

As Darynthe made her way towards the stairs, Ann called after her.

'Oh, by the way, Arthur phoned this afternoon.'

'Dad did?' Darynthe turned back anxiously. 'Is he all right? What did he want?'

'Just to ask after you. Apparently you haven't phoned him for a day or two.'

Darynthe sighed. In the six weeks she had been away from home, she had made several reassuring telephone calls and had written a weekly letter home. For the first time in her recollection, she found herself wishing her father didn't fuss quite so much.

'I'll ring him tonight,' she promised.

'He was anxious to know if I thought you were ready to go home yet,' Ann commented, intently studying her niece's reaction.

Darynthe's face expressed nothing but dismay. She knew she ought to cut her losses, get out of Caan's vicinity, but, while a faint hope existed ... while Ozanne wore no ring ...

'Oh no! I couldn't ... not yet. I ... You don't want to get rid of me, do you?' she appealed.

Ann's pleasant face relaxed, as if in sudden relief.

'As far as I'm concerned, you can stay as long as you like.'

'I'd like to stay a while longer,' Darynthe confessed, 'because . . .' she improvised rapidly, 'there's a local custom I'd rather like to see before I go back . . . the Rushbearing Procession. I've heard such a lot about it and it sounds quite fascinating. I'd hate to miss it. I love old customs, don't you?'

The words tumbled out in her eagerness to sound convincing and Ann Forster hid a smile.

'Yes, yes, of course—and, as I said, you can stay for as long as you like.'

Marcus Griffiths arrived back at the Daffodil in a very disgruntled frame of mind, and it took all Darynthe's tact and powers of persuasion to coax him out of it.

'Why didn't you tell me you had a jealous, hulking great brute of a boy-friend in the area?' he asked indignantly.

'I'll grant you the hulking great brute,' said Darynthe humorously, endeavouring to win a smile from the sulky face, 'but he isn't my boy-friend . . . and he certainly isn't jealous.'

'No?' Mark said sceptically. 'Then that was a pretty convincing imitation he gave out there.'

Darynthe was silent. It *was* hard to reconcile Caan's behaviour with the feelings she believed he entertained towards her. To him, a naturally kindhearted man, she felt sure she was just a lame dog, a disillusioned child, to be wooed back into a reasonably happier frame of mind . . . to which end he had exercised his considerable powers of masculine charm. But jealousy? She shook her head regretfully. Much as she would like to think she could inspire that sort of emotion in Caan Lorimer, she had only to think of Lady Ozanne Hanson to realise that there was no contest.

True, Caan had seemed keen enough to kiss her, and on one occasion had even seemed to be aroused himself by their proximity, but never once had he gone beyond the bounds of respectability, given way to the desire she would have expected from a man in love. Therefore, she concluded, he did not feel that way about her.

'He's not my boy-friend,' she reiterated. 'He . . . he's

sort of taken me under his wing since I've been here. I think he feels a kind of . . . responsibility for me.'

'A father figure?' Marcus jeered. 'Don't give me that, Darynthe. I saw the way the fellow looked at you. In my opinion, he's nuts about you.'

Unconvinced, Darynthe shook her head; and during the days that followed, nothing happened to change her mind. She did not see Caan, or hear from him.

The Griffiths left on the Saturday morning, as planned, in a flurry of promises to return the following year, and Marcus vowed to write to Darynthe. She supposed there would be a letter or two, until the memories of his holiday gradually faded. Perhaps there would be a card at Christmas. It was strange, she reflected, how little she cared whether he kept in touch or not. She liked Marcus, had enjoyed his company, but he was a cardboard figure when she compared him to the complex, compelling character that was Caan Lorimer.

It was the middle of the following week and a despairing Darynthe was thinking that she might just as well return home, when her aunt called her to the telephone. It would probably be her father yet again, Darynthe thought, as she descended her attic staircase. Well, if he wanted her to go home, this time she might as well say yes.

'Hallo?'

'Darynthe?' The deep, mellow tones were unexpected but heartrendingly familiar, and Darynthe put a hand to her throat, which seemed suddenly constricted.

'Caan!' she said breathlessly.

'The same! What are you doing tomorrow?' he asked without further preamble.

She should have been cool, casual, considering, but the words blurted out.

'I . . . nothing . . . that is . . .'

'Good, then that's settled. I'll pick you up at ten o'clock.'

'But I haven't . . . I didn't . . .'

The line went dead and Darynthe stood staring at the receiver still clutched in her hand, all thoughts of returning home to Corbridge effectively banished.

Caan had telephoned at last, after what had seemed an eternity, in which she had made up her mind to the unpleasant fact that he wasn't going to bother with her any more, that she would never see him again, that the misunderstanding over Marcus's identity had achieved all that her earlier hostility had failed to do.

In a passion of excitement, she clasped the receiver to her, as if it were an animate object, before replacing it upon the rest.

It was nice to know that Caan had not walked out of her life for ever, but, she thought, with mounting indignation, the manner of his re-entry left much to be desired. To telephone and issue what amounted to a command, without giving her the chance to refuse . . . even if she'd wanted to . . . or to accept, for that matter. But even indignation at this masterful treatment could not quell the mounting happiness she felt at the knowledge that, tomorrow, she would be with Caan again . . . be with him . . . but where? What did he have in mind for this occasion? Curiosity added its piquant edge to her anticipation.

It seemed essential that night, before retiring, to brush her fair hair till it shone like watered silk, to manicure faultless nails, to inspect already perfectly arched brows for the slightest sign of a straggling hair to be plucked.

After much consideration of her wardrobe, she put out a linen-look suit in her favourite colour . . . not emerald this time, but in a cool shade of mint green.

She had no idea where Caan was taking her, but as he had not seen fit to inform her, it would be his fault if she were unsuitably dressed.

When she woke next morning, for a second or two she could not account for the excited flutter in the region of her heart. Then she remembered. Caan was coming at ten o'clock. She must be ready and looking her best.

She flew to the window, but the day had not let her down; it was as warm and sunny as her mood.

Showered, perfumed, impeccably groomed to the last detail and scarcely able to eat the breakfast her aunt put before her, she was ready half an hour too soon . . . half an hour of agonising tension. Suppose he changed his mind, decided to pay her out in her own coin, didn't turn up? She felt sick with anxiety.

Ann Forster threw her a comprehending glance.

'Relax, love. You look fabulous, and he'll be here on the stroke of ten—I guarantee it.'

Ann was not obliged to eat her words. At ten o'clock, precisely, Caan strode into the entrance hall of the guesthouse, demanding Darynthe's whereabouts.

Hearing his voice, Darynthe flew to the settee, in the lounge where she awaited him, and picked up a magazine; as he entered the room, she was apparently engrossed in its pages.

'Good morning, Darynthe.'

Slowly, casually, she lifted her gaze from the print, which had swum incomprehensibly before her glazed eyes.

'Good morning,' she said, with what she hoped was a deceptive ease of manner.

He removed the magazine from hands which had developed an annoying tendency to tremble.

'I didn't know you read Norwegian?' he commented, a wicked gleam in the blue eyes, and then proceeded to survey the confusion he had wrought.

Mentally, the blushing Darynthe cursed herself for her carelessness in picking up a book left behind by a foreign visitor.

'I . . . I was just looking at the pictures,' she explained lamely. She stood up, supremely conscious of his assessing gaze.

'You wear a lot of green,' he remarked.

'It's my favourite colour.' She was on the defensive immediately.

'And very becoming too . . . exactly right for today's expedition.'

Well, that was something, she thought. It would have been more in character if he'd found her outfit unsuitable and ordered her upstairs to change.

'Yes.' He nodded again. 'That outfit is definitely calculated to inspire confidence in your bona fides as a house purchaser.'

'What?'

'We're going to look at the house I intend to buy,' he explained.

CHAPTER SEVEN

'WHERE is this house?' Darynthe asked, as Caan held open the car door for her. 'And why do you want *me* to see it?'

He did not answer until he was seated beside her, swinging the car through the narrow entrance to the guest-house car park.

'The house is just on the other side of Grasmere,' he said.

'Isn't that where your uncle Jack used to live?'

'Yes. In fact, originally our whole family came from around there. So you could say I'm coming home to roost.'

'What sort of house is it?'

He shook his head tantalizingly.

'No description of mine would do it justice.'

That sounded unlikely, she thought, coming from an accomplished writer whose lyrical description of scenery had worked its ravishing effect upon her romantic nature.

'Suppose you just wait and see,' he added.

'But why do you want *me* to see it?' She repeated her earlier question.

He hesitated.

'Shall we just say that I ... er ... would like the female view point. After all, it won't be a bachelor residence ... I don't anticipate living there alone.'

No, she thought miserably. But what makes you think my tastes and Ozanne's will have anything in common?

As Caan drove, Darynthe stole surreptitious sideways glances at him. He had commented favourably on her appearance, but he was looking extremely well-groomed himself this morning. Accustomed as she was to seeing him in jeans and sweat-shirt, or bulky weatherproof clothing, suitable for fellwalking, he seemed almost a stranger in the impeccably tailored suit in subtle shades of blue and grey, the jacket taut across his powerful shoulders.

Her appraisal had not passed unnoticed.

'Do you approve?' Caan asked, turning his head briefly towards her, so that she received the full effect of that devastating, lopsided smile.

'You . . . you look very smart,' she conceded stiffly.

And very, very desirable, she thought, with a sharp pang of very real pain. How she longed for the right to reach out a caressing hand towards him!

The car swung left, off the Keswick road and into Grasmere, passing the ancient church of St Oswald, whose yew-treed graveyard, Darynthe knew, held all that remained of the immortal Wordsworth.

As Caan slowed for the bends, Darynthe caught the tantalising aroma of freshly baked gingerbread, wafting out from the diminutive bakery by the churchyard gate.

Farther on a little country lane led out of Grasmere, between open pastures, then climbed up once more towards the drowsy summer haze of the mountains. A narrow, stony track, just wide enough for the car, led off steeply up the fellside through a wasteland of boulders and bracken, emerging suddenly into an unexpected, hidden valley, which cradled the house they had come to see.

Standing among mature trees, its backdrop was the flank of the ancient fell, with its sheep-cropped grass, criss-crossed by centuries old drystone walls.

The house itself, with its thick stone walls, was larger than Darynthe had expected. For some reason she had been picturing a cottage on similar lines to Jack Lorimer's home. But this old farmhouse was a long, double-storeyed building, with an outside stair and gallery leading to its loft, and an extra wing had been created from a converted barn, adjoining the original house.

A Range Rover was parked by the garden gate and as they approached, a man emerged and came to join them; he was, Darynthe discovered, the representative of the agency selling the house. At a nod from Caan, he unlocked the heavily studded oak door, which led straight into a

large flagged hallway, which resembled a room, with its
great open fireplace.

Beams of great age were richly dark against once white
walls, now in need of re-painting, and to one side of the
hall a splendid oaken staircase gave access to a gallery on
three sides, from which doors opened into upper rooms.

The agent led the way into the main reception room,
the door of which appeared to be very old, with the original simple wooden latch. This room boasted yet another
fine open fireplace with an inglenook, low, heavy rafters
and panelled walls.

The house, it seemed, had stood empty and unfurnished
for some time, but even so it had tremendous charisma,
and as they moved from room to room, Darynthe's enthusiastic exclamations waned and faded into depressed
silence, as she realised that this house was the embodiment
of all her dreams . . . a large, family house, full of character
and, despite its bare interior, she could sense its vast potential to become a gracious, charming home. But this was
not to be her home, but Caan's . . . Caan's and Ozanne's.

Had Ozanne seen this house? she wondered. There had
been time, before the other girl had returned to London.

Following the agent, they mounted the stairs, which
creaked slightly under their combined weight.

The bedrooms leading off from the gallery were surprisingly large and the leaded panes of the rear windows
overlooked a garden which obviously had once been
someone's pride and joy. Darynthe was sure that a few
weeks of concentrated love and attention could bring it
back to its former glory.

Their tour completed, they returned to the ground floor.
The agent looked at his watch.

'I've an appointment in Keswick in half an hour. But
I'm sure you and your fiancée would like a little longer to
make up your minds. If I leave you the keys, sir, would
you lock up and drop them off at our office in Ambleside?'

As Caan accompanied the agent out to his vehicle,
Darynthe lifted her hands to scarlet cheeks. She supposed
it was natural enough for the agent to assume that *she* was
Caan's fiancée and Caan, with his innate courtesy, would
not wish to embarrass the man by correcting his error. But

the mistake was just another twist of the knife in an already painful wound.

'Shall we take a look around outside?' Caan suggested, when he returned.

To Darynthe's relief he made no reference to the agent's mistake, and gradually her confusion began to subside.

Apart from the garden, which Darynthe had seen from the upstairs window, there were many mature trees clustered about the building, and among the more usual garden shrubs she recognised ash, holly, yew and elder.

When she commented on the unusual combination for a garden, Caan, as always, was ready with an explanation.

'Each of these trees served a purpose, in the days when this house was built,' he said. 'The ash and the holly were grown so that they could be cut for fodder in times of lean harvest ... and the elder trees provided many of the old home made remedies for various ills.'

'And the yew?' Darynthe prompted.

'Its presence arises from an old superstition,' Caan told her, 'that yew trees represent permanence and security.'

The old farmhouse certainly seemed to promise both those virtues, Darynthe thought wistfully, as they went back inside. How she longed for the reassurance of a secure, permanent home of her own! Her childhood home had been endowed with both qualities but now lacked an extra, essential ingredient ... the presence of Caan Lorimer.

'I'd thought of getting a couple of rooms habitable, then moving in the working on the rest at my leisure,' said Caan. 'What do you think?'

'It could be fun,' Darynthe agreed, wishing that she could be the one to share that enjoyment with him.

She wondered if Ozanne would find it 'fun'. Somehow she couldn't see that elegant lady climbing ladders, paintbrush in hand, hanging curtains, weeding the overgrown garden.

'Has ... has Lady Ozanne seen the house?' she ventured, waiting fearfully for the answer.

Caan nodded, absorbed in examining the panelling in the main living room.

'And what does she think of your idea?'

Caan laughed.

'She thinks I'm insane, to want to live here.' He did not seem unduly perturbed by Ozanne's view of his plans. 'She can't visualise the finished article,' he added, 'but I can.'

'So . . . so you'll move in alone, to begin with?' Darynthe asked diffidently.

He nodded, apparently unconcerned by the prospect.

'I'll be alone for a while, yes.'

For how long? Darynthe wondered miserably. How long before Ozanne joined him, before he proudly displayed the beautiful home he had created as a setting for his bride, with her exotic good looks and air of breeding?

'I want to go round all the salerooms and antique shops,' Caan explained enthusiastically, 'to furnish it the way it was originally . . . as near as I can. But we'll have atmosphere combined with modern conveniences, such as central heating and the usual electrical appliances in the kitchen.'

As he spoke, he flung a casual arm across Darynthe's shoulders, resting his cheek against her hair.

'I can just see it, in a few months' time, can't you?'

'Yes.' She found her voice with difficulty.

That was the whole trouble. She could see it, all too clearly, and she wanted desperately to be part of the picture she envisaged. Never in her life had she envied others their material possessions, but now she felt an envy close to hatred, as she visualised Ozanne Hanson living here with Caan.

'Going to help me look around for the furniture?' Caan asked, his clasp tightening on her shoulders. 'You should know a lot about antiques, from helping your father.'

She looked up to meet his enquiring blue gaze, then as quickly lowered her lids over eyes which she feared might be all too revealing.

'Surely Ozanne——' she began.

'Forget Ozanne for now,' he said impatiently. 'She's hundreds of miles away, leading a very exacting life. She wouldn't have the time to spare for a job of this size.'

And I suppose *my* time doesn't matter, Darynthe

thought resentfully. Why should she agree to spend her spare time, helping Caan to prepare a home for another woman? The more she saw of the old farmhouse and witnessed it taking on the shape Caan visualised, the more painful would be the knowledge that she would not be its eventual mistress.

'Well,' said Caan, 'when shall we make a start?'

'I . . . I may not be around much longer myself. I have to go back to Corbridge some time . . . and there's no reason now why I shouldn't go back.'

His face darkened.

'No, I suppose not,' he said harshly, removing his arm from her shoulders, and she knew he was thinking of her supposed reconciliation with her ex-fiancé; whereas there was a deeper meaning behind her words . . . no point in staying now that she knew about Ozanne; and yet—the thought was with her constantly, a tiny ray of hope—that elegantly manicured left hand had been bare of rings.

'Darynthe!' Caan's voice was husky, as he turned her to face him. 'Don't do it. Don't go back to that young idiot. He's not right for you. You must have realised it once, or you wouldn't have split up.'

If he was so perceptive, Darynthe thought, why couldn't he see that *Ozanne* was not right for *him*?

'I . . . haven't said I *was* going back to him.'

'No, but it's pretty obvious, isn't it? He follows you here . . . you break a date with me, so that you can spend time with him instead . . . and now you're talking of leaving here. If it's not to follow this Mark, what is it?'

'My . . . my father misses me, he . . .'

'Nonsense! Your aunt tells me your father has a perfectly good housekeeper, an active social life and a profession which takes him away from home quite a lot. He doesn't need you . . . and besides, he'll have to part with you some day, when you get married. He might as well get used to it. You're needed far more here, believe me.'

If only she were! If only she could believe him. If Caan would only make that need a personal one . . . his need for her because he loved her, not just because he wanted her help in furnishing his house. How willingly she would relegate her father's wishes to second place.

'I thought you liked Lakeland,' Caan persisted, 'enough perhaps to stay here?'

She met his intent gaze with something approaching despair. The great blind, senseless idiot! Couldn't he see? Of course she liked it here ... loved it. Of course she would stay ... with the right incentive. But what point was there in staying? How could she stay, unless ...

Suppose Caan *did* marry Ozanne? In such a small place, inevitably she would encounter him ... and his wife. Better by far to be hundreds of miles away. Though distance would not lessen the anguish of knowing he was married to someone else, at least she would not have a knife constantly turned in the wound, would not run the risk of exhibiting just how much it hurt to see him with another woman. If only she knew for certain what he intended, and when ... then she would know how to act.

He was still holding her by the shoulders, his hands seductively warm through the material of her suit.

'Can't I persuade you, Darynthe?' His tone was urgent and she found his words, his mood unsettling.

He pulled her closer to him and a gentle sadness made her rest unprotestingly against him, seeking to find comfort in the warmth of his embrace. What harm could it do anyone just to let him hold her like this? But contact with him seemed to light a flame inside her and melancholy was replaced by a feverish, trembling desire.

He was aware of it as soon as she, responding by shaping her body with hands that shook slightly, as his lips brushed her neck, pressed into the hollow just below her ear.

'Darynthe?'

The timbre of his voice betrayed his growing arousal and, unable to restrain herself, she moulded her slim form closely to his, reaching up to tangle her fingers in the wiry curls of his hair, lifting her lips in a blatant demand for his kiss, a kind of desperation in the joy with which she surrendered her mouth to his possession.

It was an emotion composed of both longing and despair, as if she knew that the pleasure derived from this kiss must be paid for by a lifetime of suffering. It was as though love flowered and withered, both in the same moment.

There was a growing compulsion in his kiss, his caresses, and she knew that she must be the one to withdraw, that by her open invitation she was risking a conclusion that could only result in unhappiness and shame. She must remember that he was a man ... that the fact of Ozanne's existence would not deter him from accepting what she must seem to be offering.

Trembling, breathless, she wrenched herself from his arms, retreating slightly, refusing to meet his eyes.

'It's no good, Caan. I have to go home ... to Corbridge,' she said. 'I ... I want to go home.'

At that moment it was true. She wanted to run, to hide like an injured animal, to nurse alone these new wounds of love.

'Darynthe!' He took a step forward, his deep voice pleading, seductive.

'No, Caan, please ... don't ... I mean it.'

'Is that your final word?'

Arms rigid at his side, fists clenched, lines of tension around his mouth, he seemed to be fighting some powerful emotion.

'Yes.' Eyes downcast, she whispered the word.

'You're really going back to Corbridge ... to him.'

Thinking he meant her father, she nodded wordlessly.

'Then there's no more to be said.' His voice was harsh again. 'Come on.'

They left the house in hostile silence and as Darynthe watched Caan lock up, she felt unutterably depressed. She wished he had never brought her here, that she had never seen the house, felt its welcoming aura, sensed that this was a place she could happily call home.

As they drove away down the rutted track she could not resist looking over her shoulder for one long, last look.

'You liked the house, didn't you?' Caan said abruptly.

'I loved it,' she said softly.

'Then why on earth won't you give it a try ... stay a little longer, help me to turn it into a home?' He sounded exasperated then added, more gently. 'I know your aunt would want you to stay ... not to do anything rash.'

Why did he want her to stay? she wondered wearily. It could only be because she could be of use to him, with her expertise in the field of antiques. He was doing everything he could to persuade her; hadn't he just tried the oldest trick in the world ... and to her everlasting shame, she had almost succumbed, trying to pretend for a moment that it was love which prompted his actions. She tried to recall the distaste that she had once felt at the idea of being possessed by a man of experience ... a man who had known other women ... but the shudder that ran through her was not of revulsion.

'Auntie Ann won't really need me after next week,' she said, her voice unsteady. 'My cousin will be home, fit enough to help her.'

'Well, at least that means we have another week,' said Caan.

Oh, if only she could believe in the intimacy of that 'we' ... the sharing it implied.

'We could achieve quite a lot in a week,' he urged.

Darynthe was torn. Another week of Caan's company ... should she grasp at the opportunity? After all, the memories of her stay in Lakeland, her friendship with Caan, would have to last her for many weary years; would the pain of their parting ever be dulled by time, as the pain of her break with Mark had faded? She was afraid not. She knew now that she had been in love with the idea of love, not in love with Mark himself ... otherwise surely she would have been able to forgive him anything. She knew now that she did not care how many girl-friends had littered Caan's path through life. If they had all been in the past, she would have been content with his present ... and future. But there was still Ozanne ... was Ozanne a permanent fixture? If only she *knew*!

'Darynthe?' said Caan, and she realised he was still waiting for her answer.

How could she accede to his request, without seeming to be too willing, without revealing her true reason for remaining ... just to pretend for a few more days that he was hers?

'Well, I *might* stay just a few days longer,' she conceded slowly. 'I did rather want to see the Rushbearing Ceremony before I go home. That's next Saturday, isn't it?'

Caan's features relaxed into the familiar lopsided grin, making her heart do crazy things.

'That's a deal! You help me to find my furniture and I'll take you to the Rushbearing . . . and explain the ceremony to you.'

For the next few days Darynthe accompanied Caan to every antique shop within a day's driving distance. Some of the items they purchased were very expensive, but Caan did not flinch at the prices. He must be very wealthy indeed, Darynthe thought with awe; no wonder he moved in the same circles as Lady Ozanne.

Not only could Caan afford the furniture, but he also seemed extremely knowledgeable about period and make, the names of Chippendale, Sheraton and Hepplewhite coming fluently from his tongue. Darynthe began to doubt that he really needed her help.

As well as furniture, they purchased Oriental rugs, silver, pewter and glass. It was probable that the old farmhouse had never known such luxuries, but Darynthe could not deny that Caan's instincts were right, as she viewed the results of their efforts in the main living room, the first to be completed.

Caan certainly seemed able to command prompt, efficient service, one of the benefits of wealth, Darynthe thought; for while she and Caan had been searching for the furnishings, gas central heating engineers had completed their installation and a firm of interior decorators had moved in. Beams, panels and floors had been treated with preservatives and the rough cast walls re-whitened, making a fitting setting for their purchases.

From what Caan had said, Darynthe had imagined him doing his own decorating, but she had to admit that this way faster results were achieved. At this rate the house would soon be ready . . . and what then? Don't let it be finished too soon, she prayed silently.

As she had feared, as the old farmhouse gained in beauty, so her attachment to it grew, and with it the dread of the moment when her involvement with the house would end and she must hand over the end product into the slim, elegant hands of Ozanne Hanson.

The Saturday of the Rushbearing Festival was the kind of day that a summer's day should be, the sun giving the day the benison of its full glory and Darynthe was conscious of looking her best in a dress of crisp yellow cotton, tight-waisted, with a full, flaring skirt, with matching strappy sandals; and Caan's appreciative whistle confirmed her confidence in her appearance.

Together they made their way through the crowded streets to the school near the parish church, where the procession was to begin.

'A hundred years ago,' Caan told her, 'the young women would have been up at dawn to gather reeds and rushes from the lakes; and the one chosen to be queen would plait and twist her reeds into ornate shapes. The rest would pile theirs into bundles, to be carried to the church.'

'And nowadays?' Darynthe asked.

'They still gather their rushes, but they're woven into far more complicated shapes, incorporating wild flowers and ferns from the woods, mounted on wooden frames of various designs . . . known as "bearings".'

Darynthe soon saw for herself just how ornate the 'bearings' could be, as the procession began, led by the youth of Ambleside, bearing great harps formed from rushes, tall spires decorated with flowers, crosses of all shapes and sizes interwoven with golden bracken and clover.

Then came the tiny children, the girls in bright summer frocks, the boys in crisp white shirts and shorts, bonny babies in decorated prams, followed by the men of the town, carrying the larger, heavier bearings.

Behind the bearers of garlands came brass bands, men carrying banners and finally, in fluttering black and white, the choirs and clergy of the local churches.

Caan took Darynthe's hand and keeping pace with the procession, they arrived at the market place, where the rushbearers and their procession entered a roped-off area. There was a moment's silence, then the singing began . . . the Rushbearer's Hymn.

'Our fathers to the House of God,
As yet a building rude,
Bore offerings from the flowering sod,
And fragrant rushes strewed.'

A deep bass voice, close at hand, indicated that Caan was as familiar with the traditional hymn as with the other customs of his birthplace.

'May we, their children, ne'er forget
The pious lesson given,
But honour still, together met,
The Lord of Earth and Heaven.'

The colourful scene, the excited, happy faces of the children, the music ... all affected Darynthe's always susceptible, romantic nature. Her eyes filled with tears. If only she could be here, like this, year after year ... at Caan's side, singing this old hymn with him.

The last lines of the hymn faded away.

'He makes to smile the desert place
With flowers and rushes green ...'

The bearings were lifted high, so that all the assembled crowd might see, the band struck up and the procession reformed, moving off towards the church for the short service.

'What's it all in aid of?' Darynthe asked, composure regained, as they fell into step with the marchers.

'It had very practical origins,' Caan explained, 'the old English custom of strewing earthen church floors with rushes. Some people also think it's derived from the old Roman festival, Floralia.'

'But they only did it once a year?'

'Yes. The old floor covering would be removed and burnt, the whole community assisting in cleaning the church and laying the new rushes.'

Inside the church, the sounds of revelry were hushed, and reverently adults and children set their bearings before the altar. There was not an empty seat, and throughout the service which followed Darynthe cast surreptitious glances around her, trying to imagine a wedding in this church, with herself as the central figure. She supposed Caan's wedding would take place somewhere far more splendid, probably nothing less than St Margaret's, Westminster, for Lady Ozanne. Unconsciously she sighed and Caan glanced down at her, slipping his hand through her arm.

'Bored?'

'Goodness no!' she disclaimed. 'I was just wishing ...' She stopped. Her wishes were not for publication ... not to the subject of them.

'I thought you might be fed up. Ozanne found it extremely tedious when I brought her last year.'

Darynthe tensed, moving away from him; the fact that he had brought the other girl here, had obviously been going out with her for a least a year, brought home to her the futility of her own presence here ... her folly in building up a stock of memories to haunt her, when she left Lakeland ... of thinking for one moment that she could compete with Ozanne Hanson.

Outside the church, they waited to see the children receive the traditional gift of gingerbread, then they strolled away back towards The Daffodil.

'I thought we'd start hunting for the bedroom furniture next week,' Caan said casually.

Darynthe looked at him. Had he forgotten she wouldn't be here next week?

He was watching her, waiting for her reaction, the vivid blue eyes unfathomable, and Darynthe felt herself weakening. Though she realised the heartache she risked in becoming more and more attached to this place, to this man and his future home, a small rebellious voice demanded why she did not do as her aunt had suggested ... after all, he and Ozanne were not actually engaged.

At that moment Darynthe decided to enter the lists ... she *would* fight for what she wanted. After all, the other girl was miles away in London, while she was here ... a decided advantage.

But her campaign must be a subtle one; he must not recognise her utter capitulation. She would not so far lower her pride as to reveal her feelings, until she knew exactly where she stood in his estimation.

'All right,' she said, hoping fervently that she would not have cause to regret her decision. 'Just one more week ... then I'm definitely going home.'

She hardly recognised herself these days, Darynthe thought. Was she really the same girl who had vowed never to let a man rule her life? Now she was discovering in herself a dangerous desire to give in, to actually bask in Caan's authoritative manner where she was concerned.

'I've been thinking ... the antique shops will be crowded over the weekend,' Caan said. 'How about leaving it for a weekday ... how about a complete change? Are you any good at gardening?'

'I love it,' Darynthe said eagerly. Ever since she had seen the farmhouse, she had been dying to get at that neglected garden, uncover its weed-choked glories, make it once more a fitting setting for the gracious old house.

'Eventually, I shall have the track from the road properly made up,' Caan told her next morning, as they drove out towards Grasmere. 'It's a bit hard on the car springs and not very suitable for a woman to drive over.'

Darynthe clenched her hands at her side. She wished he would let her forget, just for a few hours, that all this beauty was being restored for the woman in his life. Would Ozanne appreciate all that he had done for her? Darynthe supposed that once they were married, Ozanne would have to give up her exacting life in London. What it was that the other girl did, she had never discovered. Obviously not work of any kind ... probably just the hectic life of a rich socialite. How would such a woman settle down to the quiet life of a Lakeland village, a home miles from the nearest town of any size?

Somehow Darynthe could not see Ozanne involved in domestic chores. Probably there would be a housekeeper and a gardener, while Ozanne played the gracious lady, sitting on local committees commuting back and forth to London, when village life proved too irksome.

It was necessary to choke back a lump in her throat, as she thought how much more *she* would value the life-style that Caan had to offer his wife.

But perhaps she was misjudging Lady Ozanne. Perhaps she did love Caan sufficiently to give up her former life, counting the world well lost for love. Darynthe had no doubt which she would choose, if the chance were offered.

Unconsciously, she squared her shoulders. Well, the contest wasn't over yet!

The back of Caan's car was piled high with gardening implements that bounced and rattled, as they drove along the rutted track to the house.

Darynthe looked lovingly at his rugged profile, as he concentrated on avoiding the worst of the potholes.

'After all the professional work you had done on the house, I half expected you to get landscape gardeners in,' she commented.

Caan spared a second for a quizzical glance.

'Getting cold feet at the thought of all that weeding?'

'Not a bit,' she said stoutly. 'I told you, I love gardening.'

'Well, so do I . . . that's the reason I loathe decorating. I'm an outdoor man.'

He certainly was, she thought, as she watched him a few minutes later, dressed in a pair of disgraceful old working trousers and a short-sleeved shirt which displayed his bronzed, muscular arms, with their light, overall matt of hair.

'I'll start by pruning the trees and shrubs that are overhanging the flowerbeds, if you'll weed,' he suggested.

Darynthe stood looking around her, considering where to start. There was so much to do . . . at least a month's work, she thought gleefully. As if reluctant, she would allow herself to be persuaded into staying on a few days . . . a week at a time. Surely somehow, in that time, she could make herself wholly indispensable to Caan, get him to realise how much more suitable she would be as the wife of a countryman . . . more suitable than a girl whose life revolved around bright city lights, who probably went to bed late and rose when the best part of the day was over . . . whose well-groomed hands had certainly never done battle with recalcitrant weeds.

But she must not be diverted from her task, or he would think her useless too.

Lusty weeds choked the growth of rambler roses and pink tea roses; red and yellow poppies strove to keep their heads above the grass which had encroached on a flagged garden. She would begin here, in the front of the house, she decided, before tackling the fierce nettles which had grown up in a wild garden at the side, where rosebay willow herb, cerise-coloured campions and scarlet pimpernels had been deliberately allowed to flourish unchecked.

As she worked, she could hear Caan whistling while he pruned, sawed and hacked, and she experienced a warm glow of satisfaction. This was how life should be, working alongside the man you loved, in complete harmony, with no need for continual conversation; just the comfortable knowledge that the loved one was close by, sharing your interests, working together for a finished product, making beautiful the home where, after the work of the day was done, they would grow in intimacy, not of mind alone, but of body . . .

She stopped short, realising where her thoughts were taking her. She was allowing her imagination too much rein. Soon she would be believing that this garden, this house, this man were really hers, a dream from which there could only be a rude awakening.

Their gardening was interrupted by Jack Lorimer, who, together with Scipio, had walked over to inspect his nephew's new property.

To Darynthe he admitted that he was a little dejected at the idea that Caan would soon be moving out of the cottage.

'Still, it's better than having him miles away, in London,' said Darynthe, in an effort to cheer him. 'And I'm sure you'll still see a lot of him.'

Jack Lorimer shrugged.

'Happen. Though I daresay once he's married he won't have so much time for his old codger of an uncle, eh?'

Why was he asking her? Darynthe wondered. Surely he must know his nephew far better than she did.

'I'm sure he'll still have time for you,' she said firmly. 'Whatever his wife's like, I'm sure Caan would never neglect his favourite uncle.'

Jack gave her a strange look, but made no comment, and she supposed he must have guessed from her tone of voice that she heartily disliked Ozanne Hanson.

Disliked her? Darynthe asked herself the question cynically. Say rather that she hated her. Ozanne just wasn't right for Caan, she thought fiercely . . . would never make him happy. But would *she* do any better, an inner voice demanded, with her convictions that love should also be a mystical emotion, on a higher plane than mere physicality ... was there a man alive who would see it her way?

Yes, yes! she told herself, filled with an inner knowledge too overwhelming to be denied. At their first meeting, she had been surprised, then resentful of Caan's effect upon her, at his insistent invasion of her emotional privacy. She had been outraged both by his high-handed attempt to direct her thoughts ... her life and by her body's own treacherous denial of her most deeply held beliefs ... the belief that sensations of the flesh had no relation to the deepest meaning of love. But eventually Caan had, by the mere force and depth of his personality, subdued her rebellion against all men, quieted her mistrust of himself and by his gentle strength conquered her finally and most effectively.

She knew now that the powerful vibration of physical response which she felt at his nearness, merely gave a deeper dimension to her mental and spiritual feelings for him ... that the two things were inextricably related, interdependent.

Scipio was panting after his long warm walk and Darynthe offered to take him into the house for a drink.

Jack nodded.

'But no titbits, mind. He's in training.'

'Training? Training for what?'

'Sheepdog trials, of course. He's not just a pet, you know. He's a working dog ... and come shearing time, him and me's in much demand, bringing the sheep in off the fells.'

Darynthe regarded Scipio with new respect.

'How interesting. I've seen sheepdog trials on television, of course, but I never thought I'd meet a real live contestant.'

'Get Caan to bring you along,' Jack suggested. 'Come and see old Skip here in action ... much better than watching it on the box.'

'I certainly will,' said Darynthe with fervour. 'When are the trials?'

'Week after next.'

'Oh!'

This could present something of a problem ... or did it? She didn't really want to go home yet, that was only a pretence, to salve her pride; but Caan had said nothing about extending the week she had promised him. So, if she told him his uncle had asked her to stay ...

A secret smile curved her lips and she bent to pat the collie, to hide the gleam of pleasure in her green eyes.

'I'll be there, Jack,' she promised.

'Uncle likes you,' Caan remarked, when Darynthe told him of Jack's invitation.

'And I like him, very much,' she said warmly.

'I'm glad,' Caan said simply, but there was something in his tone, in the approval she read in those vivid blue eyes, that filled her with inexplicable happiness.

'I think he's a little upset ... about you moving out of the cottage,' she volunteered.

Caan nodded.

'I've thought about that too. He's getting on a bit to be living alone. This place,' he gestured towards the farmhouse, 'is plenty big enough to create a corner he could call his own. Somewhere where he could still be independent and yet not feel alone and cut off. What do you think?'

'I think it's a simply splendid idea,' Darynthe said truthfully. But she couldn't help thinking that Lady Ozanne might see Caan's proposal in a very different light. There had already been evidence to suggest that she and Jack Lorimer were averse to each other's company. To have them permanently under the same roof could create problems, and Darynthe knew with whom her sympathies would lie.

'I'll put it to him tonight, then,' said Caan, as he began to pack up the gardening tools.

'Is ... is that wise?' Darynthe faltered. 'I mean, shouldn't you discuss it with ... with someone else first?' She didn't want to speak Ozanne's name.

Caan elevated surprised eyebrows.

'I can't think of anyone else it could possibly concern, apart from ourselves.'

As he locked the toolshed door, Darynthe couldn't help wondering if Ozanne would agree with him. Somehow she couldn't see the other girl in the role of the complacent, dutiful wife, allowing her husband to decide alone such matters of policy.

They moved into the house, to close windows opened to air the long disused rooms.

Darynthe stood in the master bedroom, looking about her, trying to visualise it fully furnished, ready for occupation.

Caan, his round of the windows complete, came to join her, standing so close that she could feel the warmth emanating from him. Her nostrils wrinkled appreciatively at the masculine scent of him, mingled with earth smells and the resinous perfume of the shrubs he had felled.

Lightly he rested a hand on her shoulder, intensifying her tremulous awareness of him, so that she longed for him to pull her into his arms. Surely, alone up here, he would sense the strength of her desire for his kiss.

She closed her eyes, willing him to respond to her mood. It was all she could do not to turn to him of her own accord, so urgent was her need. What would he do, she wondered, if she openly invited his kiss? Oh, the blissful privileges of being married, or even engaged, so that it was not necessary to wait for your man to make the first move.

But Caan had not given her the right to take such liberties. Had he . . . would he give that right to Ozanne? Oh please, God, no, she breathed. Give him to me.

The answer came to her, from where she did not know . . . from some invisible source of power that men called God, or from within herself . . . the primeval instinct that civilisation had never really crushed.

Somehow, she vowed, she would oust Ozanne from his life. It might be a long fight, but surely there was no victory that love could not win . . . love, the most compelling and awesome force in Nature.

Tentatively she looked up at him and met his eyes, already on her in undeviating concentration. Her lips quivered into a little smile and deliberately she swayed towards him.

Now, she thought. This is it. Now he will hold me, kiss me, tell me . . . tell me what?

But the brush of his lips against her brow was fleeting and his words when they came, albeit in a voice which was slightly husky, were mundane enough.

'I'm looking forward to completing this room, aren't you?'

CHAPTER EIGHT

AUGUST, Ann Forster told her niece, was the busiest month of the year in Lakeland and, consequently, a hectic time for hoteliers and landladies. So, although her cousin Sandra was home again, Darynthe found her aunt still grateful for any help she could give.

Thus there was not much time for helping Caan, either in the garden or in his search for furniture. So she was glad when the day of the sheepdog trials came round, for she felt that her campaign to woo Caan away from his aristocratic lady-friend had been rather neglected.

The days had continued to be perfect, with unbroken, cloudless poster-blue skies enhancing the brilliantly clear Lakeland views. In fact the weather was fast approaching drought conditions.

Darynthe was not at all sure what one wore to sheepdog trials, but finally she donned a softly feminine white silk blouse, its fragile allure increased by the contrast with her figure-hugging jeans.

She felt strangely shy when she heard Caan's deep voice in the hall. It was one thing to work companionably alongside him, both engrossed in their tasks, to go fell-walking, or even hunting antiques, quite another to accompany him on a formal occasion. Also, the lapse of time since they had last been together had made him seem almost a stranger, so that she looked at him almost as if she were seeing him for the first time, his rough good looks striking her afresh, filling her with a sense of instant, magnetic attraction, as her eyes travelled from the close-cropped curls, with their tell-tale traces of grey, over the textured casual shirt, blue as his eyes, to the powerful, denim-clad hips and legs.

His appraisal was as thorough as her own and she was aware of some nameless, pulsing communication between them.

'Hallo!' she said huskily, her green cat's eyes immense with the intensity of her feelings.

'Hallo yourself!' He seemed, uncharacteristically, as inarticulate as she felt.

In silence, they walked to the car, and it was not until they were on their way that Darynthe summoned up the courage to break that silence.

'H-how are you getting on . . . up at the house?'

'Moderately well.' He glanced sideways, the corner of his mouth lifting in its familiar quirk of amusement. 'I've been missing my chief assistant.'

A glow of pleasure suffused her. So he *had* missed her.

'The bedroom is almost complete . . . except for the bed,' he continued, and now his expression was definitely, wickedly mocking. 'I was hoping *you* would help me to choose that.'

'Why me, for heaven's sake?' she queried, with an attempt at lightness.

Why not indeed? she thought, with an uncontrollable little surge of triumph. Choosing a bed was surely a very personal, intimate task, scarcely the kind of errand a woman would allow her fiancé to undertake without her. Which presupposed, Darynthe hoped, that Ozanne still did not possess Caan's ring.

'How about the garden?' she asked him.

'Progressing slowly. It's all cleared now, but it's too early for planting. That'll be something to look forward to in October and November.'

Something to look forward to . . . for whom? Would she still be here as autumn merged into winter? Darynthe wondered. She knew her father was becoming restless about her extended absence and his hints that she should now be ready to return home were getting more insistent.

The sheepdog trials, she discovered, were being held in the meadows between Loughrigg and Low Pike, and when they reached the site, Darynthe couldn't imagine how they were ever to find Jack Lorimer and Scipio.

She had never pictured anything on this scale. To her bewildered eyes, there seemed to be hundreds of black and white collies wandering to and fro, with their owners. But as well as the collies, there were foxhounds, beagles and pet dogs of every shape, size and breed.

Caan laughed at her stunned expression.

'This is quite a day for dogs!'

'You can say that again! How do we find your uncle?'

'Simple. I arranged to meet him by the judges' tent.'

He put a hand beneath her elbow, to steer her through the milling crowds of animals and humanity, and Darynthe thrilled to the proprietorial gesture, acutely aware of the strength and warmth of his fingers, through the soft, silky material of her blouse.

As Caan had promised, Jack was patiently awaiting them, Scipio at his heels, obediently motionless, except for the gleam of recognition in his intelligent eyes and the restless swish of his tail.

Darynthe thought she had never seen the elderly man looking so smart, in tweed jacket and impeccable slacks, strangely incongruous with his heavy boots and shepherd's crook.

Among the locals there was a large sprinkling of tourists, easily identifiable by their cameras.

Judging was already going on in the terrier and beagle classes, while two elderly women, in identical shapeless skirts and cardigans and battered felt hats, were arguing amicably over the pet dog section.

With so many dogs entered for the trials, it looked like being a long afternoon, but Darynthe was never conscious, even for a moment, of tedium. The elements which composed the day were, each of their kind, perfect, inducing in her an almost soporific bliss. The sun was warm on her face, she loved all animals, but dogs in particular; and added to all this, the company in which she found herself was entirely congenial. Jack, excited by the forthcoming contest, was in sparkling form, and Caan . . .

Caan had only to be there, to make her day perfect. Even conversation was unnecessary, so long as he was physically present.

'Enjoying it?' he asked her from time to time, and always she responded with an enthusiastic nod of her fair head, clear green eyes intent upon the drive in progress.

At last Scipio's turn came, and unconsciously Darynthe's hand sought Caan's, as Jack stepped forward, pulling his cap low over his eyes against the sun, Scipio trotting behind his master to the start of the outrun. There he sat down, looking up at Jack, head alert, tail wagging, one thought in mind only, to work the sheep.

A whistle from the judge and Jack gave his dog the nod. Immediately Scipio was away, racing along the side of the course on a wide outrun, to where a bunch of sheep, as yet invisible to the spectators, clustered between a clump of trees about three hundred yards away. The sheep, becoming aware of the dog's presence, moved into the open. Jack whistled once and Scipio halted immediately, right behind the restlessly shifting animals, dropping down on his stomach, then crept slowly forward to begin the lift. Guided only by his master's whistles, the collie swept the fellside in great circles, coaxing the bunch of reluctant sheep through white-painted hurdles, downhill.

'He must keep them going in a straight line, or he'll lose marks,' Caan murmured.

For a while, sheep and dog were out of sight ... at this point everything depending on the dog. Then they came into sight again, man and dog able to see each other's actions again ... a perfect partnership.

Scipio now urged his little flock into the shedding ring, where one of two sheep, distinguished by red collars, had to be separated from the others. With guidance from Jack the dog singled out his sheep from the tightly clustered bunch, separated it from the group and then gathered them all together again for the final task of driving them into the pen.

Not until all the sheep were safely penned did Darynthe realise how tightly she had been gripping Caan's hand. Now she attempted to release it, with a muttered 'Sorry' as she saw the white marks her fingers had made on the brown skin.

But he would not let her go, adding to her confusion by dropping a light kiss on the end of her nose. It was such a small intimacy, yet by its very casualness, as if it were an everyday occurrence, it meant as much as Darynthe as a more impassioned embrace.

Scipio was not placed among the finalists, but Jack had not really expected that he would be, and Caan consoled the disappointed Darynthe.

'The dog dropped a few points on the lift; but Jack just likes to keep the old fellow's eye in . . . and besides, this day out is meat and drink to Uncle . . . meeting all his cronies, talking sheep and dogs.'

'He seems a lot happier than the last time I saw him,' Darynthe commented.

Caan nodded.

'That's because it's settled now that he's going to give up the cottage. We've decided on his quarters up at the farmhouse and he's going to furnish them with his own bits and pieces.'

'I am glad,' Darynthe said. 'I was afraid he might be too proud to accept your offer.'

She wondered if Caan had been in touch with Ozanne lately, and whether he had divulged his plans for his uncle's accommodation. Her curiosity gained the upper hand.

'Has . . . has Lady Ozanne seen the house . . . since you began work on it, I mean?'

Caan nodded.

'Yes, she's been staying with friends in Keswick for the last week. She was over at the house yesterday. I think she was quite impressed.'

Darynthe's heart sank. She had been hoping either that Ozanne had dropped out of Caan's life, or at least that he would say Ozanne hated the place. But how could any woman with any sense at all fail to admire that lovely old house, refurbished and now taking on the aura of a welcoming family house. But the house and its owner together must, surely, prove an irresistible combination.

'How . . . how long is she here for?'

She tried to make her question sound casual, but she knew it was a dismal attempt and that Caan's keen ears had noted the edge to her voice.

His shrewd eyes confirmed the fact.

'Indefinitely, I believe. Her plans at present are a little uncertain.'

Fear squeezed Darynthe's heart with icy fingers. If Ozanne was in the area for an indefinite period, she would have many opportunities of seeing Caan, of visiting the house. Perhaps this was the reason for her protracted stay in the area. The other girl was finally being asked to make up her mind between London and Caan's chosen home.

'Is . . . is she very rich?' she asked, conscious of the need to say something to break the depressed silence into which she had lapsed.

'Rich?' Caan queried.

'Well, she is a "lady" . . . I thought . . .'

Caan laughed.

'Ozanne has scarcely a penny to bless herself with. For the past ten years she's been forced to work to support herself. A title doesn't automatically bestow riches, you know.'

This piece of information lowered Darynthe's spirits still further. A rich Lady Ozanne, darling of London's social life, from which she might be reluctant to tear herself away, was one thing. But an impoverished Ozanne, unable to live in the style which her title seemed to dictate, was a far more dangerous proposition.

A marriage between her and Caan could be nothing but mutually advantageous. Ozanne would be insane to turn down the chance of marrying a man who obviously possessed the money she needed. On Caan's side, as a successful author, he would have the added cachet of having connections with the aristocracy, a gracious hostess for his new home; and penniless or not, there were always those to whom a title was an irresistible magnet.

'Ozanne asked after you,' said Caan, as they made their way back towards the car, having congratulated

Jack on his dog's performance.

I bet she did, Darynthe thought darkly. Ozanne would certainly be keeping her finger on the pulse of Caan's private life and would, no doubt, be displeased to learn that she, Darynthe, was still in the neighbourhood.

'I told her you were helping me with the house . . . and the garden,' Caan continued.

And I wonder what she thought of that little gem of information, Darynthe mused. Did the other girl see it as a threat to her own relationship with Caan, or was she supremely confident of her place in his affections?

'Come out with me again tomorrow?' Caan suggested. 'We could take a picnic up on to the fells . . . and on the way, we could stop and watch old Jack exercising another of his skills.'

'What's that?'

But Caan was not to be drawn.

'Say yes, and then you'll find out. If you don't come, you'll never know, will you?' he said tantalisingly.

Darynthe hesitated. How to accept, without seeming too eager . . . how to conceal that she needed to be with Caan, far more than he could possibly need her.

She made a jest of it.

'Don't you know what curious creatures women are supposed to be? I'm intrigued, so I'll come. Besides,' she added more soberly. 'I'm very fond of your uncle Jack.'

Seated beside her in the car, he paused in the act of adjusting his seat belt, his eyes meeting hers with a challenging sexual mockery in their bright gaze.

'Only of my uncle?' he queried. 'Don't your feelings extend to his nephew?'

Helplessly she stared back at him, feeling her cheeks colouring. If only he weren't teasing her! If only it were a serious enquiry, to which he wanted an affirmative answer. As it was, she found herself at a loss for words.

With a short laugh he completed the manoeuvre with his belt and started the engine.

'No need to look so stricken,' he said, his tone harsh, as he accelerated away. 'I'm not that thick-skinned. I keep forgetting your heart is miles away in ... where is it ... Corbridge?'

Darynthe could have wept. The day had begun so well, had continued happily, until Ozanne's name had cropped up ... her own fault, of course. Suddenly, Caan had seemed to remember that they both had other loyalties ... or at least, he had ... and obviously he was still deceived into believing Marcus Griffiths was her ex-fiancé.

Neither of them spoke again, until the white sports car drew up outside the Daffodil.

'Well?' Caan said curtly. 'Are you coming with me tomorrow?'

'If you still want me to,' she said, anxious green eyes surveying his unsmiling countenance.

'Damn it!'

His good nature was certainly wearing thin more often ... and more quickly ... these days, she thought. Once it had been virtually impossible to anger him.

'Damn it!' he repeated. 'Would I bother to ask you, if I didn't want you to come?'

It was an ungracious repetition of his invitation, but it was better than nothing and Darynthe knew it was all she was likely to receive now. She couldn't afford to stand on ceremony.

'I'll come,' she said quietly.

'Good!' His manner was still abrupt and he had not even switched off his engine. 'Eleven o'clock,' he added, 'be ready!'

She slid from the passenger seat and stood forlornly on the kerb as he drove away without even a backward glance.

The air was still and humid next day, as Caan and Darynthe, both clad in the briefest of T-shirts and shorts, began their ascent of the fells.

Caan, their picnic in a haversack slung across his broad back, led the way up the hillside, and Darynthe's gaze was filled with the sight of the rhythmic movement of his hips, tapering into bare, powerful thighs.

It was warm weather for climbing, not a single cloud to obscure the scorching sun, and even the song of the birds was muted, as though their tiny throats too were parched; butterflies drifted lazily among the flowers and only the incredibly prolific tiny insects seemed active, whirring busily in the dry grass, annoying in their persistent attentions.

The track beneath their feet was dry and dusty and the almost uncanny silence was intensified by the absence of running water, for the music of many becks, once cool retreats with water sliding over rocks, dripping through ferns, tumbling among pebbles, had been stilled . . . long since dried up.

There was not a breath of wind and the searing heat seemed to flare up off the steep hillside. They were the only moving humans on the hillside, the dust disturbed by their feet drifting up to coat shoes and socks in a fine layer. Even the sheep, unkempt in unshorn fleeces, seemed listless, nosing desultorily among the tinder-dry bracken fronds and heather clumps.

At last they came upon a group of men, Jack among them, all, despite the sultry heat, toiling on the hillside and Darynthe realised what Caan had meant, when he said that Jack would be exercising another of his skills.

Over the flanks of the ancient fellsides of Lakeland zig-zagged hundreds of miles of stone walls, some of them nearly a thousand years old, boundaries between farms, parish boundaries, all craftsmen-built.

'It's all voluntary maintenance work, this,' Caan told Darynthe, as they watched a section of wall being repaired, growing rapidly under Jack's skilful, grimy hands, as he carefully selected the stones from a pile at his side, chipping into shape and placing them in position.

'It's not so long since men used to work at this twelve hours a day, for seven and sixpence a week,' said Caan. 'They used to camp up here in the fells, to be near their work.'

'It's wonderful how he seems to know just which stone

to use every time,' Darynthe commented, as Jack selected and chipped. 'I can't even manage a jigsaw puzzle.'

'The earliest walls weren't made of slate,' said Caan, 'but of cobbles . . . gathered up when a space was cleared for cultivation. The biggest boulders were rolled to the edge of the new field and left there to become the base of the wall.'

'I always thought the walls were to keep the sheep in,' Darynthe commented.

'That's partly so,' Caan agreed, 'when grazing boundaries began to be built on the fells, the wallers opened up small quarries on the fellside and brought the slate down in sledges.'

Jack was engrossed in his work, but he stopped for a cold drink and a brief explanation of the age-old technique he employed.

'A well-built wall is really two walls side by side,' he told Darynthe, 'each made of stones fitted one to the other. The gap between is filled with rubble and small fragments. Then to strengthen the whole thing a row of flat slabs is laid across from side to side joining the two outer walls. You'll often notice people using these projecting ridges as a stile . . . but that's not their original purpose.'

Jack Lorimer was obviously keen to get on with his self-imposed task, and soon Caan and Darynthe were moving on, looking for a place in which to have their picnic.

To Darynthe's relief, Caan led her lower down the opposite side of the fell they had climbed into the grateful shade of a small wood . . . a cool, silent haven.

'I can't remember when I've ever been so hot,' she gasped, throwing herself down and leaning back against the hard comfort of a tree trunk.

'Make the most of it,' Caan advised. 'The weather will break soon, mark my words.'

'I shan't be sorry,' Darynthe admitted. 'I'd almost welcome some rain.'

'I wonder if you'd be so eager for rain if you lived here all year round.'

Caan seated himself beside her, unpacking the contents of the haversack.

Darynthe closed her eyes, completely relaxed.

'I can't imagine Lakeland being anything but lovely in any kind of weather,' she said dreamily.

'You've really fallen in love with it, haven't you?'

There was an intensity in Caan's deep voice and she opened her eyes to see him leaning over her.

'I've often wondered how you would look when you're asleep,' he murmured.

She flushed, struggling into an upright position.

'Tell me, what *is* it like in winter?'

She felt decidedly breathless and slightly panicky. So often in the last few days she had longed to be alone with Caan, but now she felt nervous, afraid of revealing her almost violent reactions to him.

He shrugged, his eyes still on her square, vivid features.

'It can be very beautiful here in winter ... or very dreary. I suppose it's at its most beautiful, when there's fresh snow on the mountains: snow seems to improve the views somehow, reflecting the light, bringing distant crags nearer, making them seem twice as large.'

Darynthe watched his expressive, rugged face, drinking in his words, words similar to those she had read in his books, but given a deeper, richer meaning, spoken aloud in his low, musical voice.

'And when it's dreary?' she prompted, as he fell silent.

'Foggy days, gales, floods, blizzards ... times when a hillman can be marooned in his home for days on end ... farmhouses such as mine.' He was still watching her closely as he spoke. 'It's not all glamour, Darynthe. Can you picture it ... day after day, night after night, between your own four walls, listening to the wind shrieking around the roof, knowing that you could be there for a week, or even longer?'

'It wouldn't be so bad,' Darynthe said softly, 'if you were there with ... with someone you loved.'

'No? I wonder how many women would agree with you?'

Was he thinking of Ozanne?

They were silent again, eating their sandwiches; the

food, as always, tasting better in the open air, following strenuous activity.

Darynthe found herself wondering if Ozanne *had* considered the pros and cons of the life Caan described. She wished she had the courage to ask him outright if he meant to marry the other girl, but feared that, if his answer were in the affirmative, she might betray how much it mattered to her.

'What sort of home is *your* fiancé offering *you*?'

The question came so suddenly, so unexpectedly, that Darynthe was unable to answer for a moment, finding it a struggle to empty her inward vision of Caan's farmhouse in order to picture the house which would have been hers and Mark's.

'Oh, just an ordinary house, in a university town,' she said at last. 'You know the sort of thing . . . semi-detached, two reception, three bedrooms . . .'

How had it ever seemed so eminently attractive? she wondered. Had she really once pictured herself as a suburban housewife?

Caan echoed her thoughts.

'And you intend to return to that stultifying atmosphere, after all this?' He waved a comprehensive hand at the vista of blue skies, of encircling mountains. 'You'll be surrounded by bricks and mortar, walk city streets . . . your friends all people whose lives exactly duplicate your own.'

That was how it would have been, Darynthe recognised, if she had married Mark Little.

'A lot of people live perfectly happy lives in those surroundings,' she said evenly, careful to betray nothing.

'Only because they've never known anything better,' said Caan. 'But not *you*,' he added urgently, his hand grasping her upper arm in a hold that was almost painful. 'I've watched you these past weeks. You love the outdoor life, as much as I do. On the lake, on the fells, you come alive . . . you're at home here. Why go back, Darynthe, why?'

'I've told you why,' she said, fighting to control her voice.

The feel of his hand on her bare arm, the urgency of his voice, his accurate analysis of her feelings for the country-side, were unbearably moving. It was agony to have to prevaricate, to pretend that she had a good reason for wanting to leave Ambleside.

'I know what you've told me,' Caan said fiercely. 'You've told me that you have to go home ... you've mentioned your father, his need for your company. You've never denied it, when I've asked if you're following your fiancé ... now that you're apparently reconciled. But you've never once mentioned the word "love". I don't believe you love this Mark.'

She couldn't answer him. After all, what was there she could say? Her silence seemed to infuriate him.

'What's become of the girl I met on the Wrynose Pass, the spirited little termagant who hated all men ... feared them? You've stopped hating, I know ... and I'm glad about that. But what about your fear? Is this Mark the right one to dispel that? Will he be gentle and considerate with you? Has he the maturity, the experience?'

Again it was impossible to answer, for he was vis-ualising a completely different man. Marcus Griffiths, the man he thought of as being her fiancé, probably did appear immature and inexperienced to Caan. But what about the real Mark ... Mark Little? The irony of the situation brought a bitter twist to her full lips. No one could ever accuse Mark Little of immaturity, of lack of experience.

The memory gave a bitter edge to her tongue, as she voiced her thoughts.

'Experience! Experience? What sort of recommendation is that? Oh, it's unfair!' She turned on Caan, her eyes deepening to the intense emerald that betokened intense feeling. 'When a man marries, he expects his bride to be untouched, inexperienced ...'

'And what's wrong with that?' Caan asked grimly.

'Nothing ... nothing at all,' she said a trifle wildly, 'but why shouldn't it work both ways ... why can't a woman expect the same virtues of a man?'

Caan expelled his breath in a long-drawn-out sigh.

'So that's it,' he said, 'the truth at last. Was that what you had against your fiancé?'

She nodded mutely. It was ironic to reflect that the very thing which had destroyed her love for Mark seemed to have no importance when applied to Caan.

Although she had challenged him on the subject she knew that, if only Caan were hers, she wouldn't care about his past. When she looked at him she did not see a man so many years older than herself, did not try to reckon up his character in terms of experience. All she saw was a man strong enough to have conquered her ... all her prejudices, a man who would protect her, yet who was gentle enough to treat her with a compelling tenderness. She didn't *care* about the women in his past, if only they *were* in his past and not ... like Ozanne ... very much a part of his present.

'You little idiot!' said Caan, and there was a wealth of understanding in his voice, as, unconsciously, he echoed her thoughts. 'Don't you know that the past is dead? In any relationship, it's the present which counts.'

In the silence, as she looked at him, seeing the growing warmth in the blue eyes, she could hear the beating of her own heart. The present, he had said ... but what about the future? His present was no good to her, unless she could share his future too.

Then he was reaching for her, pulling her down beside him on the hard ground, where they lay ... and now two hearts drummed against each other.

Darynthe knew that she should thrust him away from her, that she was not yet ready for this moment ... not until he had given her some sign, some word of love ... not until she knew that Ozanne's reign was over.

But with an inherent mastery he was touching her, his hands a kneading caress, his tongue teasing apart her trembling lips, until her body's desires clouded her mind to all other thoughts than those of Caan. Never before had he gone beyond a kiss and a tentative caress. But now he held her closely moulded against his thighs, while his mouth worked its insidious seduction, creating a sweet aching void in the centre of her being.

Her brief T-shirt and shorts were no barrier to his exploring fingers, which were swiftly rousing her to the agony of physical desire.

She knew that his own need was as deep-felt as her own and every instinct urged surrender, as the pressure of his body grew in intensity.

'Caan?' She whispered the name against his lips, a question in her voice, but he smothered the sound in a renewed onslaught.

If he had spoken then, had told her that he loved her, that no other woman meant anything to him, she might have believed him, might have given way to his demands, but without those words it seemed to her that his was just a brief, sensual pleasure, a passing lust, induced by their proximity, by the warmth of the sun on their scantily clad bodies.

She must resist him, before it was too late, before she surrendered to her own wild needs. Somehow she fought him off and leapt to her feet, nervously smoothing down the shorts over her slender flanks, straightening her T-shirt, which had ridden up to expose the creamy flesh of her unsupported breasts.

'What the hell?'

His angry cry pierced her like a lance and there was anguish as well as anger in his eyes. She looked at him, dazed, still trembling.

'Come back here,' he commanded.

'No ... no, Caan, I can't ... I won't ... not here, not like this.' The words jerked out of her, painfully, as she ached with the aftermath of unconsummated love-making.

'What's wrong with making love in the open?' he demanded in exasperation. 'Don't tell me you're a prude, that you only let your hair down indoors ... or after dark?'

She wanted to cry out that he was wrong, that nothing seemed more natural, both in her nature and in his, than that they should make love under the sky, upon the earth created by a god of love.

Caan stood up to face her.

'My God, you must be made of stone! Do you feel

nothing . . . nothing at all?'

His words were spoken with such passionate intensity, that their effect on her was one of almost physical force . . . a spear turned in an already throbbing wound.

Fiercely she renounced the emotion that threatened to swamp her. Caan had no right to demand any more of her . . . and besides, believing her to be reconciled with Mark, it was despicable of him to make love to her.

No more despicable than your attempts to wean him away from Ozanne, her conscience goaded her.

'I could shake you,' Caan said huskily; his low tones were still unsteady with emotion, his mouth twisted, not in mirth this time but with anguish.

His annoyance seemed to be abating, if not his desire, and she was forced to turn away, to hide her violent awareness of him, to temper her body's treacherous longing for a renewal of his touch.

She heard him move, his feet rustling the dry foliage, and she tensed, knowing that for him to touch her now would be her undoing. It would be so easy to turn into his arms, to rekindle the fires of his passion . . . and her own.

But there was no warmth, no sensation to tell her of his nearness, and when she did swing round, it was to see him moving away from her to the far side of the copse, the haversack swinging from his hand.

He couldn't do this to her. He couldn't just walk off and leave her. He was not the only one whose needs had not been alleviated. She began to follow him, breaking into a run, as the trees hid him from sight.

As she emerged from the shade of the trees, her pace slowed. Beyond the wood was a pool, not large enough to be dignified by the name of tarn, but fairly deep, for Caan had waded in, the limpid water reaching to his waist.

As she watched, he ducked down, immersing his entire body and head, to emerge again, shaking the droplets from his face.

'Why not join me?' he suggested, his good humour now apparently entirely restored.

It was tempting. Her overwarm flesh tingled with the urge to cool itself. But the pool was too small; they would be dangerously close, the water moulding their already minimal clothing to their bodies. It would be unfair to both of them to impose yet more strain upon their hungry flesh.

He emerged from the pool and she was reminded of the morning when he had bathed in Windermere, for now, as then, he shook himself like an animal, the droplets scattering far and wide.

'Have you ever bathed in the nude?' he asked, stretching himself out on a sun-warmed rock to dry.

'N-no, never.'

'You should try it some time,' he recommended.

'Have . . . have you, then?' To picture his hard, bronzed body entirely unclothed caused a strange fluttering sensation beneath her ribcage.

'Often. There are plenty of places in the mountains, where it's possible to take a dip on a hot day.'

'But . . . but suppose someone came by?'

He shrugged.

'No one ever has yet. Tell me something, Darynthe,' his eyes were mocking now, challenging her to react, 'would you bathe in the nude . . . with a man . . . if you were in love with him?'

Darynthe felt herself going scarlet, a blush which seemed to extend to all the exposed parts of her flesh. Why did he have to ask questions of such sensual implication? *He* might have cooled his ardour by that plunge in the mountain pool, but her blood still seemed to be at fever heat, a condition not improved by the sight of him as he lay there, his still damp shorts clinging to every contour.

'Well, would you?' he persisted.

'I . . . I might . . . if I were married to him.'

He made no further comment, but rose from his rock, with a lazy, panther-like grace, and instinctively she recoiled, but he did not come near her. Instead, he retrieved his knapsack and hoisting it on to his shoulders, suggested that it was time they retraced their steps.

Darynthe was aware of a vague dissatisfaction with the day as a whole. It was the tension, she decided, the constant necessity of having to hold back, to keep her feelings in check. Her relationship with Caan was neither one thing nor the other ... neither love nor enmity ... and looked like remaining in that unsatisfactory state.

They were descending the fellside much faster than they had ascended, and Darynthe was assailed by a feeling of panic. Soon they would be back in Ambleside and Caan would be depositing her at the door of the Daffodil. Would he be so disgusted by what he considered to be her coldness, her prudery, that he would say goodbye to her, with no intention of seeing her again. She couldn't bear it if that were to happen.

'Caan,' she faltered.

He looked at her without slackening his stride.

'I ... I'm sorry that I ... I didn't ... I mean, that I couldn't ...'

He did stop then, taking her by the shoulders, looking down at her distressed face with eyes softened by concern.

'Don't be sorry,' he said gently. 'I'm not.'

With a pat on her shoulder, he urged her on her way.

But Darynthe found no comfort in his words ... rather the reverse. It sounded as if his lovemaking had been, as she had feared, an impulse, the result of propinquity and not based on any deeper emotion; and now he was relieved that it had gone no further, that he would not be involved in any embarrassing complications.

'Caan,' she said again, imploringly.

He seemed slightly exasperated by her persistence.

'Look, Darynthe. We're both agreed that what happened up there,' he nodded towards the mountainside, 'is best forgotten. Let's face it, there's seventeen years difference in our ages ... I'm far too old for you, and you had the sense to realise it. Whereas I ...'

'Too old!' Darynthe laughed, suddenly lightheaded with relief. Was that all that troubled him? 'You're *young* compared with Mark. He was forty-four ...'

She stopped, her hand going to her mouth in horror, as

she realised what she had said ... how she had given herself away.

CHAPTER NINE

'WHAT did you say?'

Caan stopped abruptly in his tracks, as though he had been struck by lightning.

Sulkily, Darynthe refused to meet his accusing gaze.

'You heard what I said,' she muttered.

'I most certainly did, and I could scarcely believe my ears.'

His rugged face was set and grim, a white line etching the contours of his mouth, as he strode on, his pace redoubled.

'Well, you know now.'

Darynthe shrugged slender shoulders, helpless in the face of his anger ... anger which she knew to be justified.

'What do I know? That that callow young man was no more your fiancé than I am ... that for some reason best known to yourself, you've been lying to me all this while. What I *don't* know is why?'

And I can't tell you, Darynthe thought drearily. I can't tell you that it was easier to let you believe that Marcus Griffiths was Mark Little ... safer to let you believe it, for the sake of my pride.

'I can only suppose you used him as a "keep off" sign for me,' Caan observed, his tone bitter.

They had reached the car by now and Darynthe could measure Caan's abstraction by the fact that he left her to get in by herself, striding round to the driver's side, slamming his door and starting the engine with an angry roar.

She couldn't deny his accusation; it was too near the truth for that; so she remained silent, knowing that by doing so, she was deepening his annoyance, but totally unable to alter the fact.

The distance to the Daffodil was covered in record time, the wheels of the little sports car spinning dangerously on the gravel of the car park, as Caan braked viciously.

Darynthe expected him to accelerate away again as soon as she was out of the car, but to her alarm, he did nothing of the sort. Instead he took her arm in a vice-like grip and propelled her before him in a manner which could only be described as a frogmarch.

'L-let go of my arm, please. You're hurting me!'

'Not as much as you deserve to be hurt,' he observed, ignoring her indignant plea.

Inside the house they came face to face with Ann Forster, who looked from one to the other in some surprise, and Darynthe realised that their faces must be all too expressive of their churning emotions . . . hers of icy fear, Caan's a white-hot fury.

Before her aunt, Caan was forced to relax his punishing grip and glancing sideways at him, Darynthe saw his white, even teeth bared in a grim travesty of a polite smile. Seizing her opportunity, she wrenched her arm free, bolting for the stairs and the safety of her room. It was an attempt doomed to failure.

A muffled imprecation from Caan, swiftly followed by a word of apology to her aunt, preceded the sound of his pounding feet on the stairs behind her.

Feeling as though her lungs must burst, Darynthe took the first two flights at incredible speed, causing the two elderly guests she encountered to flatten themselves against the wall.

If she hadn't been so terrified she would have giggled to think what their expressions must be, as Caan, hot on her heels, caused them to repeat their evasive action.

The steep attic stairs proved to be her final undoing and on faltering legs she reached her bedroom only a split second ahead of Caan, not soon enough to put the barrier of the door between them.

He pushed her into the room with such force that she stumbled and collapsed across the bed; then he slammed the door behind him, turning the key in the lock and putting it into the pocket of his shorts.

'Now,' he told her with terrible emphasis, 'now we will have some explanations.'

Drained of energy, she stared up at him as he loomed ominously above her. His large, muscular frame seemed to fill the tiny attic bedroom and if he were to move a step or two in either direction, he would be forced to duck his head to avoid the sloping rafters.

'You ... you had no right to follow me up here,' she gasped at last, her breast still heaving, as she fought for breath.

'It wouldn't have been necessary for me to come upstairs, if you hadn't been such a bloody little coward, too afraid to face the music!'

A snarl marred his normally pleasant features.

Darynthe's eyes widened. She had never seen this side to Caan's character. For a large, virile man, he had always seemed unusually placid, even-tempered and gentle. Certainly he had never spoken to her in quite this way before ... had never sworn so violently. There was nothing placid about him now; in fact he gave the impression of a tightly coiled spring, ready to expand at any moment with the force of his fury, and she had the premonition that all gentleness too might be forgotten.

'P-please go away,' she said, edging further across the bed.

He shook his head emphatically.

'Not until I get some answers.'

She attempted defiance.

'I don't have to answer your questions!'

Caan's vivid blue eyes were compelling, piercing, as if they saw right down into her innermost thoughts.

'If you have any honesty in you whatsoever, you'll admit that I have a *right* to the truth.'

He did have a right. She couldn't deny it ... to him, or to herself. But to answer his questions might involve her in telling the whole truth ... something she was not prepared to do.

Mutely she stared back at him, wishing that she had some excuse to lash herself into righteous indignation, so that she would feel capable, even justified, in defying him. But all she felt was an unutterable sadness at the realisation that their relationship had deteriorated to this extent.

As he saw that she did not intend to volunteer the information he sought, Caan's well-shaped mouth tightened and the blue eyes chilled.

'Right, since it seems we have to do this the hard way ... we'll start at the beginning. Just who was the youth with you, that day on Coniston?'

At least that was something she could answer honestly.

'Marcus ... Marcus Griffiths, a guest here at the Daffodil.'

'Yet you called him Mark,' Caan probed. 'Was he in on this conspiracy to deceive me?'

'No, certainly not!' Here Darynthe *could* feel indignation ... as though she would stoop that low, making others lie on her behalf. 'He preferred to be called Mark. All his friends ...'

'And you ... you'd never met him before?'

'No, never.'

Caan lowered himself on to the side of the bed and Darynthe tried to make herself as small as possible. The bed was only a narrow single and Caan was far too close for comfort.

'Why did you let me go on thinking that he was your ex-fiancé?'

His deep voice was flat, expressionless, but Darynthe did not deceive herself into believing that his wrath had abated.

'I don't know,' she muttered, realising that it was a feeble answer and not likely to satisfy the angry man in front of her.

'You'll have to do better than that.' His tone was scornful, giving her the goad to anger that she needed.

'All right,' she snapped, 'I was trying to spare your feelings, but since you insist on knowing, you were right ... it *was* a "hands off" sign to you. I thought it might protect me from your unwelcome attentions.'

He flinched, as though she had struck him.

'When have I ever inflicted my "attentions" on you, against your will ... answer me that?'

'Several times,' she flared back at him. 'That night on Helvellyn ...'

'I don't recall your fighting me off on that occasion.'

She ignored the interruption.

'Then there was the time on Windermere, on your boat ... and what about this afternoon?'

'On both occasions, your reactions were far from cold. In fact, I *was* beginning to think I was mistaken about you.'

'Mistaken?' A supercilious lift of her brows added fuel to the fires burning in him.

'Yes, mistaken ... in thinking that you were a frigid, immature child. I was beginning to think that after all there might be the seeds of womanhood in you.'

Aghast, she stared at him, her clear green eyes filling with unwilling tears. If only he knew how nearly those seeds had grown, blossomed under his kiss, his caress.

'For heaven's sake, don't cry,' he said irritably. 'Women always resort to tears when they know they're in the wrong ... or losing an argument.'

'That's better than a man's last resort,' she retorted, her voice something between a gasp and a sob. 'Men just lose their temper and start shouting and making hateful, untrue accusations.'

'Are they untrue?' His tone was disbelieving. 'Are you going to tell me that you're not a frigid little coward? If what you said about your fiancé was right, that he was a man in his forties, I'm not surprised he let you down. I should think your behaviour turned him right off. A callow youth like your friend Griffiths might be prepared to put up with you blowing hot and cold, but ...'

'Mark did *not* let me down ... not in the way you think. He ... he was married, going to get a divorce ...'

'Oh, so you're one of those, are you ... broke up his marriage and then got cold feet?'

'I did *not* break up his marriage! I don't mess around with married men ... or engaged ones,' she ended significantly.

Darynthe could not be sure which was uppermost now, her misery or her fury. Either way, the hot tears were coursing down her cheeks. She probably looked frightful, she thought . . . red-eyed and blotchy. This little scene was certainly going to put paid to any chance of patching things up.

Caan seemed unmoved by her tears.

'Convince me!' he said harshly.

'Mark was already planning to get a divorce before he met me. If you don't believe me, ask Aunt Ann, she . . .'

'Then why in heaven's name, did you . . .?'

'Because he didn't tell me. He let me go on thinking he was single, that I was his first . . . his first . . .'

Caan's derisive laugh stopped her in mid-explanation.

'You mean to tell me you really had the naïvety, the incredibly stupid naïvety, to think that a man who had reached that age would be as . . . as virginal as yourself?'

Darynthe was silent. She supposed she had been naïve, but, she defended herself mentally, it wasn't entirely her fault. Her life at home had been no preparation for the world . . . her parents' idyllic marriage her only guideline.

Even when friends of her own age had talked openly about infidelities, broken marriages, she had always looked upon the participants of these tragedies as being unreal, unnatural, outside her ken . . . had never dreamt that any man with whom she became involved could be anything other than the romantic love of her dreams.

Caan was shaking his head, slowly, incredulously, pityingly. How dared he pity her . . . act as if she were some kind of moron!

'You would try to find excuses for him,' she spoke the words bitterly, 'since you're probably every bit as bad yourself.'

'I am neither married nor divorced,' he pointed out, his tone even, but ominous.

'Maybe not,' she muttered, 'but . . .'

'But what?'

He was suddenly very close to her and there was no more room to retreat on the narrow bed . . . as his body trapped her between its muscular strength and the wall.

'But I bet you've had as many women as you've had hot dinners.'

She knew she was venturing on dangerous ground, but she said the words nevertheless, in a vain attempt to outface him.

'You think that, do you?' he said pleasantly, deceptively so.

'Yes!'

'Then, since you have so low an opinion of my morals, it won't surprise you if I add one more to my list of conquests!'

His meaning dawned on her a little too late for protest, as he caught her in a brutally strong embrace, his powerful body tense with violence, as he crushed his hand over one of her breasts, his mouth possessing hers totally, suffocatingly, exploring it intimately, passionately.

Against her will, she felt the sensitive peak spring to life under the torture of his fingers . . . his lovemaking rough with unleashed emotions.

Despite her very real fear, a strange desire was building up in her, a desire which she could interpret only too well, as his hard hands coaxed wholly new reactions from her quivering body.

His broad chest was rising and falling against her at a tremendous rate, his breathing ragged, as his desire accelerated, while his mouth was a blazing, consuming demand, brooking no denial.

A pulsing heat was engulfing her body, a helpless lassitude, and she felt she must suffocate if he did not soon release her.

Feebly, she tried to turn her head aside, to thrust him away, but his relentless onslaught did not slacken.

Sensuous pleasure began to give way to a shamed anger, a burning resentment, as she recognised that his caresses were totally without tenderness or sensitivity. Her lips, her breasts were bruised and tingling, the iron pressure of his mouth denied her even the right to breathe.

She had often wondered whether Caan could be roused to anger. Now she knew . . . for his fury was being displayed in this deep, driving hunger, the desire to hurt, which seemingly would never be appeased.

She had never been kissed in anger. So far, the kisses she had experienced from other men had been coaxing, tender ... meant to be enjoyed. Yet, despite Caan's roughness, she could not quell the sudden flare of passion erupting deep inside her ... even in anger Caan's kisses had a more potent power to arouse her than any gentler caress she had ever received. Soon, if she were not careful, she would be doubly trapped, by his revengeful lovemaking and by her own kindling desire.

But as the thought crossed her mind, he flung away from her, to stand over her, looking down into her face as if he hated her, the lines of compression still white about his mouth.

'Think yourself lucky, Darynthe, that I'm not the man you take me to be.'

His deep voice was thickened by passion, the words almost indistinguishable.

'You've just proved that you are.' Her ravaged mouth could scarcely form the words. 'You're a beast, a brute, an animal. No wonder you like the outdoor life ... you're uncivilised, nothing better than a savage!'

She knew as she spoke that she was being unfair, that his unbridled behaviour of the last few moments was entirely uncharacteristic of the man, provoked by herself, by her treatment of him; but she had to take refuge in anger, or otherwise her disturbed senses would make her fling herself back into his arms, begging his forgiveness, asking him to take her ... but in tenderness, not in the savagery of revenge.

'I've tried everything I know with you.' Slowly but painfully he was regaining command over his voice. 'I've tried kindness, I've tried humour ... commonsense. But there's no reaching you. When I first met you, I gave you the benefit of the doubt, because I thought you were nursing a broken heart. But you don't even *have* a heart, Darynthe, just a cold little computer, that calculates a man's worth in terms of vice and virtue. You're looking for something that doesn't exist ... a saint of some sort. Well, if you want unparalleled perfection, I suggest that you and your little computer heart get married to a robot.'

'You've tried everything?' She shouted the words at him. 'Who asked you to try *anything*? Who asked you to interfere in my life, I'd like to know ... certainly not me!'

'Believe me,' Caan said emphatically, 'from this moment on, all interference in your affairs ceases. I'm only human, Darynthe, I'm not a machine, and I can't take any more of your see-sawing emotions. I held back while I thought your engagement was on again ... though I had hoped I could persuade you, eventually, not to go through with it. Then I find you've been lying to me all the time. One thing I find it hard to forgive is being taken for a fool.'

As she stared at him, her cheeks hot with guilt and humiliation, he took the key from his pocket and unlocked her door.

'From now on you're quite safe in your ivory tower, up here under the eaves. I shan't be invading your territory again. I don't go where I'm not wanted.'

'You could have fooled me!' Darynthe spat out the words. 'You've been doing just that for the last three months. But if you're keen to go where you *are* wanted, I suggest you take up where you left off with *Lady* Ozanne.'

He regarded her grimly.

'Believe me, I might just do that.'

Without another word, he was gone, shutting the door behind him, with an exaggerated care that seemed more final than any bang.

Darynthe remained curled up on her bed, a huddled ball of misery, her fingers rubbing the livid marks on her arms, touching her bruised, throbbing lips. It would be a long time before she forgot his violating love-making. Despair engulfed her. She had lost any chance now that she might ever have had of winning his love. He'd said himself that he would never forgive her for making a fool of him. Besides, she had called him hard, cruel, unforgivable names. Any flickering feelings he might have had for her would be quite destroyed ...

stone dead beneath that shrewish barrage.

She still found it incredible that Caan of all people could be so angry, so violent. He was a big man, but she felt sure he had never used his strength in such a way before . . . and certainly not to a woman.

His scolding . . . if scolding it had been . . . had always been light, almost affectionate. Painstakingly, she began to recall every moment they had spent together, regretting, now that it was too late, her lack of total honesty with him. What would it have mattered if he *had* recognised her growing dependence on him? Caan would have been kind, gentle in rejection, and even if she had emerged from the encounter bruised and unhappy, could it have been any worse than the pain she now felt?

Unless he had said it just to punish her, Caan's words had implied an affectionate interest in her which, given time and encouragement, might have blossomed into something deeper, long-lasting, but her own actions, prompted by stupid pride, had nipped it in the bud. Now that she had lost it, she knew that what she had dubbed as his interference had been merely tender protection, and she realised how much she had come to lean on his wiser, more mature judgment.

By her deception, and now by her angry accusations, she had caused the thing she most wished to prevent . . . she had driven him into Ozanne Hanson's willing arms.

With a sudden convulsive movement, she flung herself into the still visible depression on the bed, and sobbed out her misery and desire for the man whose body had left it there . . . knowing fully the utter darkness of loneliness.

Ann Forster, coming in search of her, half an hour after Caan's departure, was shocked by the sight of her niece's ravaged countenance.

'I guessed you two had been at odds with each other, but I never dreamt it was this bad. I pictured you up here having a reconciliation.'

'Reconciliation!' Darynthe's attempt at humour brought tears to her aunt's sympathetic eyes. 'It was more like the prelude to World War Three.'

'Is there anything *I* can do to help?' Ann asked diffidently.

With difficulty, Darynthe held back the fresh tears which her aunt's kindness threatened to precipitate.

'Nothing,' she said dully. 'There's nothing anyone can do. Caan's completely finished with me. He ... he'll probably go off and marry that Ozanne now. Oh, I've been such a fool, Auntie Ann!'

Ann, perched on the edge of the bed, where so recently Caan had sat, put her arm across her niece's shoulders.

'Somehow I don't see Caan as a hard, unforgiving man,' she said slowly. 'I'm sure once his temper has cooled, he'll ... Why not give it a day or two and then go and see him?'

Darynthe shook her head.

'I couldn't, not now ... now that I've destroyed everything. If I thought he still liked me, even ... but he doesn't ... he couldn't, not after the things I said, the names I called him.'

'We all say things we don't mean, when we're angry,' Ann said consolingly. 'I'm sure Caan knows that ... and I'm certain he must have said some unkind things too? But you'll find it was only temper. At least give him a chance, Darynthe. It's no good both of you nursing your pride. He may be just as sorry ... just as anxious to make up.'

As Darynthe still looked doubtful, Ann added:

'Well, think about it anyway. You know you can borrow your Uncle Bob's car, any time you feel like driving out to Grasmere.'

For several days, Darynthe's conscience and her inclinations waged war with pride and despair. She longed yet feared to encounter Caan ... fear, on the whole, being uppermost. She did not think she could bear to see the dislike and contempt which must surely contort his rugged features at the sight of her.

But there was little time during the day for resolving her internal conflict. The guesthouse was still busy, with the last rush of autumn holidaymakers; and at night, she fell into bed with little more energy than to reflect how unhappy she was and to wonder what Caan was doing, before merciful sleep claimed her.

'You're looking very peaky, you silly girl,' Ann scolded one day, finding her niece rather listlessly stripping the bed after a departed guest. 'Tomorrow you're going to take a whole day off and do absolutely nothing.'

'Oh no, Auntie, please! I'd go mad with nothing to do,' Darynthe pleaded. 'I don't want time to think.'

'That's just what you *do* need,' Ann retorted. 'So just take yourself off for a nice long walk somewhere ànd sort yourself out. Because I tell you frankly, if you don't, you may just as well go home to your father. You're in a fair way to make yourself really ill, and I refuse to be responsible to Arthur for the consequences.'

Ann's harsh tone, her apparent lack of feeling, brought tears to Darynthe's eyes . . . tears that nowadays came all too readily, but it had the desired effect, for next day she took her aunt's advice and set off early, alone, for a walk on the fells.

She knew Ann had not intended that she should go alone and she felt rather guilty at allowing her aunt to believe she was going on an organised outing. But if she was ever to come to terms with her emotions, she needed to be wholly alone.

Ambleside was almost obscured in autumnal morning mist, as Darynthe left the Daffodil and turned her steps towards Loughrigg. It did not seem at all strange to her that she should be drawn to follow the route of her first walk with Caan.

There was not a soul in sight on the lonely heights and she walked on, deep in thought, so engrossed that she was surprised to find herself by the side of Loughrigg Tarn, 'Diana's Looking Glass', one of Caan's books had called it.

Darynthe stared into its silver ripples, as though she might find the answer to her problems mirrored on its surface.

Should she seek Caan out, apologise, risk having her overture rejected . . . or should she take the easy way out, the coward's way, and run home to her father?

The pool remained enigmatic.

A sensuous shiver invaded her being, as she recalled

Caan's talk of nude bathing in such a pool as this. What would it be like, she wondered, to bathe naked with someone you loved . . . with Caan? She had a feeling that it would be a very wonderful experience, but alas, she would never know. Would it haunt her all her life . . . that beautiful, idyllic, pagan vision?

The leaves were already lying thickly on the ground, as she continued her walk, past Skelwith Bridge and along the woodland edge of the River Brathay.

On she meandered, with no set purpose or destination in mind, through the woods to Colwith Bridge, colours fast changing from green to bronze in copses of hazel, birch and rowan.

So lost was she in her silent communing that it seemed no time at all before she was entering the village of Little Langdale and looking musingly at the sign which indicated the route to the Wrynose Pass . . . where it had all begun.

Suddenly conscious of fatigue, both physical and mental, Darynthe sank down on to a bench encircling a massive tree and leant back against the rough bark, closing her eyes. It was a mistake; for nowadays, every time she closed her eyes, a vision of Caan's rugged face swam behind her eyelids.

Hurriedly she opened them, only to wonder if the delusion was still with her, for crossing the road from the public house opposite was Caan Lorimer. But it was not merely the sight of him which brought the little choking gasp to her lips, but the recognition of his companion.

Holding on to Caan's arm, her pointed feline face alight and vivacious, her body splendid in its animal-like languor, was Lady Ozanne Hanson, and from where Darynthe sat, she could clearly see the enormous square diamond which glinted and winked mockingly at her from the third finger of Ozanne's left hand.

Her hope of remaining unrecognised was doomed to disappointment, for the couple's path to their waiting car took them right past where she sat.

It was Ozanne who noticed her first, making some little laughing remark to Caan, which immediately brought his eyes in Darynthe's direction.

She was almost certain that, left to himself, Caan would

have continued past with the briefest of chilly nods, but
Ozanne actually stopped to speak to her—probably to
make sure, Darynthe thought cynically, that she had a
good view of the ostentatious engagement ring.

'If it isn't Caan's little gardening friend!' Ozanne
purred.

She was svelte, sleek and seductive, wearing a close-
fitting jumpsuit in a trendy shade of brown mink, edged
with gold piping, the colours enhancing the tawny gold of
her slanting eyes. Her mouth with its exaggerated cupid's
bow, was curled in what Darynthe considered to be an
odiously smug smile.

Looking at the other girl, Darynthe became acutely
aware of her own dishevelled appearance, the dusty jeans
and quilted anorak which had seen better days, the woollen cap protecting her ears, making her look, she considered, like a half-witted garden gnome. Crossly she
dragged the cap off, stuffing it into her pocket.

'All alone?' Ozanne said. Her tone, Darynthe felt sure,
was one of false sympathy.

'Yes,' she said shortly.

'Have you walked far?' Caan asked stiffly, sheer courtesy, apparently, making him feel bound to contribute
something to the conversation.

'From Loughrigg.'

'So far? You must be tired.' His voice was sharp, but
did she detect a slight note of concern?

No, she must be mistaken. Caan had ceased to trouble
himself over her welfare. Unconsciously she sighed.

'We could give your little friend a lift back to Ambleside, couldn't we, darling?' Ozanne rested a proprietary
hand on Caan's arm.

'It's quite all right,' Darynthe said quickly. She particularly resented the 'little'. Since she was taller than the
other girl, she assumed it was meant in a derogatory,
condescending manner.

'I'd rather walk,' she added. 'It's a lovely day, and . . .'

'Rubbish! You're tired already,' said Caan. 'Your face
is quite pale.'

Pale . . . only because of the shock of seeing you,
Darynthe thought, and of seeing that vulgarly expensive

great ring on Ozanne's finger. Well, she'd told him to go back to Ozanne, so she had only herself to blame that he'd taken her advice. But she couldn't bear to be in the same car as the couple, not even for the short length of time it would take to get back to Ambleside.

'I'll walk,' she repeated, then found herself being marched towards a sleek grey limousine.

'Get in!' Caan ordered between clenched teeth, and after one swift look at his set face, she obeyed, sinking into the upholstered luxury of the rear seat.

To herself, she admitted that it was a relief not to have to complete the rest of the journey on foot. Somehow, meeting Caan had sapped what little strength she had left.

Darynthe was surprised when Ozanne slid in behind the wheel and soon the great car was purring along the narrow roads.

'Isn't it just the most fantastic car and the most marvellous engagement present a girl ever had?' Ozanne enthused.

Darynthe was racked by a sudden sickening wave of jealous nausea . . . not because she had the least desire to own such a car, but because it was Caan who had given it to the other girl, along with the diamond ring she flaunted. She was glad to be in the back of the car, so that neither Caan nor Ozanne could see the pain which she was certain contorted her features.

'And so divine not to have to rely on public transport any more . . . don't you agree?' Ozanne continued. 'I'm driving myself down to London tomorrow, to start shopping for my trousseau!'

She turned towards Caan, giving Darynthe the benefit of her aristocratic profile.

'Didn't you say you wanted to see your publisher, darling? Why not let me drive you down?'

He nodded.

'Why not?'

As Darynthe listened to Ozanne, her hungry eyes memorised every detail of Caan's backview . . . the grey-sprinkled, close-cropped curls, the muscular neck and broad shoulders . . . her last sight of him, once this journey was over. For she knew now what she had to do. Her decision had been made for her: she must go home. There was no longer any hope, no point in further procrastination.

Tomorrow there were two last indulgences she would grant herself and then, on the following day, she would telephone her father to tell him she was on her way.

'I must say it will be a relief not to have to work any more.' Ozanne was prattling on in her high, well-bred voice. 'Modelling wasn't really me . . . a little infra dig. Though of course,' she added hastily, 'I've always been very grateful for the strings you pulled to get me the job.' Briefly, her left hand brushed Caan's knee, a gesture from which Darynthe averted her eyes. 'So handy to know famous people, with influence . . .'

So that was what Ozanne had meant, Darynthe thought . . . when, during her first encounter with the other girl, she had remarked on all that Caan had done for her; and now he was doing even more, lifting from those narrow, elegant shoulders the necessity of supporting herself.

'You'll have to direct me, darling,' Ozanne told Caan, as they reached the outskirts of Ambleside. 'I haven't a clue where this little place is . . . the Bluebell, isn't it?'

Darynthe had the distinct impression that Ozanne knew very well what her aunt's guesthouse was really called, but she bit back the angry retort which rose to her lips, leaving it to Caan to guide his fiancée through the maze of streets.

The car stopped and Darynthe jumped out, thankful that her ordeal was over.

She felt that some comment on her part was called for.

'Thank you for the lift. I'll say goodbye, because I don't suppose I'm likely to see either of you again. I . . . I'm going home this week. Con . . . congratulations on your . . . your engagement. I h-hope you'll both be very happy.'

Then, before her feelings could engulf her, she turned and ran up the steps of the Daffodil, without a backward glance, hearing the car purr away, taking Caan out of her life for ever.

CHAPTER TEN

'OF course you can borrow your uncle's car tomorrow,' Ann Forster told her niece. She looked keenly at Darynthe's pale, set face. 'Does this mean that you've decided? You're going to see Caan ... to apologise?'

'No.' Darynthe shook her head, her generous mouth quivering slightly. 'It's too late for that.' She looked up, meeting her aunt's gaze squarely. 'He's already engaged to Ozanne Hanson.'

'Oh dear, are you certain?' Ann asked.

But even Darynthe's normally optimistic aunt had to admit that there was no gainsaying the evidence of that enormous diamond ring.

'And the car ... you say he's given her a car too?'

Darynthe nodded.

'He must have simply pots of money,' Ann sighed. 'To think, Darynthe, you might have had all that ... the ring, the car, that lovely house I've heard so much about.'

'I don't envy her any of them,' Darynthe said fiercely. 'She'd be welcome to the lot, if I could just have Caan. I don't care about him being rich and famous, and I'd live with him in a cottage like his uncle's, if I had to, if he was a pauper, or on the dole, the way I once thought he was.'

'So why do you need our car?' Ann asked curiously.

'I ... I want to say goodbye to his uncle Jack. He's been very nice to me ... and I want to take one last look at the house, before I go home. I've decided to go the day after tomorrow. I'll be sorry to leave you, Auntie Ann, to leave Ambleside, but I can't stay here and risk meeting them every five minutes.'

'Do you think they'll stay here, now she's landed Caan?' Ann asked. 'Mightn't she drag him back to city life?'

'I don't think so, somehow. She has no money of her own and I imagine she'll play things pretty much his way for a while. Besides, I don't think he's the sort of man to let a woman rule his life.'

For an instant, the picture of being mastered by Caan crossed Darynthe's ready imagination, bringing in its wake a pain so intense as to elicit a physical reaction. She sat down rather abruptly.

'Do you think it's wise to go out there tomorrow?' Ann eyed her niece with some concern. 'You'll only be rubbing salt in the wound ... and suppose you meet Caan?'

'I won't,' Darynthe said with bitter confidence. '*She* is driving him down to London tomorrow, so he'll be safely out of the way.'

'Well, I suppose you know your own business best, love.'

But Ann Forster still looked unconvinced.

It was mid-morning before Darynthe set out for Grasmere next day, by which time, she judged, Caan should be well on his way to London.

She planned to visit Jack Lorimer at his cottage first. It would have seemed churlish to leave the district without bidding goodbye to the elderly man. She hoped fervently that he would be happy at the farmhouse under Ozanne's reign, but somehow she doubted it, and her heart ached for him; and what about Scipio, with Ozanne's declared aversion to dogs?

She parked the borrowed car and, filled with nostalgia for her earlier visits, walked slowly up the familiar track towards the sturdy little cottage. It was a still but chilly autumn day, and the smoke from the chimney spiralled straight upwards; the rocky gills running through the garden gurgled cheerfully.

Although Jack would be going to the lovely old farm-house, the thought crossed Darynthe's mind that it might be hard for an elderly man to leave his accustomed home ... a place upon which he had imposed his own personality.

As usual, Scipio was on the alert, running to meet her,

assuring himself of her identity, before leading the way into the bright, cosy kitchen.

Jack Lorimer was seated at the large wooden table, a newspaper and a large mug of coffee before him. At the sound of footsteps, he looked up and his round, weather-beaten face broke up into a welcoming smile.

'Darynthe! Well, I'm blessed! What are you doing here? Is Caan with you?'

'N-no I'm alone.'

'Strange . . . I thought he'd . . .'

'I wanted to see *you*,' she said hastily, 'to explain . . .'

'Just a minute, love . . . d'you fancy a coffee?'

Not sorry to postpone the evil moment of explanation and farewell, Darynthe nodded, sitting down at the table opposite Jack.

While he moved over to the hob to make another mug of coffee, she glanced swiftly around her. Jack might be moving soon, but he had not let this fact interfere with his housekeeping. Most people moving house allowed their standards to slide, but the copper pans still shone as brightly as ever, the paintwork was clean, rag rugs and gingham curtains looked as though freshly laundered.

'When do you move to the other house?' she asked.

Jack set a large mug of coffee before her and sat down again.

'Well now, love, that rather depends. Caan asked me if I'd mind waiting until after the wedding, for a couple of weeks at least. Well, it's only fair, isn't it . . . young newly-weds, bound to want to be alone at first, eh?' He gave Darynthe a knowing wink.

Darynthe nodded wordlessly, wincing inwardly at the picture which his words conjured up . . . that of Caan and Ozanne, settling down to married happiness in the re-furbished farmhouse.

Jack drained the last of his own coffee, then leant back in his chair.

'Well now, lass, what was it you wanted to see me about?'

'I've come to say goodbye,' she said bluntly.

'Going somewhere, are you?' he said easily. 'Well, it's very nice of you, but I don't suppose you'll be gone that long, eh?' His eyes twinkled. 'Or was it Caan you wanted to say goodbye to? If that's the case, you've just missed him. He's . . .'

'No, I didn't want to see Caan,' she interrupted him abruptly. 'I don't suppose I shall ever see him again, I . . .'

'What!'

Jack came bolt upright in his chair. The expression of dismay on his chubby face would have been comical, if Darynthe had been in a humorous frame of mind.

'I said I won't be seeing Caan again. That's why I came, when I knew he wouldn't be here . . . so I could say goodbye to you.'

'But I don't understand. Have you two had a row?' Jack sounded genuinely puzzled.

'Yes . . . days ago. You mean Caan didn't tell you?' Jack shook his head.

'Oh well!' Darynthe shrugged. 'He probably didn't think you'd be that interested.'

'Not interested! Not interested, when I'm going to . . .'

'I can't stay much longer, Jack. Now that I've seen you . . . and Scipio, of course . . . I'm just going over to take one last look at the farmhouse, just to see it finished. Then, tomorrow, I'm going home . . . for good.'

Jack laid a detaining hand on her arm, as she moved towards the door.

'Hold on a minute, lass. There's something here I don't quite understand. Isn't this anything that can be put right? I'm sure if you'd just wait till Caan gets back . . .'

'No.' Darynthe shook her head. 'I'm sorry, Jack, but no. I don't want to see him, not ever again.'

The elderly man followed her to the door, his normally cheerful features a picture of distress.

'Can't you spare a minute or two longer, love?' he pleaded. 'Just to tell me what's happened. I feel so . . . so bewildered. It's all so sudden, after . . .'

'All right, I'll tell you,' Darynthe relented. 'But you're not going to think much of me when you've heard the whole story.'

As briefly as possible, she related the story of her former

engagement, her encounter with Caan and her increasing
attraction towards him; her belief that because of Ozanne's
existence, it was all quite hopeless and how she had used
Marcus Griffiths as a smokescreen for her pride.

As she spoke, the lines gradually cleared from Jack's
face.

'Then you do love him . . . it was all a misunderstanding,' he said eagerly. 'Surely all you have to do is . . .'

'There's nothing I can do,' Darynthe told him flatly.
'Caan despises me. I said some horrible, unforgivable
things to him, and told him to go back to Lady Ozanne,
and . . . and he has, so . . .'

'He *has*?' Jack asked, frowning again.

Darynthe felt slightly irritated. By his own admission
Jack knew that his nephew was to be married very
shortly.

'Well, you know he has,' she said sharply. 'You mentioned the wedding only a few minutes ago, and I've seen
Ozanne with him, just recently, saw her ring, and the car
he gave her.'

Jack began to nod, and Darynthe was extremely put
out to observe something suspiciously like a twinkle in his
faded blue eyes. But perhaps she had been mistaken, for
his face and voice were perfectly solemn as he spoke.

'Well, naturally I'm very sorry to hear that you and my
nephew are at odds, but I'm glad you came to see me . . .
very glad indeed.'

Impulsively, Darynthe bent and kissed his leathery
cheek.

'I'm sorry too, but I'll just have to make the best of it. I
hope you'll be happy at the farmhouse.'

'Oh, I'm sure I shall.'

Darynthe wished he didn't sound quite so odiously
cheerful, as though he were actually looking forward to
being under the same roof as Ozanne.

'Tell you what!' said Jack, as she gained the doorway.
'I've got a spare key here for the house. Since you're going
over there anyway, why not do it properly . . . have a
good look round inside too. I think you'll be pleasantly
surprised.'

Darynthe hesitated. It was true she had been curious to

see the completed interior, even though it might mean adding to her heartache. The last time she had been at Caan's house, only the main living room had been entirely complete. She wondered, wistfully, what sort of bed he had chosen in the end for the master bedroom.

'I don't think I should,' she said at last. 'Caan wouldn't like it, I'm sure. It would seem like awful cheek.'

'Nonsense,' Jack said briskly. 'I'm sure my nephew would say that you of all people had every right to look round. After all, you played quite a large part in its restoration.'

Temptation and curiosity won. Darynthe accepted the latch-key which Jack pressed into her hand.

'Have a good look around, love, and . . . and don't hurry yourself. After all, you've got all day, haven't you?'

'Yes . . . yes, I have.'

As she drove off, Darynthe reflected that Caan was unlikely to be back from London until late the next day, if then. She tried to picture his reaction when he learnt that she had left the district, but all she could imagine was his relief. She certainly didn't warrant any regret on his part.

As Caan had forecast, the stony, rutted approach to the house had been resurfaced; but this was all that had altered in the setting, and the sudden discovery of the house, hidden deep in its sheltering valley, struck Darynthe as forcibly as on the first occasion she had seen it.

She parked by the garden gate and walked up the flagged path, now clear of weeds, and inserted the key which Jack had given her into the lock of the heavy oak door.

Once again she stood in the large, flagged hallway. The great open fireplace was properly equipped now with a large iron firebasket, filled with enormous logs.

In the panelled living room, furniture gleamed with polish and chrysanthemums in copper bowls glowed in every corner, giving off their singularly individual scent. The house seemed to have an air of eager anticipation, ready to welcome its new occupants.

The new wing, formed from the adjoining barn, stood empty as yet, waiting for Jack's occupation, but was decorated and carpeted in a style which Darynthe guessed to be his taste.

She hesitated for a long time before ascending the wide, creaking stairs to the gallery. Then she squared her shoulders resolutely. She had come so far, seen so much that Ozanne had to look forward to, would share with Caan. Surely she could endure a little more . . . seeing the bedroom Caan and his wife would use.

Even so, she visited the other second floor rooms first, pausing to look down from the leaded windows out over the garden, now trim and orderly and glowing with autumnal colour. At the rear of the house, the fell rose steeply and up there, beyond the tree line, but still on Caan's property, Darynthe pictured the deep, tranquil waters of his own small private tarn . . . a delightful discovery they had made together.

Upstairs, as with the rest of the house, decorations and furnishings had taken into consideration the essential character of the bedrooms; and in the master suite, furniture and fabrics blended skilfully with white roughcast walls and oaken beams.

But it was the great bed, in its oasis of brown and cream carpet, that, irresistibly, drew Darynthe's eyes . . . an enormous, fourposter bed, whose tapestry hangings faithfully reproduced the style and pattern of an earlier age.

Slowly she walked around the bed, touching the hangings with reverent, caressing fingers, wondering which of the two fresh, plump pillows would soon bear the indentation of Caan's head.

She had thought it was impossible for her to shed any more tears, but insidiously the house, this room had worked their melancholy magic, and the bedroom with its magnificent furnishings wavered and blurred before her eyes.

There was the sound of a car's swift arrival, its driver apparently in a tremendous hurry; the slamming of the front door, followed by a heavy tread on the stairs, making their ancient timbers creak once more.

Panic-stricken, Darynthe looked around her for a place of concealment. There was none.

One apprehensive glance at the man who stood in the doorway, then she bowed her head, waiting for the inevitable storm to break. What mischance had brought him back here? He was supposed to be in London!

As she stared down at the carpet, two immaculately shod feet moved slowly into her range of vision and still Caan had not spoken. Unnerved by this continuing silence, Darynthe ventured a swift, upward look, catching her breath at the look in his eyes, an expression she had often imagined, but never dared to hope that *she* would see there.

But she must be mistaken. It was a trick of the sunlight that glanced through the many-faceted window-panes. It was too late for her. He had already taken the irrevocable step of becoming engaged to Ozanne Hanson.

'I . . . I'm sorry,' she said formally. 'I was just leaving. I know it was very rude of me to look over your house, without your permission, but . . .'

'Jack said I would find you here.' His voice was husky and he was still looking at her, with that strangely hypnotic softness in his blue eyes.

'I . . . I wouldn't have come, but I thought you'd be in London with . . . with Ozanne.'

'Ah, yes . . . Ozanne,' he said. 'I never had any intention of going to London today, as it happens.'

He was only inches from her now, so close that she could smell the tweedy, masculine scent of him . . . sweet torture to her senses.

'Well, if . . . if you'll excuse me . . .' Darynthe edged sideways, only to find her way barred, by a long, exceedingly strong arm.

'Not so fast!'

'I *have* to go,' she told him, desperation in her voice.

One finger of his other hand advanced, lifting her chin, as he examined her critically.

'You've been crying,' he observed.

'No, no . . . of course not,' she stammered unconvincingly.

'Oh, Darynthe, Darynthe!' he sighed. 'I suppose, knowing you, you won't even let me kiss you, until we have this unholy tangle properly sorted out.'

'I'm not going to let you kiss me at all,' she said quickly, taking a step backwards.

'Oh yes, you are, you know.' He sounded very sure of himself and Darynthe, knowing his strength, his determination, felt that she was surely lost.

'But first things first,' he continued. 'I've just come from Ambleside . . . where your aunt informed me that you intend going home tomorrow.'

Darynthe nodded, not trusting her voice.

Two large hands imprisoned her slender shoulders, sending a sensuous, responsive quiver through her entire body.

'Why were you running away again, Darynthe?'

Still she did not . . . could not . . . answer.

'Mrs Forster told me you'd gone to my uncle's, to say goodbye to him. Did you intend leaving, without saying goodbye to me?'

'Please . . . please, let me go,' she begged. 'Stop torturing me!'

Caan shook her gently, contriving at the same time to bring her closer to him.

'I'm not torturing you, you silly child. Can't you see, I'm just trying to get at the truth?'

'I am *not* a child!' she snapped, with a little of her old fire. 'I'm a woman and I . . .'

'Yes?' His question was eager.

But her eyes evaded the piercing blue of his again and she shook her head.

'Then *I'll* tell *you*, shall I?' he said softly. 'Tell you what both *your* aunt and *my* uncle told *me*?'

'No . . . no . . .' Darynthe panicked. 'They had no right . . . they . . . they don't know what they're talking about. They're just trying to . . .'

But Caan went on inexorably.

'They both told me that you were running away from me. Because,' his voice deepened, 'because you love me. Darynthe, is this true or not? I want to hear it from your lips.'

She threw up her head defiantly, her eyes glittering emeralds.

'All right! If that's what you want. My aunt . . . your uncle shouldn't have told you that . . . that I . . .' Her voice faltered.

'You mean it isn't true?'

His grasp on her shoulders slackened and he sounded suddenly weary. Looking at him, Darynthe fancied she could see new lines about his mouth, at the corners of his eyes.

'I mean they shouldn't have told you, because it's true,' she said quietly. 'They might have left me my pride . . . I didn't want you to know, to feel sorry for me.'

His grip tightened once more, his hands sliding down now to encompass her upper arms.

'Why on earth should I feel sorry for you, when I . . .?'

'Because, in spite of everything, I believe you're a kind man. How could you help feeling sorry for **me,** since you're engaged to Ozanne and I . . .'

'I'm *what?*'

'En-engaged to Ozanne.' She looked at him doubtfully. 'Well, you are, aren't you?'

'Like hell I am!'

The words came explosively and now he did not hold back, but hauled her into his arms, swearing softly against the silkiness of her hair.

'You silly, crazy, little idiot! I have never, ever, had any intention of marrying Ozanne Hanson. There was a time, I believe, when she thought otherwise. But I soon disabused her of that idea, once I'd met you . . . took her out to lunch, you may remember, so that I could tell her so.'

Darynthe strained back in his arms, to meet his eyes, her own enquiring, anxious.

'You're telling me the truth? You really aren't engaged to her?'

'Not even a little bit,' he assured her gravely, the smile that she had never thought to see again quirking his mouth up in that engaging sideways twist. 'That ring she wears is not mine.'

'Oh, Caan!' Eyes shining, Darynthe stood on tiptoe, brushing her lips against his. 'Oh, Caan, I . . . I don't think I've ever been so happy in my life!'

Whereupon she promptly burst into tears.

With a strangled sound in his throat, he bent and sweeping her off her feet, carried her over to the massive bed, setting her down with a kind of gentle reverence, covering her wet eyelids, damp cheeks and quivering mouth, with a series of burning kisses . . . gentle, yet with an underlying fervour that spoke of strong emotions, barely held in check.

Feverishly Darynthe returned his kisses, tangling her fingers in his wiry hair, exploring the muscles of his neck, running her hands inside his jacket, to feel the hardness of his chest, the rapid beat of his heart. This was heaven . . . a heaven she had never thought to know.

A sudden doubt occurred to her and she evaded his lips, holding him off.

'What now?' he groaned, his eyes clouded with desire.

'You . . . you made me tell you that I love you, but you . . . you never said . . .'

'That *I* love *you*?' His laugh was low, exultant, as he pulled her close again. 'Can you doubt it? Oh, Darynthe, if I were to spend time in telling you how much I love you, whole precious hours would be lost . . . hours in which I could be demonstrating the fact in a far more satisfactory fashion.'

'But . . . but the other day, you said you'd never interfere in my life again . . . when you walked out, I thought you'd gone for ever.'

'I was angry, my little love, but I knew even as I said it, I wouldn't be able to keep away from you for very long. I thought,' he sighed, 'I thought I'd give you time to miss me. I don't know if you did, but I certainly missed you. I went through hell.'

Reassured, she allowed herself to be drawn even nearer, and now they were lying side by side on the great bed, her pliant, slender body moulded closely to every hard contour of his. Loving Caan, living with him, was going to be a warm and wonderful experience, she thought dreamily. There might be frequent emotional storms . . . they were both strong-willed people, but such constant stimulation would only intensify the powerful vibrations of physical response each aroused in the other.

'Caan . . .' once more she evaded his lips, 'you do . . . you do want to . . . to marry me?'

'I'm counting on it,' he said softly, his blue eyes surveying her rosy face, warm with love. 'I want you beside me at night when I go to bed. If I wake in the night, I want to know that you are there, and I want your face to be the very first thing I see when I wake up.'

His kisses were satisfying proof of his words. Then a low rumble of laughter, deep in his chest, made her look at him indignantly.

'What are you laughing at?'

'I'm just picturing the consternation poor old Jack must have felt when you told him you were leaving . . . just as he was all set to move in with us.'

'With us? But how . . . I mean, he didn't . . . you hadn't asked me to . . .'

'But I fully intended to. I'd always intended to marry you . . . and once I knew your act with young Griffiths was just a blind, I was determined to make you love me as well, even if it took me a lifetime.'

'But Ozanne . . . that ring . . .' she faltered.

'Ozanne, my love, after shilly-shallying for the past two weeks between two suitors, has finally made up her mind, and she is currently engaged to a very rich man . . . far richer than I shall ever be . . . and who stands to inherit a title some day.'

'But she *was* your girl-friend, once?'

His face was suddenly stern.

'Darynthe, let's get this straight, once and for all, shall we? Yes, Ozanne was my girl-friend for a time . . . as many other women have been. Damn it, Darynthe, I *am* thirty-eight. It would be a lie if I said you were my first girl-friend. But they're all in the past. There'll never be anyone else for me now but you. You are my present and my future . . . and the present can't be touched by yesterday; it's gone . . . forgotten. Do you agree?'

'Yes,' she whispered submissively. 'Yes, Caan . . . oh yes!'

Finally she knew that she could accept the fact that Caan had made love to other women, but she would not enquire now, or ever, into the depth of those relationships. As Caan had said, the present was hers . . . and the future.

'I love you,' she murmured.

'We're wasting time again,' said Caan, his voice unsteady, turning her to him once more, shaping her body with his hands, slowly, unhurriedly, sensuously, pressing against her with his full weight, so that she could feel the throbbing desire that racked him.

As the heat of longing scorched through her own body, mentally she threw aside the last of her inhibitions, prepared to submit now to his possession, if he demanded it of her; but this time it was Caan who drew away, albeit reluctantly, his shrewd eyes regarding her quizzically.

'You'd rather wait until after we're married, wouldn't you, my old-fashioned darling?'

For a moment, from the depths of her own need, Darynthe thought that she could deny the truth of his statement, but he knew her too well and she recognised that he respected as well as loved her for her principles. She nodded.

'Yes. Yes, please. Th-thank you, Caan.'

With a wry smile he stood up, hauling her off the bed.

'Come on, then, while I still have the strength of character to agree with you.' Then, his mood changing suddenly to one of playful exuberance, he swung her round and round, in a crazy, head-spinning waltz. 'Let's go and tell everyone!'

'Everyone?'

'Well, everyone that matters . . . my uncle, and your aunt.'

'And I must telephone my father,' Darynthe reminded him soberly. 'He'll be rather surprised . . . but he must be here to give me away.'

'You don't want to be married from Corbridge, then?' She shook her head, green eyes sparkling.

'No, I want to be married here . . . the parish church at Ambleside, the first church we ever entered together.'

'Even though you hated me then?' he said teasingly.

'Oh, Caan!' She looked at him, unutterable promises in her clear eyes. 'I've got so much to make up to you. I hope you won't ever be bored by my loving you so much.'

'Darynthe Browne with an "e" . . .' His deep intake of breath shook the whole of his massive frame. 'Come away from here, before I break my resolution!'

*

Two weeks later Darynthe achieved her heart's desire, walking down the aisle on her father's arm, in a cloud of satin and lace ... the perfume of flowers; with eyes only for the tall, broad-shouldered man awaiting her.

To her relief, her father and Caan had liked each other instantly, her father admitting that while he would be sorry to lose her, he felt easier in his mind about her marriage to Caan than he had done when she had been contemplating life with Mark Little.

He had also confessed, with some embarrassment, that he was thinking himself of remarrying ... his future wife herself a widow of some years' standing and an old friend of Darynthe's mother.

'You don't mind?' he had asked her anxiously.

'Goodness, no!' She assured him. 'Now I needn't feel guilty about you being lonely. I hope you'll be very happy ... as happy as I'm going to be.'

On one occasion during the previous days, Caan had asked Darynthe where she wanted to go for a honeymoon, but she had answered simply, 'Home', looking at him with so much love and longing in her eyes that his had blazed with the fire caught from hers and once again he had been hard put to it to keep his promise.

So, after a small family reception at the Daffodil, and where Darynthe also changed into a becoming, figure-hugging woollen dress of emerald green, they drove away through Grasmere in the rapidly descending dusk of a late, but unseasonably warm, autumn evening.

'I'm glad we haven't a long journey before us,' Caan said huskily, his strong hand resting for an instant on Darynthe's knee.

'So am I,' she whispered, as she quivered responsively to his touch.

The house seemed to close protectively about them, like welcoming arms, as Caan carried her over the threshold. Closely linked, they entered the living room, where, despite central heating, a log fire was set ready for lighting.

With his usual efficiency Caan soon had it burning, then turned to Darynthe, the glow in his eyes owing nothing to the firelight.

'Come here, Mrs Lorimer,' he ordered.

Willingly she surrendered herself into his arms, glorying in her new status, as he kissed her, languorously at first, so that a tremor ran over her whole body. Then his hands began to move over her, lingering, caressing, stirring her to full life, so that she craved physical fulfilment . . . and yet she had a dream, unrealised.

'Shall we go up now?' he murmured, his kisses becoming a searching sensuous need. 'Or shall we stay here in front of the fire?'

'Not, not yet. Caan, could we . . . could we go for a walk first?'

She sensed his disappointment, his tense disapproval, but she knew that she had to persist.

'Please, Caan!'

'Very well.' His tone was curt.

Outside, a full moon sailed serenely over the mountain tops and behind the house, the fell curved up smoothly, then dropped again to a valley, enclosing the small but beautiful tarn.

'Darynthe?' Caan's voice was stiff with restraint. 'You're not afraid . . . of me, of . . .' His hand came out to touch her, but it was too soon . . .

She began to run, hearing him curse softly, but she did not slacken her pace until she reached the water's edge. There, with a few swift movements, she let the simple, clinging dress she wore drop around her ankles, revealing her clad only in two scraps of lace.

As Caan reached her side, she slipped soundlessly into the water, gasping a little at the coolness, then plunging her shoulders beneath the moon-silvered ripples, she swiftly discarded her remaining garments.

Seconds later Caan joined her and she saw, for the first time, his powerful body, as naked as her own, as he trod water, reaching out for her.

'You remembered,' he said softly, as he held her, no barriers between them now save the soft caress of the waters; and Darynthe was deliciously aware of her smooth, damp flesh moving against his.

'Yes,' she whispered against the sweetness of his mouth, 'and ever since, I've longed to bathe like this . . . with you.'

Her words, her every movement against him, were a deliberate provocation and she did not resist when he lifted her, carrying her to the bank, covering her with his body, their bed the cushioning turf of the hillside.

She ventured only one small half-stifled protest in that last second before their flesh became one.

'It seems such a pity . . . that glorious fire, that magnificent bed . . .'

'The night isn't over yet,' said Caan, and she trembled at the promise in his voice, the promise of more joys yet to come, as together they stilled the aching longing of their senses; together they touched not just the roots of heaven . . . but heaven itself.

Harlequin® Plus

A POEM FOR THE LAKE DISTRICT

Darynthe's aunt named her guesthouse "The Daffodil," after a poem by William Wordsworth, a romantic nineteenth-century poet who made England's beautiful Lake District his home. On page 16 Caan quotes from this famous poem. Here it is in its entirety.

I wandered lonely as a cloud
That floats on high o'er vales and hills,
When all at once I saw a crowd,
A host, of golden daffodils;
Beside the lake, beside the trees,
Fluttering and dancing in the breeze.

Continuous as the stars that shine
And twinkle on the milky way,
They stretched in never-ending line
Along the margin of a bay:
Ten thousand saw I at a glance,
Tossing their heads in sprightly dance.

The waves beside them danced; but they
Out-did the sparkling waves in glee:
A poet could not but be gay,
In such a jocund company:
I gazed—and gazed—but little thought
What wealth this show to me had brought:

For oft, when on my couch I lie
In vacant or in pensive mood,
They flash upon that inward eye
Which is the bliss of solitude;
And then my heart with pleasure fills,
And dances with the daffodils.

ALL-TIME FAVORITE BESTSELLERS
...love stories that grow
more beautiful with time!

Now's your chance to discover the earlier great books in Harlequin Presents, the world's most popular romance-fiction series.

Choose from the following list.

17 LIVING WITH ADAM Anne Mather

20 A DISTANT SOUND OF THUNDER Anne Mather

29 MONKSHOOD Anne Mather

32 JAKE HOWARD'S WIFE Anne Mather

35 SEEN BY CANDLELIGHT Anne Mather

36 LOVE'S PRISONER Violet Winspear

38 MOON WITCH Anne Mather

39 TAWNY SANDS Violet Winspear

41 DANGEROUS ENCHANTMENT Anne Mather

42 THE STRANGE WAIF Violet Winspear

50 THE GLASS CASTLE Violet Winspear

62 THE MARRIAGE OF CAROLINE LINDSAY
    Margaret Rome

66 CINDY, TREAD LIGHTLY Karin Mutch

67 ACCOMPANIED BY HIS WIFE Mary Burchell

70 THE CHATEAU OF ST. AVRELL Violet Winspear

71 AND NO REGRETS Rosalind Brett

73 FOOD FOR LOVE Rachel Lindsay

75 DARE I BE HAPPY? Mary Burchell

78 A MAN LIKE DAINTREE Margaret Way

ALL-TIME FAVORITE BESTSELLERS

Complete and mail this coupon today!

Harlequin Reader Service

In the U.S.A.
1440 South Priest Drive
Tempe, AZ 85281

In Canada
649 Ontario Street
Stratford, Ontario N5A 6W2

Please send me the following Presents **ALL-TIME FAVORITE BESTSELLERS.** I am enclosing my check or money order for $1.75 for each copy ordered, plus 75¢ to cover postage and handling.

☐ #17	☐ #35	☐ #41	☐ #66	☐ #73
☐ #20	☐ #36	☐ #42	☐ #67	☐ #75
☐ #29	☐ #38	☐ #50	☐ #70	☐ #78
☐ #32	☐ #39	☐ #62	☐ #71	

Number of copies checked @ $1.75 each = $ _____
N.Y. and Ariz. residents add appropriate sales tax $ _____
Postage and handling $ .75
TOTAL $ _____

I enclose _____
(Please send check or money order. We cannot be responsible for cash sent through the mail.)
Prices subject to change without notice.

NAME _____
(Please Print)

ADDRESS _____ APT. NO. _____

CITY _____

STATE/PROV. _____

ZIP/POSTAL CODE _____
Offer expires August 31, 1983   30556000000